She resented his control even as she envied it

"I take it you and your mother aren't close?" Ross asked.

"If you were from here, you wouldn't even have to ask that." And Layne wasn't about to fill him in.

"You haven't spoken to your mother in almost a year?"

"September twentieth. Nineteen ninety-three."

If he was surprised, she couldn't tell. Couldn't read him in the best of times, let alone when her emotions were jumbled, her thoughts confused.

She prided herself on her ability to see situations…people…clearly. Being unable to do so with him only served to infuriate and, yes, intrigue her. Damn him.

What if her mother had changed her mind and hadn't wanted to leave her family? What if Layne hadn't said those things to her that night? What if she'd tried to stop her mother from leaving instead of telling her to go and not come back?

Dear God, what if her mother was dead? And it was all her fault?

Dear Reader,

Writers are often asked where we get our ideas. The truth is, I have no clue how I come up with my stories. Sometimes it's from something I see on TV, others it's a line or two from a newspaper article or even lyrics from a song. All I know is that my books usually start with a character, one who grabs my attention, who has some fatal flaw to get past or an emotional wound that needs healing. Once I have that character in mind, I focus on writing a story that pushes them to grow and change and earn their Happily Ever After.

It wasn't that way with The Truth about the Sullivans trilogy. As a matter of fact, the premise for all three stories came from one simple quote: The truth will set you free.

It's a simple concept, but also one that can be very powerful. At least, that's what I found out when I wrote these stories. I had to know what would happen if three sisters discovered that their mother, the woman they'd thought had abandoned them, had actually been murdered.

The answers surprised me. For Layne Sullivan, the eldest daughter and heroine of *Unraveling the Past,* discovering what had really happened to her mother meant a complete reevaluation of everything she'd always believed. It also meant facing some hard truths about herself, the resentments she'd held on to all these years and her ability to forgive—others and herself.

I had a great time writing Layne and Ross's story and I hope you enjoy it, as well! I love to hear from my readers. Please visit my website, www.bethandrews.net, or drop me a line at beth@bethandrews.net or P.O. Box 714, Bradford, PA 16701.

Happy reading!

Beth Andrews

P.S. Look for book two of The Truth about the Sullivans series, *On Her Side,* available in August 2012.

Unraveling the Past

BETH ANDREWS

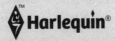

TORONTO NEW YORK LONDON
AMSTERDAM PARIS SYDNEY HAMBURG
STOCKHOLM ATHENS TOKYO MILAN MADRID
PRAGUE WARSAW BUDAPEST AUCKLAND

Recycling programs
for this product may
not exist in your area.

ISBN-13: 978-0-373-71782-8

UNRAVELING THE PAST

www.Harlequin.com

Printed in U.S.A.

ABOUT THE AUTHOR

Romance Writers of America RITA® Award winner Beth Andrews lives with her husband and three children in northwestern Pennsylvania far from the ocean, Boston accents and New England Patriots fans. The middle of three daughters, she knows a thing or two about the dynamics between sisters—a skill that came in handy while writing The Truth about the Sullivans. When not writing, Beth spends too much time in the kitchen and too little time on the treadmill. Learn more about Beth and her books by visiting her website, www.BethAndrews.net.

Books by Beth Andrews

HARLEQUIN SUPERROMANCE

Other titles by this author available in ebook format.

For Montgomry

ACKNOWLEDGMENT

Special thanks to Assistant Chief Mike Ward of the Bradford, PA, Police Department.

CHAPTER ONE

W<small>HEN</small> J<small>ESSICA</small> T<small>AYLOR</small> lost her virginity three months and six guys ago—after fiercely guarding it for fifteen years—she'd been stone-cold sober.

She hadn't made that mistake again.

Her stomach rolled. From the Jack Daniel's, she assured herself. She should've stuck with beer. It always gave her a nice, mellow buzz without making her want to puke. Mostly because she knew her limit. Whiskey was a new beast, one she hadn't figured out her tolerance to yet.

But Nate had been so sweet when she'd arrived at the party a few hours ago, teasing her into trying J.D. and Diet Coke, making sure her glass was always full, adding more soda when she choked, her eyes watering at the first taste.

Yeah, he was a real prince.

A cold sweat broke out along her hairline. Her stomach churned again. Because of the alcohol. It had nothing to do with her being on her back in the middle of the freaking woods.

She stared up at the moon peeking through the branches of the trees and pretended she was somewhere else, anywhere else, doing anything except what she was doing. That she wasn't wasted—yet again. And that Nate Berry, with his floppy, pop-star hair and tight circle of friends, really liked her. Cared about her. That he wasn't using her.

That she wasn't letting him use her.

Her skin grew clammy. Prickled with the cold. Nate's fingers clenched her hips, his face pressed against her neck. He was just another boy. And this was just another meaningless, drunken hookup in what was quickly becoming a long line of meaningless, drunken hookups.

Tears stung the backs of her eyelids and she squeezed her eyes shut. No. No feeling sorry for herself. She had every right to have sex with whoever she wanted, whenever she wanted. It was her body after all. Her choice to give it to some guy or not.

She was in control.

Her back and butt scraped against the rough earth. Her neck was stretched back, her hair caught between the crown of her head and the ground, pulling painfully each time he moved. She just wanted it to be over. Wanted to pretend it had never happened in the first place. Just like all the other times.

Clutching his arms, she lifted her hips to keep from getting the mother of all brush burns, to stop the contents of her stomach from sloshing. She inhaled deeply, breathed in the scent of Nate's cologne and the pungent smell from the bonfire in the clearing outside the trees. His grip tightened, his nails digging into her skin as he groaned hoarsely and shuddered then finally— finally—stilled.

Thank God.

He collapsed on top of her, surprisingly heavy for a guy who looked as if he'd never heard of carbs, let alone ate any. His heart beat frantically against her chest, his breath hot and ragged against her shoulder. They had connected in the most elemental way. And still she felt alone. Always alone.

Her throat closed. Without a word, without a kiss or a murmured endearment or even an outright lie about how fantastic it'd been, how fantastic she was, Nate climbed to his feet. He turned his back and adjusted his clothes.

The cool night air washed over her bare skin. She shivered but couldn't find the energy or the care to cover herself. After she'd lost her virginity to a smooth-talking college freshman, she'd stopped believing guys' lines. Had quickly learned they'd do and say anything to get into a girl's pants.

Yeah, she'd learned. But she hadn't stopped hoping, couldn't stop wishing that each time would be different. That, when it was all over, the guy she'd been with would think she was…special. Instead, once she gave them what they wanted, they all thought she was trash.

She was starting to wonder if they were right.

As she yanked up her jeans, shouts of excitement from the party still going strong reached them. The bonfire illuminated the colorful graffiti on the huge rocks that formed a barrier between the woods and what passed for civilization around here. Flames shot high into the air—probably from someone tossing gasoline onto the fire.

What a bunch of idiots.

"Come on," Nate said, facing her as he stuffed his hands into his jean pockets. "Let's go. Sounds like the party's getting wicked wild."

Jess snorted. "Yeah." She lurched to her feet and swayed. He held out a hand to steady her but she slapped him away. She didn't want him touching her again. "I'm sure it's a crazy wild time," she continued, her words slurring. "At least by this town's standards."

"Mystic Point not good enough for you?"

Okay, so she'd pissed him off, either with her comment or her slap. Good.

She rolled her eyes—and immediately wished she hadn't when she almost tipped over. "Relax. God, why is everyone so defensive about this place?"

"Maybe we don't like outsiders slamming our town."

Outsider. That was her. And she was glad. She didn't want to belong here. She just wanted to go home.

"There's a whole big world out there," she said, waving her arms. "Places where parties are held in actual houses instead of in the middle of nowhere surrounded by some stupid rocks."

She'd much preferred last week's party at the secluded part of the beach. The one and only thing she liked about Mystic Point was its proximity to the water. She loved the sound of the waves crashing on shore, the smell of salt water, the power of the ocean. But word had spread that the local cops had gotten wind of the underage drinking going on there and were going to increase their patrols of that area.

Which is how she ended up at some old quarry at the edge of town.

"If you hate it here so much, why don't you go back to Boston?" Nate's tone was snide, superior, as if he knew damn well why she was stuck here.

He thought he was better than her because he had a normal family, a mom who didn't spend all her time so strung out she barely remembered she even had a kid. A dad who not only acknowledged him, but spent time with him.

Jess's mom couldn't even say for sure which of her lowlife boyfriends had knocked her up.

Her hands curled. He was right. She did hate it here. And she hated Nate, too. Him and all his friends with their small-town attitudes and stupid cliques. They'd all heard about her past—nothing was sacred in a small town, after all. They'd discussed her. Judged her. And found her lacking. Even if she'd wanted to fit in, she'd never had the chance.

Several car headlights flashed twice then remained on, the brightness cutting through the trees. Jess squinted against the glare.

"What's the matter, Nate?" a male voice called. "Having problems…performing?"

"Dude, I bet she knows all sorts of tricks to help with that," another guy yelled.

"She should," a girl added gleefully, "she's had enough practice. She spends more time on her back than her feet."

Laughter erupted and a moment later, the lights shut off. But not before she saw the grin on Nate's face. Saw how little he really thought of her.

Bastard.

With a low growl that, if she wasn't careful, could easily turn into a sob, Jess picked up his sweatshirt and threw it at his face.

He caught it before it could make contact. "What's your problem?" he asked. "They're just joking around."

"I don't have a problem." But everyone else did. They were too small-town boring and uptight. She started walking deeper into the woods.

He grabbed her arm, stopping her so fast, the entire world tilted. She clamped down on the urge to vomit.

"The party's this way," he said.

Once the trees stopped spinning, she jerked away. "Get off me." No one touched her unless she wanted them to, and he'd lost that right. "I'm leaving."

Her voice broke and she prayed he didn't notice.

"All right," he said slowly, as if trying to calm her down, "if that's what you want." This time, he reached for her hand. "Come on, I'll take you home."

She crossed her arms. "Why?"

He sighed heavily and glanced back at the party. "Because you're drunk and shouldn't be wandering around the woods at night."

"What's the matter? Afraid I'll die of exposure or get attacked by a wild animal and you'll be blamed?" Though she gave him plenty of time to deny it, he didn't. All he cared about was getting into trouble if something happened to her. "Go back to the party. I'm sure you're dying to tell everyone what a stud you are." She raised her voice. "But you might want to leave out the part about how it lasted a whole five minutes."

"Everyone was right about you," he said. "You really are a bitch."

Bitch. Slut. Loser. All names she'd been called before. Whoever said words couldn't cause pain had obviously never gone to high school.

"And don't you forget it," she said with her patented sneer. And she walked away.

This time, he let her go.

Good. She didn't want him chasing after her pretending he cared about whether she made it home safely or not. Oh, sure, he'd been all charm when he'd called and invited her to the party, had layered it on even more when she got there, flirting and joking around, but it'd all been an act. She wasn't sure who she was angrier with: him for not being different, for not living up to her hopeful standards.

Or herself for sleeping with him anyway.

She squinted at the narrow path cutting through the woods. If she kept walking, she'd end up in the clearing near the quarry's entrance.

She hoped.

Too bad the farther she got from the clearing and the fire, the darker it got, the trees seeming to have multiplied to cut off any and all light from the moon. But it still beat going back the way she and Nate had come. She knew what would happen if she rejoined the party. The girls would freeze her out with their bitchy comments and accusing glares, blaming her for giving the boys what they were too frigid to. The guys would exchange smirks and elbow nudges and Nate would end up avoiding her the rest of the night.

And she was too wasted, too emotionally messed up at the moment to pretend it didn't bother her.

She took out her phone and pressed the speed dial for Marissa, her best friend back in Boston. Holding it to her ear, she began making her way through the woods again, her steps unsteady, her head spinning.

"Come on," she muttered when Marissa didn't pick up. "Where are you?"

Despite her best efforts, tears streamed down her face. She angrily wiped her cheek with the back of her hand. Her toe caught on a tree root and she pitched forward. Her phone flew from her grip and she landed hard on the ground on her hands and knees.

Tears and snot dripped from her face as she fought to catch her breath. To not puke. Her palms stung, her head swam. She straightened her leg, felt material rubbing against her knee and realized she'd ripped a hole in her favorite jeans.

God, but this place sucked. She hated it here.

Patting the ground around her for her phone, she crawled forward. Something rustled behind her. She froze, holding her breath as she listened. When only silence surrounded her, she continued her search, inching forward along the forest floor, the sharp twigs scratching her.

"Shit," she whispered.

"You can say that again."

Her head jerked up and she fell onto her rear, squinted against the harsh glare of a flashlight. But she didn't need to see who had spoken, didn't need a light to know a cop stood before her. No, not just a cop, but Mystic Point's new chief of police.

"Hi, Uncle Ross," Jess said. Then she reared forward and threw up at his feet.

Police Chief Ross Taylor couldn't breathe. Didn't dare move. If he so much as blinked, he might lose all control. And that wouldn't be good. Not when his instincts screamed at him to wrap his hands around the puny neck of the kid he and Assistant Chief Sullivan had dragged into the woods to help search for Jessica.

The kid who'd admitted he'd let her go stumbling off by herself in the dark. The kid who hadn't had to admit what he and Jess had been doing while the rest of their delinquent friends drank and whooped it up in the clearing. The empty cups and the used condom Ross had walked past had made it all too clear they hadn't been stargazing.

He exhaled heavily. *Son of a bitch.*

Ross knelt next to his niece. "Are you okay?" he

asked quietly, well aware Layne Sullivan and the kid made a rapt audience to this little family drama.

Jessica stared up at him, her face illuminated by the flashlight Sullivan shined in their direction. Jess's eyes—light blue like her mother's—were huge. And unfocused, the pupils dilated. "No."

Then she threw up again.

Behind him, the kid gagged. Ross pointed his flashlight on him and, sure enough, the boy's face was pale. "Don't even think about it," Ross said harshly.

The kid swallowed hard. "Yes…yes, sir."

Satisfied, Ross turned back to Jess. She sat back and wiped her hand across her mouth.

"Finished?" he asked.

"I hope so." Her voice shook.

He helped her to her feet, keeping a firm hold of her upper arm so she didn't fall. And so she couldn't take off should the idea enter her head. Her pale, shoulder-length hair was matted and tangled, her clothes wrinkled and stained with puke and dirt. Tears leaked unchecked from her eyes, leaving trails of mascara down her cheeks.

She looked like every other underage drunk girl he'd ever arrested. He had to remind himself that she was just a kid. A rebellious, self-destructive kid. She was also his responsibility.

One he wasn't sure he wanted. Wasn't sure he could handle.

"What in the hell are you doing out here?" he asked.

What was she doing getting drunk, rolling around with some pimply faced kid, when she was supposed to be safely tucked away in her bedroom? Damn, he really wasn't cut out for this guardian stuff.

She wiped the moisture from her cheeks. "You're

the one who told me I needed to give Mystic Point a chance. That I should put myself out there and make friends. Nate and I got very friendly. Didn't we, Nate?"

Her tone was spiteful, almost…gleeful. But her eyes… When he searched her eyes he saw the truth. Anger. Regret. And such pain, he wasn't sure he could fix it. Could fix her.

"We weren't…" the kid blurted. "I mean…we didn't…"

Ross glanced over his shoulder, his quick glare shutting the kid up.

"Sullivan," Ross said quietly, "would you please escort this young man back to the fire?"

Three years younger than Ross's thirty-five, Layne Sullivan was ambitious, levelheaded and had been the front-runner for the position of chief until Ross threw his hat into the ring. He had no doubt she'd enjoy spreading around the tale about how he couldn't even control his niece. How inept he was when it came to dealing with a rebellious teenager.

"Yes, sir." But she didn't move.

"Is there a problem?" Ross asked.

"No…no problem. But what do you want us to do with the kids?"

When Ross, Sullivan and patrol officer Evan Campbell had pulled up to the bonfire, most of the kids had taken off into the woods. But a half dozen had been corralled and were being watched by Campbell—a rookie cop barely old enough to drink himself.

"I want you to do your job," Ross managed to reply in what he considered a highly reasonable tone. "Check IDs. Those under the legal drinking age—" and from what he'd seen, they were all underage "—will be cited. If they're under eighteen, take them back to the station and hold them there until they can be released into their parents' custody."

"You're going to call our parents?" Nate asked, his voice hitching on the last word. "Oh, man, my dad is going to kill me."

Ross's flat gaze had him hunching his shoulders.

"Can I have a word with you, Chief?" Sullivan asked. "In private."

Without waiting for an answer, she walked down the trail, the light from her flashlight bobbing on the worn path.

Ross jabbed a finger at Jess. "Don't. Move." She saluted him—her middle finger clearly visible. He ground his back teeth together. "You," he barked at Nate, "sit."

The kid collapsed into a sitting position as if Ross had swept his feet out from under him. Ross glanced from Sullivan's back to Jessica. If only everyone could take orders so well.

Sullivan waited for him a good twenty feet from the kids. She was tall. Long-legged. Sleek and sexy even in uniform, her face more interesting than beautiful, her dark hair pulled back into a long tail that reached the middle of her back. Attraction flared, quick and hot in his gut.

He ruthlessly squelched it.

She was surly, defensive and wore her resentment toward him as blatantly as she wore the badge on her chest. More important, she was his subordinate. Which put her so far off-limits, she may as well have been on another planet.

"What is it, Captain?" he said, stressing her rank. No crime reminding her who the superior officer was. Especially when she clearly needed that reminder.

"Usually, in situations like this, we make sure no

one who's been drinking is driving then let them go with a warning."

"And how many warnings do they get before they're held accountable for breaking the law?"

"Chief Gorham always thought it was in everyone's best interest to let this type of thing slide."

"Gorham is no longer chief of police—"

"Believe me," she murmured, "we all know that."

"Therefore, we will no longer be doing things the way he did them. Or letting his actions as chief dictate the decisions I make."

She flipped her long, dark ponytail over her shoulder. "We can certainly do things your way—"

"I appreciate the permission."

Her face was hidden by shadows but he'd bet a year's pay she rolled her eyes. "But if you cite those kids, you'll rile up a bunch of parents."

"Part of the hazards of the job."

Sullivan stepped closer, holding the flashlight between them so it illuminated the lower half of her face. "I realize you don't understand how things work in a small town," she said softly, as if imparting some hard-won wisdom, "but believe me, you're not going to win any points for hauling these kids in. What'll happen is they'll all get slapped with fines, lose their licenses—if they have them yet—and be ordered to perform community service. Fines," she continued pointedly, "that their parents will more than likely have to pay for. Community service that their parents will have to take time off of work to take them to. Just like they'll have to drive them to every practice, school function and social event until they get their driving privileges restored."

Ross fought for patience. For the past month he'd

been careful not to step on any toes, to be respectful of the veterans of his department who were less than thrilled at being ordered around by an outsider who'd taken the position from one of their own.

He'd been especially cautious around Sullivan. She'd had her fellow officers' support in her bid for the position of chief, she had their respect. She was also, as far as Ross could tell, a damn fine cop.

But it was past time they all realized he was in charge now.

"I appreciate your input." He kept his tone mild, not giving away the frustration eating at him. "While I may not have much experience with small-town living, I do know that it's illegal for a person under the age of twenty-one to purchase or consume alcoholic beverages in the state of Massachusetts. It's not up to us to interpret the law or decide when and where to enforce it. It's black and white."

"A good cop knows there are always shades of gray. sir," Sullivan added, making the sign of respect sound like anything but.

"Not on my watch. Not in my department. There's right and there's wrong." She didn't have to agree. She just had to do as he said. "Give anyone eighteen or older the choice to take a Breathalyzer test. If they pass, they're free to go. The rest get cited."

"Even your niece?"

He ignored the skepticism in the captain's husky voice. "She broke the law. She'll have to face the consequences like everyone else."

And if that made him the bad guy then so be it. Over the past three months he'd gotten used to playing that role with her. Just as he'd played it with her mother—

his younger sister—his entire life. He glanced at Sulli-van, noted her disdain for him in the twist of her mouth.

Hell, now he got to be the bad guy at home and at work.

Funny how doing the right thing could be such a pain in the ass.

"It's quite a coincidence," Sullivan said, "you show-ing up right as Evan and I pulled in."

"I heard the call."

"Well, aren't we lucky you just happened to be lis-tening to the police radio at one-thirty in the morning."

Hard not to listen to it since he'd been driving around looking for Jess after discovering she'd snuck out. Which Sullivan must suspect or else she wouldn't be taking this little fishing trip. "Glad I could offer my assistance."

Her mouth flattened. "Come on, Nate," she called and the kid scrambled to his feet. "Let's go."

They walked away. Ross checked on Jess and found her back on her hands and knees.

"Get up." He crossed to stand over her. Jess, of course, didn't so much as glance at him. She excelled at doing the opposite of what she should. "I said—" he took a hold of her elbow and tugged "—get up."

Once on her feet, she pulled away from him, the ef-fect ruined when he had to reach out to keep her from falling flat on her face.

"I have to sit down," she said. "I don't feel well."

And for a moment, Ross got sucked in. Sucked in by her pale face and big eyes, by the trembling of her voice. By how young and scared and...alone she looked.

He gave his head one quick, hard shake. She didn't need coddling. She needed a swift kick in the ass. It was the only way to get her to straighten out. He was pissed and embarrassed and at the end of his rope with her. Just thinking about what she and Nate had been doing made him want to rail on that boy, shake some sense into her and then send her to a convent for the next twenty years or so.

"You can sit in the back of my squad car," he told her, taking her by the elbow again and leading her—carefully—back to the path. "And if you puke in there, you're cleaning it up."

She stopped, forcing him to halt midstride. "My phone."

"What about it?"

"I dropped it." With her free hand she gestured vaguely behind them. "Over there."

He started walking again, dragging her along. "Too bad."

She dug in her heels, tried peeling his fingers from her arm. "I have to find it! I need it."

"Then I guess you shouldn't have dropped it in the middle of the woods at night."

"Ow!" Jess cried suddenly. "Uncle Ross, stop. You're hurting me."

What the hell? "I'm barely touching—"

"I'm sorry." She started sobbing. Loudly. Loud enough for everyone in the clearing to hear. "I won't do it again. Please don't hurt me."

"Seriously?" he asked. "You're going to play games with me now?"

The radio at Ross's hip crackled to life. "Everything okay, Chief?" Sullivan asked.

With a sigh, Ross unhooked the radio, pressed the button to speak. "Everything's fine."

"You sure?" she asked, humor evident in her tone. "You need backup?"

"Negative," he ground out. "I'll be there in a minute." He put it back, never taking his eyes off Jess. "You should join drama club when school starts again. Put those acting skills to good use."

She lifted a shoulder, her expression smug. "I'm not leaving without my phone."

She was stubborn. Sneaky. Manipulative. And until she turned eighteen, she was his problem. His responsibility. And he had no idea how to handle her. Damn it.

"You have three minutes." He held out the flashlight so that it shone up, lighting their faces. She grabbed the bottom but he held on. "At the end of those three minutes, you're going to accompany me out of these woods willingly and, most important, quietly. Whether or not you've found your phone. Understand me?"

"Whatever," she muttered.

He let go of the flashlight and she staggered back toward where he'd first found her. And it hit him. He'd given in. She needed rules and discipline and to learn how to obey orders and he'd let her get her way because she'd caused a scene. Because it was easier than dealing with the drama she created.

He tapped his fingers against his radio. Glanced toward the clearing. Not that he could see anything other than the faint glow from the fire. He trusted Sullivan had the situation there under control. And was handling it how he wanted it.

"Time's up," Ross called. Jess had her head bent as she searched the area by a large evergreen. "Let's go."

"That wasn't three minutes."

"Sure it was. Come on." She didn't move, just held the flashlight so its beam was on the ground, her eyes downcast. Probably plotting other ways she could make his life difficult. "Jess. Now."

Still staring down, she slowly crouched and reached out her free hand only to snatch it back as if something had snapped at her. Made a sound like she'd been kicked in the stomach.

"Damn it, Jessica," he growled, picking his way through the thick undergrowth to stand over her. "Don't make me handcuff you and haul you out of here."

"Loo—look," she said in a strangled voice.

He followed her trembling, pointing finger to the end of the beam of light.

And the human skull half-hidden under a fallen log.

CHAPTER TWO

"KATY PERRY, HUH?" Layne asked, her pen poised over her notepad as she took in the petite blonde in front of her. "That really what you're going with? You don't want to try something a little more…oh, I don't know… creative? Like Amelia Earhart or Bette Davis or maybe Carly Simon?"

And by the blank look in the teen's eyes, she had no idea who any of those women were.

What did they teach kids in school these days?

"My name is Katy Perry," the girl insisted, lifting her adorable, turned-up nose.

"Have any proof of that?"

She shrugged, a bored expression on her pretty face. "I left my license at home."

"Uh-huh."

"I did." She added a foot stomp to go with her pouty tone. "I don't even care if you believe me or not. I'm telling the truth. I'm Katy Perry. Katy," she said, stretching the name out as if speaking to someone who'd recently been hit on the head with a rock. She looked pointedly at Layne's notebook. "Like…do you need some help spelling it? It's *K-A-T—*"

"Thanks, but I think I can sound the rest out."

Layne wrote the name down and put the notepad into her back pocket. A light breeze blew smoke into her eyes and picked up a few strands of hair that had escaped her ponytail. She smoothed them back. The wood pallets in the fire behind her crackled. Sparks shot into the night sky.

Chances were, the elderly gentlemen who'd called the station to report suspicious activity never would've known the kids were partying out here if they hadn't had flames reaching thirty feet high.

She glanced toward her squad car. Evan, his brown hair cropped close to his head, his dark blue uniform hanging on his thin shoulders, tried to calm down the pudgy brunette who'd been sobbing since they'd pulled into the clearing. Out of the six kids they'd corralled, only two had proof they were eighteen and both had passed the Breathalyzer, leaving the brunette, Nate and the other boy—with longish hair, baggy jeans and a T-shirt advertising the store where it'd been bought—standing in a row illuminated by her car's headlights. While the girl bawled, the boys wore similar smirks, Nate having found his cocky bluster upon returning to the company of his buddy.

Layne rubbed at the headache brewing behind her temple. Ah, the joys of youth. Rebellion. Recklessness. The certainty that nothing bad could ever happen. And the arrogance to believe that if, by some crazy coincidence you did get busted, an endless supply of smart-ass comments or, better yet, copious tears and hysteria, would get you out of trouble. All you had to do was stick with it long enough to wear down the dumb adult trying to force you to obey their archaic rules.

She and Evan were stuck dealing with two of the little darlings each—while their intrepid leader only had to take care of his niece.

"You know," she said conversationally to the blonde, "being a police officer means being able to read people and situations. For example, see that Audi over there? The red one?"

"What about it?" faux-Katy said in a snotty tone that reminded Layne of when her sister Tori had been sixteen. Come to think of it, Tori still used that tone with Layne.

"Well, if I had to hazard a guess, I'd say that car belongs to you."

"I never said that," the teenager said quickly.

"No, you didn't. But this is where my detecting skills come in real handy. You see, a car like that? It has 'you' written all over it." If only because it went so well with the girl's expensive, dark jeans, silk top—silk, at a bonfire in a quarry—and expertly applied highlights. But really, that silver Princess vanity plate gave it away most. "Which means that, since I've already written down the license plate number of every vehicle parked here, all I have to do is plug those numbers into my computer to find out who, exactly each vehicle is registered to. Katy."

The girl paled, her expression no longer quite so confident that she'd put one over on some stupid cop.

Layne bit back a smile. "You can rejoin your friends."

She did, but not before glaring at Layne as if she could incinerate her on the spot. Such was one of the consequences of being on the side of law and order.

Evan divided the teens, putting the girls into the back of Layne's cruiser, the boys in his, then walked toward Layne, his short hair sticking up on the side as if he'd run his fingers through it. Repeatedly.

"I didn't know someone could cry that much," he muttered, the fire casting shadows on his round cheeks. "At least not without becoming dehydrated or passing out from lack of oxygen."

"The human body is capable of many amazing and wondrous feats. Especially when helped along with massive quantities of alcohol."

"Do you think you should search for the chief? He's been gone awhile now. Maybe he got lost."

"It's been fifteen minutes," she said. "And how could he be lost? All he has to do is walk toward the lights."

"Maybe…" Evan ducked his head toward her. "Maybe something happened. You heard his niece scream. Maybe the chief…snapped."

Layne snorted. "He has too much control to snap. Besides, she's just messing with him."

But Evan was completely serious. Nervous. God, had she ever been that young? That earnest?

"How can you tell?" he asked.

"Let me explain it to you, grasshopper. Once, many moons ago, I was a teenage girl myself. Plus I raised my younger sisters who, at one time or another, were also teenage girls." And thank the dear Lord those years were over. "Believe me, that scream wasn't real."

It was a cry for help, though. One she doubted Chief Ross Taylor would heed.

Not her problem, she assured herself. She'd raised her sisters, had taken care of her family. She'd done her time.

"Captain?" Taylor's voice came through her radio as clearly as if he stood beside her.

"See?" she said to Evan as she unhooked the radio. She lifted it and clicked the talk button. "Yes, Chief?"

"Turn them loose."

Her jaw dropped. "Excuse me?"

"The kids. Give them a warning and let them go."

"And here I thought we were going by the precept of the law being black and white."

"Let. Them. Loose. Have Campbell escort anyone you suspect of drinking home. They are not to drive. Am I clear on that, Captain?"

"Crystal," she managed to say. As if either she or Evan would let some kid—or anyone else—get behind the wheel after they'd been drinking. "Anything else? Sir."

"I want Campbell to walk each child to their doors and make sure they are remanded into the custody of their parents. As soon as you've given him his orders, get back out here with me. Bring some flares, a blanket and a camera."

Flares? A blanket and camera? She could feel Evan watching her curiously. She flicked the radio's button. "Uh, Chief, I'm not sure what you think you and I are going to do with a blanket and a camera—"

He growled. The man literally growled at her. "Get out here. Now."

Yet one more item to add to his growing list of faults. No sense of humor.

When the radio remained silent for three heartbeats, she clipped it back to her belt. "You heard him," she told Evan. "We have our orders."

She helped Evan transfer the girls into his car, the brunette still sniffling. Poor Evan. Layne didn't envy his job, dealing with four teens and their parents.

But she did thank God—and Chief Taylor—she didn't have to do it.

She returned to her cruiser for a blanket, flares and the camera she kept in the trunk. Looping the camera's strap around her neck, she tucked the blanket under her arm, turned on her flashlight and headed back into the woods.

Whatever had happened must be big for "there's

right and there's wrong" Chief Taylor to let those kids go with a warning. Or maybe Evan had it right. Maybe spending so much time in a town so small it didn't even have a Starbucks, combined with his niece's wild ways and running a department of officers who didn't want him there, had finally gotten to Taylor and he'd cracked. At least enough to dislodge that stick he had up his ass.

Or maybe he decided to listen to her good sense on this one.

And that was as likely as Layne handing in her badge to follow in her father's footsteps. Or, even more impossible, her mother's.

Okay, maybe there had been plenty of times when she'd thought Chief Gorham should've been less... flexible...with the law. It was a danger having kids partying and then getting behind the wheel of whatever car mommy and daddy had bought for them.

So, no, she couldn't honestly say she didn't back Chief Taylor. She just wouldn't. Say it, that was. To him or anyone else. Not when she should be the one calling the shots, not some hotshot detective from Boston.

Twigs and dead leaves crunched under her boots as she approached the spot where she'd left the chief and his niece. Still a good fifty yards away, she heard them before she saw the glow of the chief's flashlight.

"—found it in the first place," the girl was saying, her words not quite as slurred as they'd been earlier.

"For the last time, you're not getting a reward," Taylor said gruffly. Impatiently. "Drop it."

"You suck," the girl snapped but underneath the bite in her tone, Layne heard the threat of tears. And wouldn't it be interesting to see how Taylor handled an angry, drunk, weeping teenager?

But he didn't handle it. He didn't make any response

at all. No attempt to either reprimand or soothe the girl. He continued searching the ground by the end of a fallen tree as if his niece hadn't even spoken. As if she wasn't even there.

No chance of this guy winning Uncle of the Year.

He must've heard Layne's approach because he turned, the light from his flashlight skimming over her before he lowered it. "We have a situation."

"I gathered." She stepped over a rock and handed him the flares. "What's up?"

He aimed his flashlight so the beam hit the ground at the end of the log. Illuminating a dirt-encrusted skull.

Layne's eyes widened. "Yes, I'd say that is definitely a situation." And not what she'd expected. Not in Mystic Point.

She knelt next to the skull, discerned it was human and, as far as she could tell in the dark, very real. Chills broke out on her forearms. "How'd you even see it?"

"Jess stumbled upon it looking for her phone."

"Which he's holding hostage," the girl—Jess—said, slouched on the far end of the log.

Taylor didn't even glance her way. "Not the time, Jessica."

Layne pulled her cell phone from her pocket. "I'll contact the state forensics lab…have them send a team out here."

"Already have one on the way. I've also contacted all available officers. We'll get some lights out here and start a search for the rest of the remains."

"I'm not staying while you hunt for more bones." Jess wrapped her arms around her legs, her entire body shaking. "I want to go."

"We will," Taylor said. "Soon."

"I'm cold," Jess whined in a tone guaranteed to make dogs howl. "And I don't feel good."

Taylor's jaw moved, as if he was grinding his teeth to powder. "Then I guess you shouldn't have been drinking." But he took the blanket and wrapped it around her shoulders. Surprise, surprise. Maybe he wasn't a heartless cyborg after all.

Jess shrugged him off, the blanket sliding to the ground. "I want to go home." Her voice cracked on the last word, her eyes shimmered with tears she tried to blink back. "Could you tell him to let me go home?" she asked Layne. "Please?"

Layne couldn't help it, though Jess had no one else to blame for the vomit on her clothes, the dirt in her hair, the drying blood on her knees—Layne's heart went out to the kid. She seemed so...lost.

Layne remembered that feeling entirely too well.

"I'm sure the chief will get you home as soon as he's finished here," Layne said, having no idea if that was true or not. God knew the new chief was an enigma. A frustrating one.

Jess's smirk was more sad than cocky as she laid her cheek on her knees. "Yeah, right."

Layne inclined her head meaningfully at Taylor then walked away, stopping next to a scraggly pine tree.

"Another problem, Captain?" he asked in the flat Boston accent that grated on her last nerve.

Though it was past midnight he was, as always, clean-shaven, his flat stomach a testament to his refusal to indulge when one of their coworkers brought in doughnuts. His dark blond hair was clipped close to the sides and back of his head, the top just long enough to start to curl. He had a high forehead, thick eyebrows and eyes the color of fog over the water.

The private, female part of her admitted he was attractive—in an earthy, overtly male way.

The cop in her resented the hell out of him for it.

"If you want to run her home," she said quietly, "I can get things moving here."

"She doesn't want to go home—to the house we're renting. She wants to go back to Boston."

"Oh." She had nothing else to add to that. Didn't want to get involved in his family problems. "Still, I have this under control if you want to get her out of here."

"You ever handle a case like this?"

She rolled her shoulders back like a fighter preparing to enter the ring. "Not exactly like this. No."

"You get a lot of missing persons' cases in Mystic Point?"

"People don't go missing from Mystic Point." Although plenty of them left. "But this isn't some Utopia. We have our share of crime, including battery, burglary, rape and occasionally, murder. All of which I have investigated."

"Still, I think I'll take the lead on this one."

And then he walked away.

Layne curled her fingers into her palms and followed, her steps jerky, the camera bouncing against her chest. "Is it because I'm a woman?" she called.

He picked up a flare, lit it then stuck it in the ground, his back to her the entire time. "You're going to have to be more specific."

She stopped behind him, her fists on her hips. "You want specific, sir, how about this. Is the reason you're not handing this case over to me—the only detective on third shift, your second-in-command and the person who should be assigned it—because I don't have a penis?"

"He's a total misogynist," Jess said with the exaggerated seriousness only the inebriated could pull off.

They both ignored her.

Taylor straightened slowly, the flare casting an orange glow over the hard lines of his face. "Tread carefully, Captain, or you might overstep."

But she'd never been one to play it safe. Bad enough he'd come into her town and taken the position she was meant to have, now he wanted to screw with how she did her job?

"I don't think it's overstepping to clear the air, Chief. So let's lay it on the line, right here, right now. You have something against having a woman on your force? Or maybe it's just me you have a problem with?"

Lights flashed, bounced off the trees as a car drove toward the quarry but Taylor didn't take his attention off her. She wanted to say having his cool gray eyes watching her so intently didn't unnerve her but she'd never been a good liar.

"The decisions I make as chief aren't personal." She didn't doubt he used that placid tone because it made her seem out of control in comparison. "I assign cases based on experience and expertise." He stepped closer. "You don't have to like how I run this police department," he added softly. "You don't even have to agree with me, but if you feel the need to question every decision I make, perhaps the Mystic Point Police Department is no longer the right place for you."

Her vision blurred, her throat burned. "Is that your oh-so-subtle way of threatening my job?"

He moved closer, so close she picked up a hint of his spicy aftershave, felt the warmth from his big body.

"For over a month you've fought me, skated the line of insubordination—"

"Hey now—"

"And have generally been nothing but a pain in my ass." How he kept any and all emotion from his voice, she had no idea. But she almost respected him for his control. Almost. "Now, you can continue along that path and force me to take action. Or you can accept that I'm now in charge and start working with me. So, no, I'm not making threats against your job." He tipped his head close to hers, his breath caressing her cheek. "I'm giving you the choice of what happens next."

By 5:00 A.M., ROSS'S EYES were gritty, his fingers tingling with cold and his head aching. He walked toward his cruiser, the rising sun's rays reflecting off the large rocks surrounding the water, turning the sky pink and gold. The damp air smelled of burned wood and dirt.

Once the forensics unit from the state had arrived on scene around 2:00 a.m., Ross had coordinated the search for more remains. It hadn't taken long and by three, they'd found badly decomposed bones near the area where Jess had discovered the skull.

Now, the remains were on their way to the state's lab for testing while Campbell and Patrick Forbes, one of the department's part-time officers, packed up the spotlights. Sergeant James Meade, a middle-aged man with thinning hair and a perpetual jovial expression that hid what Ross had already deduced was a keen cop's mind, stood talking with Sullivan by the still-smoldering ashes of last night's fire.

Ross lifted his hand, indicating he was leaving. Meade, taking a sip from his take-out cup of coffee, nodded. Sullivan kept her gaze on the ground. With his free hand, Ross pulled his cell phone from his pocket and hit speed dial. Jess's phone rang. And rang. He tucked the phone between his ear and shoulder and opened his car door, tossed the evidence bag onto the seat.

His call went to voice mail. "It's me," he said. "Call me."

Not that she would. Ever since he'd been granted custody of his niece, she'd been nothing if not steadfast in her determination to do anything and everything in her power to make his life more difficult.

He glanced back at Sullivan. Sort of like someone else he knew.

He just hoped neither one ever figured out what a good job they were doing of it.

He tried the house phone. No answer. Damn it. He needed to get the necklace they'd found near the body—the one piece of concrete evidence they had—back to the station so it could be processed. He could ask Meade to do it. Or, he could bite the bullet and do what he should've done in the first place.

"Sullivan?" he called. "Do you have a minute?"

"Can it wait until we get back to the station, Chief?"

Christ, but nothing was easy with her. Not even a simple request. "No, Captain, it can't."

Her mouth thinned but after saying something to Meade, she started toward Ross, taking her sweet time getting there. He bit back on his impatience. His edginess. Edginess she caused with her constant antagonism and smart-ass mouth. With her slow, saunter and the determined, confrontational glint in her hazel eyes.

Her dark ponytail swung behind her, the light blue, MPPD-issued windbreaker she'd put on at some point during the past four hours blowing open over her uniform. Showing the sway of her hips, how her breasts bounced under the loose material.

Interest, male and elemental, stirred. He hissed out a breath through his teeth. Shit. He must be more tired than he thought.

"Yes?" she said when she finally reached him, her tone belligerent, dark circles under her eyes.

"Jessica's not answering her phone."

She raised her eyebrows. "You let her have her phone back?"

Warmth crawled up his neck. He refused to call it embarrassment. "So I could get ahold of her. Yes."

"Uh-huh. And how's that working out for you?"

His jaw tightened. He was tired, cold and hungry. And in no mood to, once again, get into it with his most abrasive officer. "You took her home?"

"As per your orders."

"And you saw her go inside?"

"No. I pushed her out of the car as I drove past," Sullivan said dryly. "But don't worry, I told her to tuck and roll when she hit the ground." When he just stared, she sighed. "I walked her inside myself. I'm sure she's fine. She's probably sleeping it off. Besides, from what I saw, she threw up most of what she'd had to drink. And possibly a kidney."

He stiffened. "I fail to see the humor in that particular situation."

Sullivan waved at Meade as the sergeant drove away. "Yeah, well, a sense of humor comes in awfully handy when dealing with teenagers. Keeps you from losing your mind. And it has the added benefit of pissing them off. Win-win."

He tipped his head side to side but the tension in his

neck remained. "All I have to do is talk to Jess and she gets pissed at me."

Why the hell had he admitted that? He didn't share his thoughts easily, especially with a subordinate officer. Better to keep work and his personal life separate.

"I realize your shift is over in—" He checked his watch. "Less than five minutes, but I need you to take the evidence to the station to be processed."

"If you're really worried about her, I can call a friend of mine who's an EMT. I'm sure he'd be happy to stop by and check on Jess."

"That won't be necessary," he said more gruffly than he intended. "Besides, I'm not worried she's slipped into an alcohol-induced coma or succumbed to alcohol poisoning. I want to make sure she hasn't taken off again resulting in me wasting time going after her, not to mention pulling my concentration from this case."

Like she was doing now.

Sullivan's mouth turned down. "Wow. That's really…" She shook her head. "Never mind."

He almost asked her to finish her sentence. But he could easily guess what she'd been about to say and he didn't need to hear her low opinion on his guardianship skills. Not when his parents had warned him he'd be in over his head if he took Jessica on.

But she needed him. He had to save her. Somehow.

If he didn't end up strangling her first.

"After you drop off the evidence," he told Sullivan, "I'd like you to check the missing persons' files, see if any are still open."

She smiled tightly. "And here I thought you'd stick me behind a desk so I could field more questions from the press for the duration of this investigation."

In Boston, the press meant reporters from various

media outlets: TV, newspapers, radio and magazines. All vying for a quote, a new side to the story they could run with, the more sensational the better.

Fortunately the *Mystic Times* had only sent one reporter out to the quarry last night. And he'd seemed more than happy to hang around all night, flirting with Sullivan instead of digging for information about the human remains found outside of town.

Because the paper went to press shortly after midnight and printed a morning edition, the story wouldn't break until tomorrow. Although Sullivan had warned him—in her you-don't-know-anything-about-small-towns-and-don't-belong-here way—that everyone in Mystic Point would hear about it by lunchtime anyway.

"As I understand it," he said mildly, "you've been MPPD's liaison to the press and the public since you were first hired."

She held Ross's gaze, her hip cocked to the side. "Been studying my personnel records, Chief?"

"Just doing things the way Chief Gorham did them. Isn't that what you want?" While he paused to let that sink in, her mouth opened. Then shut.

And if the sight of her finally being rendered momentarily speechless gave him a strong sense of satisfaction, no one had to know.

"Okay, you got me. Things weren't perfect under Chief Gorham. But at least he trusted us to do our jobs."

Damn, but she was stubborn. And, in this instance, possibly right.

Besides, he'd made his point. No need to drive it home with a hammer over her head.

"Fair enough," he said, earning himself one of her suspicious glares. "After you drop off the evidence, why don't you take a few hours, grab a nap and a bite to eat. We'll meet back at the station at eleven for a debriefing."

"A debriefing?" Sullivan asked as if Ross had told her to bring a bikini, a case of whipped cream and her handcuffs and meet him at a motel. "What type of debriefing?"

"The kind that will give me a chance to present the facts—as we know them now—about this case to the detective working on it with me." Now she looked shocked. Good.

"Let me get this straight. You're putting me on this case?" He nodded. "Why?"

"Because you were right. You should be in charge of it." He'd let his animosity and irritation toward her goad him into letting his personal feelings dictate his professional decisions.

And personal feelings had no place on the job. Ever.

He leaned into the car, reaching across the seat for the box of plastic gloves. He put one on and straightened, the evidence bag in his other hand. "The sooner we're on the same page, the sooner we can start investigating who this person was, how she—or he—died and came to be out here. And hopefully this will point us in the right direction."

This being a tarnished, dirty silver chain that could've belonged to anyone, which wasn't going to make their job any easier. Using his gloved hand, he pulled it from the bag. The charms—three small, intricately scrolled hearts, one in the center of a larger, open heart, the other two on either side—glinted in the sun.

Sullivan made a sound, somewhere between a gasp and a whimper, her hand going to her chest before she lowered it again, her fingers curled into her palm.

"Something wrong?" Ross asked, frowning.

"No." But her face was white, her voice thin. Uncertain. She cleared her throat. "It just…hit me. What we're dealing with. We've had homicides before, usually related to bar fights or occasionally domestic violence but…" She shook her head slowly. "Nothing like this. Where…where did you say the necklace was found?"

"Close to the skull."

"But it could be that it doesn't actually belong to our victim. Maybe the victim stole it or someone lost it. Someone not connected to the victim."

"Anything's possible but it's highly doubtful. Besides, at the moment this—" he dropped the necklace back into the bag before handing it to her "—is our only clue to our victim's identity. And once we discover who she was, we can focus on finding out who killed her."

LAYNE'S HEAD SNAPPED BACK as if Taylor had slapped her. His eyes, always watchful, never missing a freaking beat, narrowed. Studied her. Trying to figure out what she was hiding from him. What she hadn't told him.

Oh, God.

"You sure you're all right, Captain?"

"Yeah. Sorry. Just tired. I'll head back to the station. Get this processed." And because she didn't want to sound as if she couldn't wait to get away from him, she didn't move. "Unless there was something else you need me to do?"

"No. That should cover it." He took off the glove and tossed it onto the seat. "If you need me before eleven, call my cell."

"Yes, sir." Keeping her stride unhurried, she walked toward her cruiser, her pulse drumming in her ears. She kept the bag pressed against her chest with both hands, the plastic slippery against her damp palms.

"Sullivan?"

Her breath caught. Fear enveloped her, coated her skin in a thin sheen of sweat. She licked her lips and faced him, her eyebrows raised in question.

She prayed he couldn't see how unsteady her hands were.

He jingled the keys in his hand. "Good job last night."

The air left her lungs making speech impossible so she nodded. She'd overheard him say the same thing to the other officers who'd worked the scene but having him say it to her stunned her.

Almost as much as it scared her.

She didn't want to care what he thought of her or how she did her job. Couldn't afford to change her mind about him. Not now.

She went around to the trunk and pretended to organize the items back there. Chief Taylor sat behind the wheel of his patrol car, his head bent. The engine was running but he didn't seem in any hurry to leave.

It was all Layne could do not to press herself against his back bumper and start pushing.

Finally, thankfully, he pulled away.

She lurched to the open passenger-side door of her car and collapsed onto the seat. Lowering her head between her knees, she breathed deeply, battling the sense of urgency, of panic spiking in her blood. She squeezed the top of the bag, her nails digging into her palm through the plastic.

Tears blurred her vision but she refused to let them fall. She couldn't cry, couldn't afford that weakness or that luxury. She had a case to solve.

Her head still down, she stared at the necklace.

And wished she didn't recognize it.

CHAPTER THREE

"I DON'T KNOW HOW the Boston P.D. does things," Ross's secretary Donna Holliday said in her precise tone, "but in Mystic Point we tend to start our workday at 8:00 a.m. Sharp."

Ross tucked his cell phone between his ear and shoulder as he climbed out of his car and shut the door. Donna, like the car, the beat-up metal desk in his office and the animosity from his entire department, had come with the police-chief position.

He'd love nothing more than to give all of them back.

"I'll be there in fifteen minutes," he told Donna, deciding not to mention how he'd been working all night—which she damn well knew—because she'd probably point out how most of the department had been up all night and were already at work. "Twenty, tops."

"Better stick with fifteen. Between that body popping up and you busting a kiddie party, we've been inundated with calls and visitors. We've had everyone from conspiracy theorists who are certain the bones belong to Jimmy Hoffa, to parents calling for your badge for having their little darlings brought home in a police car. And if that's not enough to light a fire under your rear—"

"As always, I'm astounded by your professionalism," he said dryly.

"The mayor's assistant called," she continued, ignoring him—nothing new there, "to say His Honor will be gracing us with his presence at nine sharp."

"Fine. Fifteen minutes."

He ended the call, slid the phone into his pocket and jogged up the steps to the back door, the bushy, overgrown shrubs on either side of the stairs scratching his arms. Inside, he tossed his keys on the counter and headed straight to the refrigerator. Mustard, ketchup, a carton of eggs he didn't remember buying, milk and leftover pizza from two nights ago. Or was it three?

With a shrug, he pulled out the box, grabbed the slice inside and bit into it. And almost ripped his teeth out in the process. Definitely three nights ago.

He took another bite as he hurried upstairs to his bedroom. Holding the pizza in his mouth, he stripped off his shirt and tossed it toward the open hamper in the corner of the room where it landed on the edge to dangle by a sleeve. He took out the last uniform shirt in his closet and shoved his arms in, leaving it hanging open while he finished his breakfast.

He needed groceries. And to throw a couple of loads of laundry in the washing machine. The yard hadn't been mowed in two weeks. He threw the pizza crust into the plastic garbage can next to his bed and buttoned his shirt. He'd put them all on his To-Do List, right after Identify Remains, Solve Mystery of Yet Unknown Person's Death and Straighten Out Rebellious Niece.

At least he could cross one item off this morning—though it was the last thing on the list he wanted to tackle.

Tucking in his shirt, he went out into the hall. Jessica's bedroom door, as usual, was closed, the whiteboard hanging off it sporting her flowing script in red: *Abandon hope all ye who enter here.*

Ross squeezed the back of his neck. Guess a Keep Out sign would be too subtle.

He knocked. "Jess?" Nothing. No sound of any kind from the room. He tapped his forehead against the door several times. He really didn't have time for his niece's games. Lifting his head, he used the side of his fist to pound against the wood. "Jess! Open the door."

Still nothing. Trying the lock, he raised his eyebrows when it turned easily. As with it usually being closed, the door was also often locked. He opened it wide enough to see inside. Sunlight filtered through the slats of the blinds covering the two windows, illuminating a lump on the single bed.

"Get up," he said, flipping on the overhead light. Jess stirred then snuggled deeper into her pillow. Ross shoved the door open. It hit the wall with a resounding bang.

Jessica jackknifed into a sitting position with a gasp. Breathing heavily she twisted from side to side as if to locate what had woken her. She shoved her tangled, dirty hair from her eyes and blinked rapidly.

Ross leaned against the doorjamb. "Good morning, sunshine."

She hit the bed with both hands. "What is wrong with you? Were you raised by psychopaths or something?"

"Is that any way to talk about your papa and Grammy?" And if his active, sixty-year-old mother ever heard him call her Grammy, she'd hit him upside the head with her tennis racket. "It's time to get up."

"It's not even nine!"

"From now on, you'll be up and out of bed each

morning by eight," he said, kicking clothes out of his way as he crossed the floor to one of the windows. He opened the blinds. "Which shouldn't be a problem since your new bedtime is 9:00 p.m."

"You're kidding," she said flatly.

"Not even a little." He opened the second set of blinds and she winced, holding her hands up like some vampire trying to ward off the brightness.

Going by how many times she'd puked last night, she probably had one hell of a hangover. She groaned and flopped back onto the bed, one arm covering her eyes, her face pale. Sweat dotted her upper lip, dampened the hair along her forehead. Sympathy stirred. If he was a good uncle, a more caring guardian, he wouldn't want her to suffer. Would offer her pain meds to stop the pounding in her head. Ginger ale to soothe the dryness of her mouth and ease the churning in her stomach.

A good uncle wouldn't think she'd gotten exactly what she deserved for not only disobeying him and breaking the law, but following in her mother's footsteps.

He stood at the foot of her bed, his hands on the curved wooden footboard. "You have piss-poor decision-making skills, no sense of right and wrong and way too much unstructured free time."

She lowered the arm from her face. "Go. Away."

"And while I can't do anything about the first two, I'm taking control of the third." He checked his watch, saw he had less than ten minutes to get to the station. If he used his lights and siren, he could make it there in three. "Which is why today you will mow the grass, sweep and mop the kitchen floor and do the laundry. And since all that shouldn't take long, you can also clean out the garage."

"Screw you," she spat. "I'm not your servant."

"This isn't about servitude. It's about taking responsibility and doing your fair share around your home."

"This isn't a home. It's a prison!"

Ross scratched the side of his neck. Sweet God but she was as dramatic and rebellious as her mother had been at that age. And he was as clueless now as he'd been then as an eighteen-year-old watching his kid sister spiral out of control.

"Fine." You couldn't argue with certain segments of people. Stoners, sociopaths and teenagers. None of them listened to reason. "It's a prison. And after today it's going to be a clean prison with a neatly mowed yard."

"That's why you took me in, isn't it? So you could have someone to clean up after you."

His jaw tightened. He didn't expect much from her. Obedience. Respect. Maybe a bit of gratitude for how he'd rearranged his entire life for her.

He'd settle for one out of three, and at this point, he didn't even care which one it was.

"I took you in," he pointed out, "because it was the right thing to do. And because you had nowhere else to go."

Her lower lip trembled. Great. What the hell had he said now?

Before he could figure it out, her mouth flattened and she went back to glaring at him as if she wanted to carve his heart out with a spoon.

"After you're done with the chores I've assigned you," he said, "you are to spend the afternoon pounding the pavement."

She pressed both hands against her head. Probably trying to keep it from exploding. "What?"

He headed toward the door. "Get a job."

She scrambled onto her knees, tugging the material of her oversize T-shirt out from under her. "It's summer vacation."

"It's summer," he agreed, his hand on the handle as he stood in the doorway, "but vacation time for you is over. Working will help you realize what it's like out there in the real world. Plus, last night's little adventure proved how much you need some structure to your life."

"You should be thanking me instead of being such a di—"

"Careful," he warned darkly.

"—douche bag," she spat. Not exactly a term of respect but better than what she'd started to call him. "I found that body," she pointed out. "If it wasn't for me, you never would've even known it was out there."

This must be why some animals ate their young. So they didn't turn into teenagers.

"Part of the reason we moved here was so you could get a fresh start. Instead you snuck out of the house and disobeyed my direct order not to engage in any reckless or criminal activity." Though his hand tensed on the handle, he kept his voice mild. "But you're right about one thing. If it wasn't for you, I wouldn't know about the body. If it wasn't for you, I'd still be in Boston, not trying so damned hard to make things work for us here."

She looked so stricken he immediately wished he could take his words back. That he could tell her he didn't mean them. But while Jessica was rebellious and mouthy, she was also bright and had a way of seeing through people's bullshit. No way she'd buy an apology from him. One he wasn't even sure he'd mean.

He cleared his throat. "I'll be home for dinner at six. Seven," he amended, figuring he'd have to put in a hellishly long day. "Be here."

He stepped into the hall and had no sooner closed the door when something hit the other side of it with a loud crash. He tipped his head back and blew out a heavy breath. He didn't know if he'd ever be able to get through to her. If he'd ever be able to save her from herself.

Some days he wondered why he even bothered trying.

LAYNE BACKED INTO HER SPOT in the police station's paved parking lot. She stepped out of her cruiser only to reach back in for her aviators. The dark lenses hiding her eyes, she shut them long enough for the edginess in her stomach to smooth out. For her nerves to calm and her scattered thoughts to settle.

She doubted herself, the decisions she'd made, which she'd never done before. Couldn't afford to do now. So she stood there, the bright, midmorning sun warming the top of her head as she inhaled deeply, the familiar briny scent of the sea filling her senses. She held her breath. When she exhaled, she opened her eyes and strode toward the entrance as if her moment of weakness had never happened.

She didn't do weak. She had too many people depending on her. Counting on her to take care of them.

Sure, sometimes she wondered what it would be like to worry only about herself. To put her own needs first without thought or care for anyone else. To be manipulative and selfish and egocentric.

Like her mother.

But she was so much stronger than Valerie Sullivan had ever been. So much better.

And if she kept telling herself that, if she pretended that this morning had never happened, that she'd never seen that necklace, maybe she'd actually start believing it.

For the first time in her life, she had no idea what was real and what was fiction. What if her suspicions were right? What if the past eighteen years were nothing but a lie? Worse, what if she was to blame?

She pressed her lips together and yanked open the door so she could step into the dimly lit, cool hallway. No. It wasn't her fault. None of it was. The blame lay with one and only one person—Valerie. All Layne had ever done was keep her family from falling apart.

She'd keep doing it. No matter what.

Before turning the corner that would take her to the squad room, Layne stopped long enough to crack the knuckles of each finger then shook her hands out. Her expression composed so none of her doubts, her guilt, showed, she entered the room and went straight to the desk she'd kept despite her promotion a year ago.

Across from her, Jimmy Meade glanced up from where he pecked at the keyboard of his computer. He frowned. "I thought you were going home to get cleaned up."

"I got sidetracked," she said, hooking her foot around her chair leg and pulling it out. As she sat, she felt him watching her. "What?"

He leaned back in his chair, linked his hands together on his protruding stomach—now half the size it had been thanks to his wife insisting he cut back on the sweets in case the new chief decided to fire anyone who could no longer fit into their uniform. "You have something on your mind?"

Her throat clogged. Jimmy had always been on her side, from the moment she'd first been hired. One of her uncle Kenny's old school buddies, he'd kept an eye out for her, mentored her. And she was about to look him in the eye and lie.

God, she hated this.

"Nope." She booted up her computer, watched the monitor as if her next breath depended on her wallpaper—a picture of her nephew Brandon in his baseball uniform—loading properly. "Any new developments in the case?"

"Haven't heard of anything." He straightened and reached for his favorite coffee cup. "Chief's been in a meeting with the mayor for almost an hour now."

Whatever happened in town, Mayor Seagren wanted to be involved.

"It must be my birthday," Evan breathed as he came in from the break room—obviously the chief had him working overtime, too. "Because I'm about to get a present." He nodded toward the double glass doors that overlooked the foyer.

The foyer where Layne's sister Tori laughed at something Officer Wilber—currently manning the booth—said, her head back. All the better to show off her long, graceful neck.

"Oh, I am not in the mood for this," Layne muttered as Tori sort of…slinked…toward the squad room, a plastic take-out box in her hand. Then again, her black skirt was so tight—and short—normal walking was probably out of the question. And how she waited tables all day in those strappy, high-heeled sandals, Layne had no idea.

Thankfully Tori's bad attitude and questionable fashion sense weren't Layne's problems anymore.

Just a few of the many crosses she had to bear.

"For God's sake, have some pride," Layne told Evan. The kid was practically drooling. "And you—" She turned to Jimmy. "You're a happily married man. And a grandfather."

He didn't even have the grace to look abashed that he'd been caught gawking. "Carrie and I have an agreement. I can look all I want. And she pretends I have a chance in hell of letting some beautiful young woman steal me away from her."

Evan scrambled off his desk and practically tripped over his own feet to open the door. "Morning, Tori," he said, sounding like a chipmunk going through puberty.

"Good morning," Tori said, all bright and shiny as a new penny. "Hey, was that you I saw out on Old Boat Road a few days ago?" she asked Evan. "I didn't know you had a bike."

"It's not a bike," Jimmy and Layne said together, repeating what Evan had told them repeatedly. "It's a Harley."

"And his mom bought it for him," Jimmy added.

Evan flushed. "She loaned me the down payment. That's all."

"A Harley?" Tori asked, seemingly impressed. Though with her, you never knew what was truth and what was for show. She shook back her dark, chin-length hair and winked at him. "Moving up to the big leagues, huh? Who knows what you'll be ready to tackle next."

"Okay," Layne said, pushing her chair back and standing, "I just threw up in my mouth a little, so if you don't mind could you please play Cougar and Innocent Cub somewhere else? We're trying to work here."

"That's why I'm here. I heard you pulled an all-nighter out at the quarry." She raised the take-out container. "Thought you all could use some sugar to help get you through the rest of the morning."

Layne picked up a pencil from her desk. Squeezed it. "You heard about that?"

"About the body?" Tori set the box on Layne's desk and flipped up the top exposing neatly packaged blueberry scones and cinnamon rolls. "Sure. It's all everyone's been able to talk about."

Tori worked as a waitress at the Ludlow Street Café, Mystic Point's most popular restaurant.

Layne scraped at the paint on the pencil with her thumbnail. "Really?" she asked, keeping her voice neutral. "I figured it'd take at least until lunchtime for word to get around."

Tori stepped aside while Jimmy helped himself to both a scone and cinnamon roll. "In this town? Please. People are already taking bets about who it is."

Jimmy harrumphed but Layne's blood ran cold.

"Who...who do they think it is?" she couldn't help asking.

Jimmy shot her a questioning look but she ignored it, watching her sister's face, so similar to her own, carefully. If Tori suspected, Layne couldn't tell. Then again, her sister had always been excellent at hiding her true feelings.

"Most people think it's that hiker that went missing a few years back," Tori said, picking up Layne's nameplate then setting it back down. "A couple people insist it's the gangbanger who escaped prison back in '08. Me, I have ten bucks on the hiker theory."

"It wasn't a hiker," Evan said around a mouthful of scone. He swallowed. "The body was found—"

"I hadn't realized we were at liberty to discuss an ongoing investigation," Layne snapped.

Evan looking at her as if she'd slashed the tires of his

new Harley only made her feel crappier. Perfect. She sighed. "What do you want?" she asked Tori.

Her sister laid a hand over her heart. "Can't a grateful citizen bring a few treats to Mystic Point's finest without being accused of wanting something in return?"

"A grateful citizen can, sure. But you? No."

"That hurts." She hitched a hip onto Layne's desk, causing her skirt to rise up, showing several more inches of her toned, tanned thigh.

"Get your ass off my desk before I'm forced to arrest you for indecent exposure," Layne said. "And if that's what you wear to work, Celeste needs to seriously consider instituting a dress code at the café. It is a family restaurant after all."

Tori slowly slid to her feet, her grin razor-sharp. "Funny, but no one else complains about my clothing." She looked down at Layne—only because those stupid shoes of hers added several inches to her height—and sneered. "At least mine are clean."

Layne didn't have to glance down at herself to know she had a streak of dried mud running from her right shoulder to her left hip. Or that her shirt was wrinkled and she had still-damp mud stains on both knees. "Yes, well, searching for human remains is a messy job. Unlike pouring coffee."

"You have a dead leaf in your hair."

Layne reached up and…yep…sure enough, found a leaf. She picked it out of her hair and let it float into the trash can. "Well, since you've done your good deed for the day and all, I guess you'll be wanting to get on your way. I'm getting a soda." She'd kill for some sugar and caffeine and she was afraid Tori would end up being her victim. "You want anything?" she asked Jimmy.

He lifted the last bite of his cinnamon roll. "I'm good."

She picked out a scone. "Thanks for dropping by," she said to Tori.

She circled her desk and walked down the short hallway to the break room. She'd no sooner popped the tab on her Coke when Tori came in.

She should've known her sister wouldn't get the hint and go on her merry way. Tori was nothing if not stubborn. One of the few traits they shared.

"Can we expect the pleasure of your company tonight?" Tori asked. "Or are you planning on skipping it like you did last year?"

Crap. Now was probably not the time to admit she'd been so caught up in the investigation and the necklace that she'd forgotten today was Brandon's twelfth birthday.

"I didn't skip anything," she said, adding ice to a plastic cup and pouring in half the soda. Took a long drink. "I was working. Just like I'll be working tonight." But she hated missing her nephew's party. "Tell Brandon we'll head into Boston sometime next month." When, hopefully, her life would be settled again. When any and all investigation into the remains would be long completed. "Catch a Red Sox game."

"I'll do that. You know," Tori said, one hand on her cocked hip, the other gesturing to Layne's hair. "It wouldn't kill you to use a brush once in a while. Especially since you have a new boss to impress and all."

She bit into the scone. "I'm not out to impress anyone."

"Obviously," Tori drawled, staring pointedly at the crumbs collecting on Layne's shirt.

Layne brushed them away. "What. Do. You. Want."

Tori fluttered her eyelashes. "Your black boots."

Layne slowly set her cup on the table. "You want my black boots? My designer, over-the-knee, cost-me-an-entire-paycheck black boots?"

"Just for tomorrow night. Randy Parker's taking me out to dinner and your boots would be perfect with this great little black dress I—"

"No."

"Why not?"

"How about because it's the middle of summer? Or hey, how about because you shouldn't be dating already. The ink on your divorce papers is barely dry."

Tori inhaled sharply. "First of all, I hardly think I'm going to take fashion advice from a woman who hasn't worn lipstick in over ten years and usually dresses like a man."

"I don't dress like a man. I dress like a cop." As the only woman on the force, she had to work twice as hard to be accepted. To be treated as an equal. To prove herself. And if that meant forgoing makeup and jewelry, then so be it. She'd gladly shove beauty off a steep cliff if it meant she'd be taken seriously at her job.

"Secondly," Tori continued as if Layne hadn't spoken—she'd always been good at ignoring things she didn't want to hear, "my divorce was final six months ago. Six months. And obviously Greg didn't get your little memo about the proper amount of time between divorcing and dating since he's been seeing Colleen Gibbs for over a month now."

"And whose fault is that? You're the one who let him go."

Tori edged closer until they were toe-to-toe. "My marriage, my divorce and my decisions, are just that. Mine."

"Maybe, but you aren't the only one affected by your decisions. Or did you plan on taking Brandon along on your date?"

"Brandon will be at his father's house tomorrow night. God! What is your problem?"

"You want to know what my problem is?" Layne asked, her voice rising despite her best effort to keep her rioting emotions under control. She tried to hold back but the words poured out of her, fueled by her anger and resentment. Her fears. "You, Tori. You're my problem. You and your selfish attitude. All you care about, all you've ever cared about is yourself. You were tired of being married so you got a divorce. You want to date so you leave your son with his father so you can go out and have a good time."

Tori's eyes, light brown like their mother's, narrowed dangerously. "I'm not leaving him on the side of the highway sixty miles outside of town. It's Greg's weekend to have him. Why shouldn't I go out and enjoy myself?"

"Because you're a mother," Layne cried, tossing her hands into the air. "You need to think about what's best for Brandon, do what's right for him."

"Don't you ever—" Tori jabbed her finger at Layne, stopping a hairbreadth from drilling a hole into her chest "—ever accuse me of not putting my son first."

Layne laughed harshly. "You've never put anyone first but yourself. Your wants. Your needs. I mean, a prime example is how you were with Evan. Flirting with a kid who's ten years younger than you, all for what? So you can feel good about yourself? So you can pretend you're special? The way you dress…how you act… You're…" She snapped her lips shut and shook her head in disgust.

"I'm what? A tramp? A slut?" Tori's voice was low. Shaky. But under the tremble, Layne heard the resolve that told her to step carefully.

She heard it. She just chose to ignore it.

She was terrified. Scared of what the next few days would bring and while she and Tori weren't exactly close in the best of circumstances, their snarky spats rarely took on this edge. She should shut up. Better yet, she needed to apologize. Blame the stress and her going over twenty-four hours without sleep for making her so bitchy.

But she couldn't. Not when Tori stood there pushing Layne's buttons simply by wearing her snug, revealing clothes and a bring-it-on smirk.

"Worse," she said, meeting her sister's eyes unflinchingly. "You're just like our mother."

CHAPTER FOUR

THE ARGUMENT IN THE break room grew louder and, from what Ross could tell as he stormed toward the room, more heated.

Meade stood. "Chief, I don't think—"

Ross didn't even slow, just held up a hand. The other man shut his mouth and sat back down.

Smart call.

As he opened the door, Ross heard the unmistakable sound of a splash and a gasp.

Then Sullivan said in her husky voice, "Truth hurts, doesn't it?"

"Go to hell," a woman snapped as he stepped inside.

After a beat of stunned silence, Sullivan—wiping liquid from her face with both hands—noticed him. "Perfect," she snapped. "Just freaking perfect."

"Ladies." Behind him, he heard the scrape of chairs and then footsteps as Meade and Campbell maneuvered closer in the hopes of catching part of the upcoming conversation. Ross shut the door and spoke quietly, hoping it would encourage the women to do the same. "Is there a problem here?"

Sullivan used her inner forearm to wipe soda from her chin. Her shoulders were rigid, her face white except for two bright spots of color high on her cheeks. Damp hair clung to the sides of her neck and the front of her shirt was soaked.

"Everything's dandy," she said stiffly.

Ross glanced from her to the life-size brunette Barbie, and back to Sullivan again. The resemblance between them was striking. Though Sullivan's face was clean of any paint and the other woman's features were made up—smoky eyes, slick red lips—the shade of their dark hair, the shapes of their mouths and the sharp angle of their jaws were the same. They were both tall and had legs that went on forever. And they were both seriously pissed off, with neither showing any sign of backing down.

He inclined his head toward the other woman. "Your sister?"

Sullivan's mouth pinched. "One of them."

"Tell me, Captain, how is it you thought having a family argument in my police department was a good idea?"

Sullivan pulled her shoulders back causing the damp material of her top to hug the curve of her breasts. "We weren't arguing. Sir."

"No? Because not five minutes ago I was three doors down in my office with Mayor Seagren discussing the department's—" he flicked a gaze at the civilian "—current investigation—"

"Is 'current investigation' official cop code for the body discovered out at the quarry?" the sister asked. "Because half the town already knows about it."

Another similarity between the women. Their smart mouths.

"—when we were interrupted by shouting coming from this room. Care to explain that?"

She pursed her lips for a moment, as if considering his question. "No, sir, I don't."

He pinched the bridge of his nose. Turned his attention to her sister. "And you are…?"

"Leaving." But when she stepped toward the door, he shifted to block her exit. She jammed her fists onto her hips. "Really?"

"Ma'am, are you aware of what the penalty is for assaulting a police officer?" he asked.

She shook her hair back. "Nope. But say…how long do they send you away for tossing a carbonated beverage in a cop's face? Five years? Ten?" She waved her hand as if wiping it all away. "Whatever it is, it was worth it."

"There was no assault," Sullivan said, shooting her sister a warning glare. "I apologize for our behavior and any embarrassment it may have caused the department."

Not the most sincere apology he'd ever heard but it would do. "Next time you decide to have a family disagreement, do so outside of work. Being a good cop means being able to keep your personal life and professional one separate."

If looks could kill, Layne Sullivan wouldn't need to carry a sidearm. "It won't happen again."

"See that it doesn't." He opened the door and gestured for Sullivan's sister to precede him. "Ma'am. Let me walk you out."

She smiled, but it didn't hide the calculating gleam in her eyes. "Thank you, Chief Taylor. You're not nearly the asshole Layne said you were."

Behind him, Sullivan snarled.

Ross fought a grin. "I appreciate that, ma'am," he told the sister.

He also appreciated that when he glanced back at Sullivan as he stepped out of the room, she held his gaze. She didn't try to make excuses or claim she'd never said any such thing.

He respected that.

Besides, he didn't need her or any of the other officers below him to like him. He just needed them to obey him.

Walking beside Sullivan's sister through the squad room, he couldn't help but notice the changes in her demeanor. Her expression softened, her body lost its stiffness as she crossed the floor in a hip-swaying walk too rehearsed to ever be called natural. And enticing enough for most men not to care.

"Bye, Jimmy," she said to Meade, giving him a little finger wave. A finger wave Meade started to return only to freeze when Ross glanced at him. "Evan, you be careful on that new Harley."

Ross held the door for her and she went into the lobby where Officer Wilber shoved the hunting magazine he'd been reading under the counter. "Chief," he said in greeting as the phone rang. He slid the clipboard holding the sign in/out sheet to Sullivan's sister. "All set, Tori?"

"You bet." She wrote the time next to her name— Tori Mott—while Wilber answered the phone. "So nice of you to walk me all the way out here," she said, shooting Ross a glance from underneath her thick lashes.

"My pleasure, ma'am."

This time when she grinned, it was less sultry, more genuine. "Oh, I doubt that." She tipped her head to the side and studied him. "We both know you only did so you could make sure I left without causing more trouble."

"If that was the case, I would've had to escort your sister out, too."

"Please. Layne's the original good girl. She spends all her time making sure everyone else is keeping their noses clean."

"Including you?"

"Well, I do try...." She skimmed her gaze over him, her meaning, and invitation, clear. "But somehow Old Man Trouble always comes along and nudges me off that straight and narrow path." She stepped close enough for him to notice her eyes were a shade darker than Sullivan's, her forehead wider. "You interested in walking down that road with me sometime?"

Her voice was throaty, and as smoky and sexy as classic jazz. But beyond the seductive act, he saw glimpses of humor and intelligence. She was mysterious and smart and hot enough to melt a man's brains— and his good intentions—in her painted-on black skirt and snug, white top, the top three buttons undone. And she knew it.

She could bring a man to his knees with a single look. She also knew the score, knew exactly what men wanted from her. A few hours of dark pleasure. Nothing more.

If they'd been back in Boston, he might have been tempted enough not to care that she was a magnet for mayhem and heartbreak. He would've walked her to her car. Asked if she'd be interested in going to dinner. But this was Mystic Point and he had Jess to think of, had an example to set for her.

Plus, he wasn't kidding about keeping his professional life separate from his personal one. And while asking out the sister of one of his officers didn't necessarily step over that line, it blurred it.

He liked things—rules and his own moral code— to be crystal clear.

And when he looked at her, he saw Sullivan. Compared her blatant sexuality, her coyness with the captain's blunt, what-you-see-is-what-you-get attitude. In that comparison, Tori came out lacking.

He deliberately stepped back. "Have a good day, ma'am."

She didn't seem disappointed by his lack of response toward her. Which made him wonder if she really had been interested or if it'd all been part of some show he hadn't been invited to.

"You do the same," she said. "And good luck solving your first big case as chief." She picked up the set of keys from the plastic bin provided for visitors' keys, cell phones and other devices that would set off the metal detector they needed to pass through before entering the squad room.

Her key ring was a plastic frame with a picture of a dark-haired boy in his baseball uniform, a bat over his shoulder as he smiled for the camera. A member's benefit card for a local grocery store was hooked onto the frame along with a small, silver heart hanging from a thin chain.

A small, silver heart that looked very familiar.

Son of a bitch.

"Those are yours?" he asked abruptly. "That's your key ring?"

"Yes and yes." She frowned. "Why? Is there a problem?"

Though his brain screamed at him to haul her ass back inside and toss her into a holding cell until he got to the bottom of what was going on, his instincts told him otherwise. Tori may have a missing piece of the puzzle but she couldn't answer the questions running through his head. The growing suspicions.

"No. No problem. Have a good day, ma'am."

He went back into the squad room. Sullivan was on her phone while Meade and Campbell both worked on their computers. Ross crossed to her desk. "I need to speak to you in my office."

She held up a finger for him to wait then spoke into the receiver. "Yes, this is Assistant Chief—"

Ross snatched the phone from her hand and handed it to Meade in one smooth motion.

She reached for the phone. "Wha—"

"My office," Ross said, leaning down, both hands on her desk as he crowded her against her chair. "Now."

He straightened and stepped back far enough to give her room to stand. Her expression set, her movements stilted, she rose and walked ahead of him out of the room and down the short hallway.

"Take a coffee break," he ordered Donna as he passed her desk.

She looked from him to Layne then took her purse out of the bottom desk drawer. "Sure thing. I'll be back in ten minutes."

Ross followed Sullivan into his office and closed the door.

No sooner had the latch clicked shut when she whirled on him. "I've already apologized for my unprofessional behavior," she said through barely moving lips. "And I don't appreciate you treating me with such a lack of respect. Especially in front of my coworkers."

"Is that so?" he murmured, taking her in. Her arms were straight, her hands clenched. He had to give her credit. She didn't give anything away. She met his gaze steadily, no guilt, certainly no remorse on her face.

But she would regret lying to him.

"Yes." She raised her chin, revealing a thin silver chain around her neck. "That's so."

He thought of the shorter piece of chain attaching the heart charm to her sister's key ring. Remembered how, when he'd first shown Layne the necklace found with the remains, her hand had gone to her throat. At the time he'd thought it an innocent gesture.

Fury had him closing the distance between them in two long strides but he didn't let it rule him. He never let his emotions rule him.

Still, his expression must not have been as calm as he'd thought because her eyes widened. But she held her ground. "What do you think—"

"You don't appreciate being treated with a lack of respect?" he repeated. "Well, I don't appreciate being lied to."

He hooked his forefinger under her necklace and tugged it free of her shirt.

And discovered the same heart Tori had on her key chain.

An exact replica of the smaller hearts from the necklace they'd found with the remains.

"WHAT THE HELL is going on?" Taylor growled. He smelled of coffee and mint. Her necklace was wrapped around his finger and his knuckles brushed against her collarbone. His skin was warm. His tone cold enough to make her shiver.

To Layne's horror, tears pricked the backs of her eyes. She found herself wanting to tell him everything. Her fears and suspicions. Not because she was afraid of him or worried about the safety of her job or her professional reputation. Although, she realized with a jolt, she should fear for both.

She wanted to share her burden with someone. Or better yet, let someone else take care of things for her.

Which was so unlike her she almost pinched herself to see if this whole crappy experience wasn't some nightmare.

She was the strong one. The responsible one. She'd stepped up and taken care of her family when her mother bailed. Had given up her childhood to ensure Tori and their younger sister, Nora, were safe and cared for. She'd protected them. Always protected them.

But, oh, God, she wanted, badly to be the one taken care of. Just one time.

Pressing her lips together, she jerked back and for a second, she didn't think he'd let go. But then he eased away, letting the charm fall back to bounce once against the top button of her uniform.

"Nothing's going on." Her tone betrayed none of her uncertainty, her guilt. "It's a coincidence."

At least that's what she'd been trying to convince herself of all morning.

"You and your sister both have charms identical to the necklace we found with a set of human remains. Remains you and I are both very aware could belong to the victim of a violent crime, and you want me to believe it's a coincidence?"

"Yes."

He regarded her intently, trying to get a read on her. Just like a good cop did when talking to a witness.

Or a suspect.

"Then why not mention it earlier?" he asked.

She shrugged, trying to make the gesture casual but figured she looked like she was having a seizure. "I meant to…" Even someone who valued honestly above all else could be forgiven for a little white lie every so often. "But I didn't see any point."

"Where is it?"

"Where is…?"

"Captain, what did you do with the evidence I gave you earlier this morning?"

Offended, she narrowed her eyes. "What do you think I did with it?"

But she knew. He wasn't worried she'd accidentally lost or misplaced it. Oh, no, he thought she'd hid it. Or destroyed it.

"Where is the necklace?" he repeated sharply.

"Processing has it."

As soon as she'd handed it over the guilt weighing on her shoulders had lightened. Yes, it had taken her a few hours to make the right decision but when push came to shove, she'd done the right thing.

He circled his desk. Picking up his phone, he glanced at her. "Sit down."

Her mouth went dry. If she had to endure his calm, controlled reprimand accompanied by one of his sub-zero looks, she'd do it how she did everything in her life. On her own two feet. "I'd rather stand, thanks."

Except he didn't go with the iceman routine. Instead his hot stare just about blistered her skin.

She sat. And disliked him even more for being un-predictable.

He dialed a number. "Officer Campbell," he said into the phone, but kept his eyes on her, "I need you to go down to Processing and check on the status of the evidence found at the quarry."

Her face burned. Anger and resentment sizzled in her blood. He had no right to treat her this way, as if she couldn't be trusted. She'd made a mistake. A mistake she planned on correcting at the earliest convenience.

And here she'd thought that, after being chastised for fighting with Tori, she couldn't possibly be more humiliated.

Man, she hated being wrong.

Hated even more that, like what happened with her sister, this was her own damn fault. She'd dug herself a deep, smelly hole and now she had to figure out how to claw her way out.

Tapping her fingers against her knee, she checked out the office. The furniture—two wooden chairs facing a metal desk, a banged-up, four-drawer filing cabinet and a bookcase—were left from Chief Gorham. The freshly painted beige walls were bare. A lamp, two neatly stacked piles of folders, a mechanical pencil and a coffee cup the only items on his desk. There were no framed commendations or knickknacks. No nameplate. No personal photos, not even a snapshot of the niece who was living with him—and what was up with that?

The room was like Taylor himself. Unreadable. There was nothing to give a person any type of clue as to what—if anything—went on beneath the chief's starched surface.

Being a good cop means being able to keep your personal life and professional one separate.

Maybe he was a damned good cop. But he obviously had a few things to learn about being an actual human being.

"You're sure?" Taylor asked Evan. "You saw the necklace? Not just that it had been entered into the evidence logbook?" Pause. "Good."

And he hung up.

"What did you think I did with it?" she asked, unable

to stop herself or keep the bitterness from her voice. "Tossed it into the ocean?"

He linked his hands loosely on top of the desk, his mouth a flat line. "What are you hiding?"

Her breathing quickened. She worked to remain calm—and not hyperventilate. God, she'd been so stupid. She should've mentioned, oh-so-casually, how she happened to have a charm like the ones on the necklace.

"I panicked," she admitted. "I jumped to conclusions without having all the facts."

And what a dumb, rookie mistake that had been. One that could possibly come back and take a nice-size chunk out of her ass.

Taylor seemingly remained unaffected by her confession. "Do you know who that necklace belonged to?"

Layne ran her damp palms down the front of her thighs. "My mother. She had a necklace similar to the one that was found."

He watched her out of hooded gray eyes. "How similar?"

"Identical," she said, as if admitting that didn't have the possibility of ripping her world apart.

Her father had given it to Valerie for Valentine's Day the year Layne was twelve. The large heart symbolized their relationship, with three smaller hearts for each daughter. He'd then given Layne and her sisters replicas. She never took hers off.

Mistake number one.

Chief Taylor took a legal notepad out of a drawer and picked up his pencil. "Mother's name?"

"Valerie. Valerie Sullivan."

"Does the necklace we found belong to her?" He held up a hand when she opened her mouth. "Just yes or no."

She shifted, gripping the chair's arms so tightly, her

fingers ached. "I can't give you a yes or no answer. There could be hundreds…thousands…of those necklaces sold yearly."

"Have you spoken with your mother recently?"

Her lips were dry but she didn't lick them. Didn't want to give anything away, especially nothing that would give him the impression—the wrong impression—that she was nervous. She just hated talking about her mother. Didn't answer questions about her or let herself wonder what Valerie was doing, where she was. If she regretted her choices.

Didn't want to think about what could've happened to her. That the remains they'd found could be her mother. Not after Layne had spent half her life trying to forget Valerie Sullivan had ever existed.

"No." A bead of sweat formed and trickled down between her breasts. Reminded her that her uniform was dirty and wrinkled and—thanks to Tori's temper—wet. Her hair a tangled mess, her face and chest sticky. And there he sat, behind his desk like a king about to send her to the guillotine, all calm and composed and dry.

She resented his control even as she envied it.

He made a note. She craned her neck but they were too far apart for her to see more than the darkness of his neat print. "I take it you and your mother aren't close?"

"If you were from here, you wouldn't even have to ask that."

But he wasn't from Mystic Point. He hadn't grown up hearing the rumors, hadn't been around when Layne's family had been the subject of gossip and speculation. He didn't know what her mother had been like.

And Layne wasn't about to fill him in.

"When," he asked, "specifically, was the last time you spoke with your mother?"

She inhaled deeply. "September 20. Specifically."

"You haven't spoken to your mother in almost a year?"

"September 20. Nineteen ninety-four."

"That was eighteen years ago." If he was surprised, she couldn't tell. Couldn't read him in the best of times let alone when her emotions were jumbled, her thoughts confused.

She prided herself on her ability to see situations… people…clearly. Being unable to do so with him only served to infuriate and, yes, intrigue her. Damn him.

"And you didn't even need a calculator," she said. "No wonder city council snatched you up for the chief's position."

"Your mother hasn't contacted you at all?" he pressed, ignoring her lame attempt to divert his attention. Or, better yet, make him show some sort of emotion.

Twisting her fingers together in her lap where he couldn't see the betraying motion, she shook her head. "My mother left when I was fourteen without so much as a goodbye. There were no calls or letters or emails. No birthday cards or presents at Christmas."

"That must've been tough."

"We survived." She and her sisters had done fine without Valerie in their lives. Probably better than if their mother had stuck around. At least, that's what she'd always believed, but now…now she didn't know what to think. Her entire world had been thrown off balance. It was all she could do to keep her footing. To not let herself slide down into a quagmire of doubts and fears and what-if's.

What if Valerie had changed her mind and hadn't wanted to leave her family? What if Layne hadn't said those things to her that night? What if she'd tried to stop her mother from leaving?

Dear God, what if her mother was dead? And it was all her fault?

"Did it ever occur to you," he asked, "in all that time that something could've happened that prevented your mother from contacting you?"

"No. Why would it? Everyone thought she ran off with Dale York, the man she was having an affair with." Chief Taylor made a note, probably of her mother's lover's name. "We had no reason to think there was any other possibility of why we never heard from her again."

"You've admitted your mother had a necklace identical to the one found with the remains. You've also stated that you haven't heard from her in over eighteen years. Do you know of anyone who has been in contact with your mother since she left? Your sister? Or your father?"

"Not that I'm aware of."

He tapped his pencil on the desk twice then tossed it aside. "Surely once you saw the necklace you had to have considered the possibility that the remains discovered at the quarry belong to your mother."

Her scalp prickled. A roaring filled her ears. She slowly shook her head but her thoughts remained jumbled. She had to be careful. Had to stick to the truth as closely as possible without giving him anything that he could twist for his own purposes.

Just like she would if she was questioning someone about what would undoubtedly end up a murder investigation.

"It occurred to me," she said slowly. "Yes."

"And yet you didn't say anything."

She leaned forward, all earnestness and sincerity.

"Because I didn't want the investigation to start off on the wrong track. Look, there could be any number of explanations for that necklace being there. It might not even be hers. Or, if it is, she could've lost it or had it stolen from her. Or, more than likely, she pawned it before she took off."

"Those are all possibilities. Or maybe you know more than what you're telling me." His voice softened though his expression remained fierce. "What are you afraid of?"

"Nothing," she said quickly, her hands gripping her knees, her nails digging into her skin.

"Then help me figure out the identity of the body we found." When she hesitated, he raised his eyebrows. "Unless you don't care that it could be your mother?"

"Of course I care," she said shakily.

She just didn't want to believe it was Valerie.

"I'll need the name of your mother's dentist," he said.

So he could get a warrant and check Valerie's dental records against the skull they found.

"Dr. Simon. His office is on Park Square." Her underarms grew damp, her stomach turned. She swallowed a surge of nausea and lurched to her feet, breathing through her mouth until the sensation passed. Oh, God, she had to escape, had to get out of here before she lost what little control she had left. "If that's all, sir…"

"It's not." He opened a drawer and pulled out a paper and a large plastic bag. Her heart stopped. "I'd like a sample of your DNA to test against the remains."

"Covering all your bases, aren't you?"

They both knew that dental records were enough to identify the remains. But juries loved DNA matches, and in law enforcement, more was better. And if this case ended up a murder investigation, as they both obviously expected, Taylor would want irrefutable proof that the person found in those woods was her mother.

She didn't blame him. She wanted that proof, as well.

He slid the paper toward her and gave her a pen. While she signed the release form, he opened the kit and removed a long swab from the tube. "Rub this firmly against the inside of your cheek for thirty seconds."

She snatched it from him so he couldn't tell her hands were shaking. "I know how to collect a DNA sample."

When she finished, she placed it in the tube and snapped the long handle in two. The swab fell into the tube and she put the cap on. Taylor put it back into the bag and wrote her name and the date on it in bold, block letters.

She bit her lower lip but couldn't stop the words from pushing past her throat. "I know what you're thinking."

"Do you?"

"You don't know me so you probably don't realize this, but I'm actually big on honesty."

You could always count on the truth. It made life easier to be honest about your thoughts and feelings, your wants and needs. Easier and much less messy.

She'd had enough messy to last a lifetime thanks to her mother's lies and manipulation.

"For someone who values the truth so much," Taylor said, "you don't seem to have any problems stretching it to suit your own needs."

She grimaced. And that's what stung the most. Not his bad opinion of her—though she could admit to having a slight twinge over that, as well. No, what really hurt was that she'd acted like her mother. And that was completely unacceptable.

"I had a momentary lapse in good judgment," she said. "It happens to the best of us."

Taylor sent her a look that clearly said it didn't happen to him. "I don't like being lied to," he said, obviously not hearing a word she'd said. Or choosing to ignore it like he'd ignored his niece's pleas to go home last night. "What I like even less is having a cop in my department I may not be able to trust."

Her chest hurt. He was wrong about her. She was Layne Sullivan, for God's sake. She'd never, not once, cheated on any test, her taxes or any of the boyfriends she'd had over the years. She didn't lie—usually. She was as trustworthy as a Girl Scout. Or a nun. Or a nun who'd once been a Girl Scout.

"For obvious reasons," he continued, "you are no longer to be associated in any way with this case."

"If it's not my mother—"

"Doesn't matter. Not now. Not after this," he said flatly. "You are relieved of your duties until your regular shift Monday."

She blinked. Opened her mouth. Shut it. "You're suspending me?"

"I'm giving you a few nights off. Time for you to think about—"

"You want me to think about what I've done?" she asked incredulously. "What is this? Kindergarten?"

"Time," he repeated, "for you to decide what's in the best interest of your career. Unless you'd rather I file a formal suspension of your duties?"

The knot in her chest loosened. He wasn't reprimanding her. At least, not formally. He could, she realized. She'd lied—by omission, yes, but it was still a lie and they both knew it—about information pertinent to an ongoing investigation. At the very least she'd abused the authority of her position. At the most, she was guilty of interfering with an investigation or obstruction of justice. She could lose her job. Even if she didn't there would be speculation about how she did that job. And her integrity.

By giving her time off, he was protecting her reputation. And keeping what she did between the two of them. She didn't deserve it, wasn't sure she'd have done the same if their positions were reversed, but that didn't mean she couldn't latch on to this slight reprieve as firmly as possible.

It didn't mean she couldn't be grateful.

"Thank you. I know how this looks but my mother, she's not..." She could barely say it let alone think it. "That body...it's not her. She's not...dead. She can't be."

"I guess we'll see about that." But his voice was almost compassionate. Which made her feel worse. She didn't want or need his compassion. All she needed, all she wanted was for that body to be someone else.

He picked up the phone. "You're dismissed, Captain."

She walked to the door, her legs unsteady, her mind whirling. Her mother wasn't dead. Because if she was, her family would be torn apart.

And Layne was afraid she wouldn't be able to hold them together this time.

CHAPTER FIVE

IF IT WASN'T FOR YOU, I'd still be in Boston.

Filling out a job application at the front counter of the Quik Mart, Jess's fingers tightened on the pen. God. Bad enough she had to live with her uncle, now she couldn't get his voice out of her head.

Talk about torture. Hearing him in her subconscious sucked worse than the relentless pounding in her skull thanks to her hangover.

He had it all wrong, too. He'd dragged her to this lame town. Not the other way around. He'd ruined her life—and seemed happy to keep right on ruining it.

Asshole.

But it'd all be over soon, she assured herself, neatly printing her address on the application. She was going home.

She sipped from a bottle of ginger ale, the only thing she'd been able to keep down so far today other than the four ibuprofen she took before leaving the house.

She'd almost taken off this morning after Uncle Ross had left. Had even packed a bag and checked bus schedules online. But when she'd tried to pay for the ticket, her uncle's credit card number—the one she'd written down one night while he'd been in the shower—had been declined due to the account being canceled. Worse, the bank envelope filled with cash had disappeared from his sock drawer.

It was like he didn't trust her at all.

Didn't matter. She'd get out of here on her own.

And if that meant working some low-paying job for the next two months so she could save up enough to get back to Boston, then that's what she'd do. Even if Uncle Ross would think she'd caved in to his bullying.

A little boy raced up to the candy display next to Jess and grabbed a king-size chocolate bar. When he turned, a huge, satisfied grin on his face, his monkey backpack brushed against the shelf, knocking candy to the floor.

"David, please be careful," a woman said sharply enough for Jess to hear her over the music playing on her iPod. The lady hurried up to David, a gallon of milk in her hand, another kid, a younger, rounder one, on her hip. "Pick them up and put that candy bar back. And hurry or we'll be late getting Daddy."

David's lower lip jutted out. He clutched the candy to his chest as if his mother couldn't snatch it away from his pudgy little hands. "I want it."

The mom, her perfect makeup and glossy golden hair at odds with the orange stain on the shoulder of her white shirt, hefted the baby higher. "I said no."

But Jess—and probably the kid—sensed she was already wavering. Either because she was in too much of a hurry to argue or because she was a pushover.

The baby babbled then patted his mom's face. Hard. The lady smiled at him then looked back at David but couldn't quite pull off a stern expression. "Fine," she said with a sigh, "you can get it but you are not eating it until after supper."

Definitely pushover.

Jess bet the kid had the candy gone within the next ten minutes.

"Now come on," the woman said, setting the milk on the counter, "clean up that mess."

"It's okay," Jess said, gathering the candy. "I'll get it."

"Thank you so much." The baby babbled along with his mom, blowing spit bubbles. Drool slid down his dimpled chin. Gross. "David, tell the nice girl thank you."

"Thank you," he said, tearing into the candy's wrapper.

The smell of chocolate made her stomach roll.

"You're welcome," Jess mumbled, hoping to send them on their way before she tossed up the soda. To make sure neither of them decided to keep talking to her, she ducked her head and turned up the volume of Eminem and Rihanna's "Love the Way You Lie."

Painful to her aching head, yes, but better than having a conversation with some cute kid and his nice mother.

She put the candy back on the shelf while the woman checked out. When the lady left, she picked up the tail of the monkey on the kid's back and Jess realized it wasn't just a backpack. It was a leash.

Jess smirked. Uncle Ross probably had one on order for her. All the better to keep her under his control.

Straightening, she jumped to find a guy standing behind her by the cappuccino dispenser. A seriously cute guy with light blue eyes, curly hair the color of wet sand and a dusting of facial hair a shade lighter. He looked like he could've lived in ritzy Beacon Hill with his pretty, pretty face and just-this-side-of-slouchy white pants and designer blue shirt, the sleeves shoved up to his elbows.

His lips moved then he grinned, showing even, white

teeth and a dimple on the right side of his mouth. A dimple! Jeez, she would've melted at his feet if she hadn't been made of sterner stuff than that. And cynical enough not to trust some gorgeous guy just because he smiled at her.

He pointed to his ear.

Her cheeks heated. Yeah, she was an idiot, standing there staring at him like it was the first time a guy had talked to her. She took the earbuds out. "Sorry."

"No problem. I was saying I thought you might want to reconsider trying to get hired here."

She narrowed her eyes. "How do you know I'm applying for a job?"

He scratched the back of his head. "I sort of noticed the application here—" He gestured to the paper on the counter and lowered his voice. "Trust me, you don't want to work here."

"Oh?" she asked, picking up the application in case he was some deranged stalker. Hopefully he hadn't read her name or address on it. "Why not?"

"For one thing, you put the Reese's cups in with the Kit Kat bars. And that Snickers is upside down." His deep voice was amused and, unless she was mistaken, interested. He made a *tsking* sound. "I'm sure that kind of shoddy work isn't acceptable at the Quik Mart."

Her mouth twitched. Okay, so he was hot—in a preppy way—and funny. Maybe she wouldn't cut him off at the knees. Yet.

She tipped her head to the side and studied him. "You don't work here…" When he arched his eyebrows at her, she indicated his clothes. "No Quik Mart shirt or matching visor—"

"Man, I would love one of those visors."

"For all you know, there could be some sort of candy bar orientation to ensure the highest standards."

He edged closer. "Actually I had a friend who worked here last summer. She had some…issues…with the manager."

Jess followed his pointed glance at the potbellied man behind the counter. Caught him watching her, a predatory gleam in his eye. She hunched her shoulders and wished she had on more than a tank top and shorts. "Yeah, he's a bit…creepy. I thought maybe it was the porno mustache giving me that vibe, though."

The guy's grin was fast and appreciative. "Trust your instincts. He's bad news and the last thing you want is to be stuck working a late shift with him."

"You're probably right. But," she said, picking up the pen and filling in the next line on the application, "as far as I can tell, this is one of the few places hiring that's close enough for me to walk to."

"You don't have a car?"

Did he sound condescending? Surprised? "I didn't need one in Boston," she said, unable to hide the defensiveness in her voice.

Not that having a car would've made a difference since she wouldn't be able to get her permit until her birthday next week. And then it would be another six months before she could take her road test. If Uncle Ross even let her drive. And really, what kind of town doesn't have public transportation? No buses or even taxis. It was so completely stupid.

Cute Guy took a large cup from the stack and set it under the French Vanilla spout. "You're from Boston?" He pressed the button. Steaming liquid filled his cup. "I just finished my third year at B.U."

Of course he did. "Let me guess." She let her gaze

drift over him. "No socks. Short hair. No discernable piercings or tattoos and a love of bad, convenience-store coffee. Premed?" Weren't all rich, preppy guys premed?

"Law," he said, putting a lid on the cup. And she gave him major points for not saying he wanted to play doctor with her. "You?"

"Me what?"

"I'd ask what's your major, but I'd hate to be accused of resorting to cheesy pickup lines."

She blinked. Oh. Ohhh. Well, what do you know? Guess she looked even older than she realized. "I'm still undecided. I'm going into my second year at Northeastern." My, my, my. Hadn't she become quite the accomplished liar in a short period of time?

He took a sip of his chemically enhanced drink. "What brings you to Mystic Point?"

A strung out mom, overbearing uncle and a court system blinded to her needs and feelings.

"My mom. She's…out of the country. I'm staying with my uncle until school starts again."

"I'm a native. Maybe I could show you around town sometime."

Her heart about leaped out of her chest. "Was that a cheesy pickup line?"

"Only if it worked."

She couldn't help it. She laughed. It sounded rusty and felt weird but it also felt sort of…nice. "Yeah. Maybe."

"Listen, all attempts to get you to go out with me aside, if you're looking for a job, you could try the Ludlow Street Café. My cousin is a waitress there and when I stopped in this morning, she mentioned they have a part-time position opening up. They haven't even put it in the paper yet so if you go down there today, maybe you could get a jump on the competition."

"I could. If I knew where it was."

"Here." He set his cup down, took the application and pen from her and wrote something then handed it back to her, pointing to what he'd written in the corner. "That's the address. All you do is take a right at the light—" He nodded at the intersection visible through the glass door. "Go down two blocks then take another right on Winter Street. You can't miss it."

"Is this the phone number?" she asked, squinting at the scrawled numbers. "Is that a four?"

He bent his head close to hers to see. His cologne was spicy and woodsy and probably expensive. But at least he didn't bathe in it like the guys her age did.

"Seven," he said, straightening and meeting her eyes. "And it's not the café's number. It's mine. In case you wanted to call to thank me for helping you land a great job."

She folded the paper and stuck it in her back pocket. "There's no guarantee they'll hire me."

"Tell Celeste—that's the owner—I sent you."

"Good idea. Who are you?"

He shook his head. "Right. Sorry." He held out his right hand. "Anthony Sullivan."

"Jessica," she said, shaking his hand. His palm was slightly rough, his skin warm. Best of all, he kept his gaze on her face instead of dropping to check out her boobs.

"You know," he said, still holding her hand, "we could skip the whole call-me-later thing and make plans right now."

Her stomach flipped. Whoa boy. He was gorgeous

and charming and completely out of her league—not to mention her age bracket. "Confident, aren't you?"

"More like hopeful," he murmured, scanning her face as if she was beautiful. Special. And worthy of an obviously wealthy, smart guy who seemed truly, sincerely nice.

She wasn't. If her life kept going in the direction it had been for the past few months, she probably never would be. But how was she supposed to resist him?

Why on earth would she want to?

"What did you have in mind?" she asked, reluctantly removing her hand from his.

"Dinner," he said quickly. "Tomorrow night?"

Dinner. Like a real date. It sounded so…mature. And too good to be true. Sort of like him. "I don't think that's a good idea."

He took out his iPhone. "At least give me your phone number so I can try to convince you. Come on," he added, that damn dimple flashing. "What do you have to lose? I promise I'm trustworthy. I could even supply a few references if it'd make you feel better."

He was sweet. But hadn't she thought the same thing about Nate last night? Look how that had turned out.

Still, she couldn't be blamed for wanting, hoping, this time would be different. That Anthony was different.

"Can I see that?" she asked before she could talk herself out of it.

If he thought the request odd, he didn't show it. Just handed his smartphone over. What a trusting soul. She could use that, she realized. Was using it. Her fingers faltered as she unlocked the phone. Her stomach pinched with guilt.

She ignored it.

It wasn't like she planned on knocking him out and stealing his wallet. Besides, he'd come on to her. And he'd assumed she was older. She was just playing along. Having a little fun.

Holding the phone out, she snapped a picture of herself, added her number and saved it in his contacts.

"Don't say I didn't warn you," she told him, handing the phone back.

Then she walked away, adding more sway to her stride than usual. She smiled. Maybe the next two months wouldn't completely suck after all.

THE LAST THING ROSS EXPECTED when he got home after such a complete shit day was to discover that Jess had obeyed him. The yard was mowed, the kitchen floor spotless and a basket of folded towels sat on the end of the couch.

No, he thought, setting the plastic grocery bags on the end of the counter, the very last thing he expected was to find the table set and a pan of something simmering on the stove releasing the scents of chicken, onions and peppers in the air.

He did a slow turn to make sure he hadn't somehow stumbled into the wrong house after being up for almost forty-eight hours. Brand-new flat screen TV on the living room wall, brown leather armchair and sofa, and the wagon wheel coffee table Jess had declared so ugly it should be doused with gasoline and torched—after someone had taken an ax to it. The mail scattered on the counter was addressed to him and sticking out from underneath a Chinese takeout menu were the sunglasses he'd been looking for for the past two days. He picked them up, hooked the earpiece on to the V of his shirt.

It was definitely his house.

He hurried upstairs, locked his service weapon in the gun box he kept on the high shelf of his bedroom closet. Stepped out into the hall as Jess came out of her room.

"You're home," she said, her hair held back on either side of her face with sparkly butterfly clips. "About time. I'm starving."

She walked down the stairs ahead of him in a T-shirt and baggy sweats, the word *sexy* scrolled across her ass. He stopped as if he'd hit an invisible wall. Sexy. Jesus.

Next chance he got, those pants were going to mysteriously disappear. Just like that T-shirt—the one proclaiming her to be a "hot bitch"—had.

Being a cop didn't mean he couldn't be sneaky when the situation called for it.

He checked his watch as he reached the kitchen. Eight-fifteen. "You didn't eat yet?"

"I was waiting for you." She lifted the lid from the pan releasing a puff of steam. "Do you want peppers and onions in your quesadilla, or just chicken and cheese?"

A jar of salsa and a container of sour cream sat on the table along with an open bag of tortilla chips. Shredded cheese was in a bowl on the counter next to a package of flour tortillas.

"What is all this?"

"Uh…dinner. Duh." She set the lid down, tore open the flour tortilla package. "Do you want onions and peppers or not?"

"You made dinner? What did you do now? It better not involve any felonies."

"Nice," she snarled, tossing a handful of shredded cheddar cheese onto a tortilla. "Real nice. I do everything you want me to do—including getting a stupid job—and all you can think is that I did something wrong."

He squeezed the back of his neck. He was so far over his head here and drowning fast. What the hell did he know about living with—raising—a teenage girl?

"You can't blame me for being surprised." Although she probably would anyway. "When I left this morning, you were far from enthusiastic about anything I'd had to say."

Shrugging irritably, she added chicken, onions and peppers to the tortilla then folded it over. "I had time to think."

He waited but she didn't elaborate, leaving him to wonder what she thought and how it got her to obey him. If he knew, maybe he could repeat it and make sure it happened again. "I'm almost afraid to ask but, how did you pay for all of this?"

"That cop didn't tell you?" she asked, adding the quesadilla to a heated pan.

"What cop?" In the act of unloading groceries from a bag, he lifted his hand. "And please don't say the one who busted you for shoplifting."

She rolled her eyes. "The old guy at the station. The fat one? I stopped by to get money from you so I could pick up some groceries but you weren't there so he gave me some cash. Said he'd square it away with you when you got back."

He slammed a can of tomato soup onto the counter harder than necessary. "Damn it, Jess. I don't want you taking money from my coworkers," he said, humiliated at her going around with her hand out like some charity case.

Like he had no idea how to take care of her.

"Sure. No problem." She flipped the quesadilla—

and when did they get a spatula? "Next time I get hungry, I'll walk down to the beach…harpoon myself a fish for lunch."

Holy shit, she was right. Again. He'd left her here this morning with no food and no money. He pulled out his wallet. "Here."

She eyed the two twenties in his hand warily. "What's that for?"

He set them next to the coffeepot. "It's your allowance. For helping around the house," he added, feeling like an idiot.

"I thought that was about taking responsibility and doing my fair share."

He should be pissed she'd thrown his words back at him but at this point he was just glad she'd listened to him. "It is. And as long as you're doing it, you'll get an allowance."

Maybe if he'd done this when she'd first come to live with him, he wouldn't be out five hundred dollars in credit card charges, not to mention the one hundred and fifty bucks she'd taken from his dresser drawer.

"But this money is not to go toward any alcohol, drugs or drug paraphernalia," he said. "Understand?"

"There goes that pretty bong I'd had my heart set on."

"I hope you're joking."

"Yes, Uncle Ross. That was a joke."

Good. Although maybe he needed to start giving her random drug tests, just to be sure. "I didn't know you could cook."

And wasn't it interesting that after all these months of living with him, she decided to make dinner now, tonight? He'd like to say that the why and how of her sudden turnaround didn't matter, but he wasn't that gullible.

"Yeah, well, I learned pretty early that if I wanted to eat something other than cold cereal for supper I needed to learn at least the basics."

He shifted uncomfortably as he pulled out one of the three boxes of cereal he'd bought from a grocery bag. Not that he'd planned on feeding her Honey Nut Cheerios for supper. He thought he'd make grilled cheese if she hadn't eaten yet.

"Heather didn't cook?" he asked of his sister.

"Mom's…schedule…didn't really mesh with mine."

He paused as he put the cereal in an upper cabinet. "What does that mean?"

Jess's expression was carefully blank, her movements jerky as she transferred the quesadilla to a plate. "It means she couldn't cook dinner because most days she was usually passed out by 4:00 p.m. When she wasn't, she was too strung out to be trusted around sharp utensils and a hot stove." She faced him, her hands on her hips. "So do you want one of these or not?"

"Yeah," he said, carefully shutting the cupboard door instead of slamming it like he wanted. "I'll take one."

He finished putting away the groceries then leaned against the counter, watching while she fixed his food. Jesus. All these years he and his parents had known Heather was using but she'd traveled so much, dragging Jess up and down the East Coast, from city to city and state to state, they hadn't realized how bad it had gotten. Hadn't been able to help.

His parents had tried. They'd paid for Heather to go into rehab twice; once right after Jess was born, underweight but otherwise healthy. The second when Heather was picked up for possession when she and Jess had been living in Fort Lauderdale with one of Heather's low-life boyfriends.

It wasn't until Heather got busted eight months ago after she'd returned to Boston that Ross was able to step in and do what was right. Now it was up to him to take care of Jess, to make sure she was healthy and safe. And, most important, that she didn't end up like her mother.

Jess added his quesadilla to the one already on a plate then handed it to him. "You can put this on the table." He sat down, setting his cell phone next to his full water glass while she got a drink from the fridge then took the seat across from him.

And he realized it was the first time they'd shared a meal since she'd moved in with him. She flipped open the tab on her soda and took a sip.

"Should you be drinking that for dinner?" he asked.

"What else would I drink?"

"Milk." Weren't kids supposed to drink a lot of milk? "It's good for you."

Her answer was another of her vision-impairing eye rolls.

He added sour cream and salsa to his plate, cut into his quesadilla with the side of his fork and took a bite. "This is good. Really good."

"They're easy," she said as if it was no big deal. But the tips of her ears were pink. She mixed her sour cream and salsa together on her plate. "I could make you another one if you want."

"That's okay," he said, though he'd plowed through half of his already. "You go ahead and eat yours first before it gets cold."

She cut hers into three triangles, picked one up and

dipped the tip into her sour cream/salsa mixture. They ate in silence but it wasn't uncomfortable, more like… wary. As if neither of them wanted to do or say anything that would jinx the undeclared truce they seemed to have going on.

Which worked for him. He preferred the quiet.

He'd cleaned his plate when she cleared her throat. "So, in case you were wondering," she said, setting her drink down, "I start tomorrow."

Wiping his hands on a paper napkin, his mind blanked. "Start what?"

She set the remainder of a triangle down and stood. "My new job. The one I told you about?" She turned the stove back on and frowned at him over her shoulder. "God. Do you even listen to anything I say?"

"I listen. You didn't mention what this new job is, though, or where it's at."

"I'll be waitressing," she said, putting together another quesadilla. She laid it in the pan then wiped her hands on the towel hanging from the oven door handle. "At the Ludlow Street Café."

Ludlow Street Café. He knew of the place, had been in there once or twice. Big, two-story building downtown. Blue paint. Great burgers. "That's—"

His cell phone vibrated, caller ID flashing the name and number of the dentist in Boston where Ross had sent Valerie Sullivan's dental records.

"Chief Taylor," he said, pushing his chair back as he listened to Dr. Roberts give his findings. "You're sure? Okay. Thanks for getting to it today."

He ended the call and got to his feet. Went upstairs for his weapon, clipping it in his holster as he came back down. After glancing around, he spied his keys by the empty grocery bags on the counter, grabbed them and skirted the table.

"Where are you going?" Jess asked.

"I have to go out, make a death notification."

"Now? I thought you wanted another quesadilla."

"I did. Do. Stick it in the fridge and I'll eat it when I get home." He opened the door and paused to look back at her. Why she seemed so disappointed and peeved when she couldn't stand to be around him for more than two minutes, he had no idea. Then again, he didn't understand much about her—or females in general.

"Do not leave the house," he ordered. "Understand?"

"Whatever," she muttered as he stepped outside and shut the door behind him.

TREE BRANCHES SCRATCHED Layne's arms, stung her face and neck as she raced through the woods. The dark surrounded her, crept in on her like a shadow, threatening to swallow her alive, to pull her into its depths. Terror coated her throat, dried her mouth.

Unnamed urgency propelled her forward until she stumbled into a sudden oasis of light and greenery. Brilliant moonlight shone down, warm and golden, illuminating the three figures in the clearing. A man, his thumbs hooked in his front pockets, his hair dark and tousled. His lips curved slowly into a grin, one sexy and dangerous that didn't reach his deep green eyes. Across from him her father waited, tall and proud, his legs apart as if he was still on board a ship. A cap covered his short, graying hair; his face was weathered, worn and wrinkled from a life spent at sea.

And in between them, her beautiful face tipped up, her arms outstretched as if she could somehow gather the moon's rays in her embrace, stood her mother.

Oh, God. A sob rose in Layne's throat. She swallowed it. But Valerie was just as wildly, gloriously beautiful as always. Her long dark hair streamed behind her in a breeze Layne couldn't feel, her lips upturned in a sly, secretive smile. Always secrets. Always lies.

Valerie looked longingly at the dark-haired man then faced her husband. She reached her arms out to Tim Sullivan. Begged him to forgive her. To take her back.

Of course he would, Layne thought numbly. Even after all this time, after everything Valerie had done to him, he'd do anything, give up everything that mattered to him, to make her happy. He'd put her first, just as he always did. Above his daughters. Above his own pride.

Tim held out his hand but before Valerie could step forward, the dark-haired man was there, his fist wrapped around Valerie's hair as he yanked her head back.

No, Layne shouted, but her words were stolen, snatched in that unfelt wind and carried away before anyone could hear. Her legs were heavy, her head fuzzy. For a moment, she couldn't move and desperation seized her. She had to save her mother.

She had to stop him.

But no matter how hard or fast she ran, she never got any closer. Could do nothing when her father joined the dark-haired man and Valerie, her mother reaching for her husband even as she laughed. And laughed. Secure in the power she held over both these men, over all those who wanted her. Who loved her. Squeezing her eyes shut, Layne covered her ears with her hands but the sexy sound of her mother's laughter only got louder, filling her head until she heard nothing else, until her own thoughts seemed to dissolve into that husky sound.

A shot rang out and Layne jerked, opened her eyes

to find she no longer stood at the edge of the woods but in the middle of the clearing, a gun in her shaking, blood-covered hands.

And at her feet lay her mother's crumpled, motionless body, a bloodstain blooming across Valerie's chest. Her lips were blue, her eyes…Tori's eyes…Layne's own eyes…open but unseeing.

The gun slid from her numb fingers as she dropped to her knees and screamed.

CHAPTER SIX

SOMEONE SHOOK HER. HARD.

Layne bolted forward, smacked her forehead with a sharp crack against what felt like a concrete wall. Her eyes swam.

"Ow," a familiar, male voice said. "Damn it. Wake up, Layne."

Her heart racing, Layne glanced around frantically. She was on the recliner in her sister's living room, the Red Sox game flickering on the muted TV in the corner, sounds from her nephew's birthday party floating in through the open windows. Lying on the back of the couch, Tori's cat Fang, a calico with enough attitude to rival his owner's, lifted his head then stood and stretched before leaping to the floor.

A dream. It'd all been a dream.

Her cousin Anthony stood before her, one hand rubbing his forehead, the other holding a plate loaded with a huge piece of lasagna and three slices of garlic bread.

Not a concrete wall, she thought as she lightly touched the ache above her eyebrow. Her cousin's hard head.

"Anthony." Her hands were unsteady as she shoved the hair out of her face. "You scared the hell out of me."

"That's no reason to give me a concussion," he griped, pushing aside an unlit scented candle so he could sit on the coffee table.

"Guess you should've thought of that before you shook me so hard my back teeth are still rattling."

"What else was I supposed to do?" he asked, forking a big bite of lasagna into his mouth. He chewed and swallowed. "I called your name—several times— but you kept on twitching and moaning. Bad dream?"

"No, I try to get a workout in while I sleep," she said dryly, helping herself to the plastic cup he had beside him. "It's called multitasking."

"Funny."

She took a long drink, still so freaked out by the dream she didn't even realize what she was drinking until she'd drained half the glass. "Tori let you have beer? And in front of your parents?"

He took the cup back, frowned when he saw how much she'd had. "Want to card me? Last time I checked, twenty-one was the legal drinking age."

Oh. Right. He'd had his twenty-first birthday in March. "I still can't believe you're old enough to drink. I just got used to the fact that you're taller than I am."

"I've been taller than you for six years."

"Yeah, but I've only recently accepted it." She had to look up to meet his eyes when they were standing; he had a scruffy beard and a man's wide shoulders. When had that happened? "My God, I used to change your diapers."

"I hate when you remind me of that."

"Why do you think I bring it up so often?"

"I never should've said yes when Dad asked me to get you," he said, scooping up more lasagna.

"You said yes so you could sneak more food."

"True."

Guess that second helping he'd had when they'd eaten dinner over two hours ago hadn't been enough to fill him. She lifted the bread to her own mouth, re-membered her dream, the sight of her mother lying in a pool of blood. Tossed the bread back onto his plate.

He studied her, his expression contemplative. It was all she could do not to squirm. "What's wrong?"

"Nothing."

He wagged his fork at her. "Now you're lying to me."

Did she have a huge sign over her head, the word *liar* all lit up and pointing right down at her? "Anthony," she said in the same tone she'd used when she'd bab-ysat him and wanted him to quit bugging her and go to bed already. "I'm fine."

"Not buying it. For one thing, you're not usually so jumpy—"

"I'm not jumpy. I was sleeping."

"And you look like hell."

Fighting the urge to smooth her hair, she batted her lashes. "Sweet-talker."

He touched her arm. "I'm serious. Everything okay? Come on." He grinned, all charm and confidence. "Tell Uncle Anthony all about it."

"I'm fine." And because he obviously still didn't be-lieve her, she forced a smile. "Really."

"Then why are you hiding in here while everyone else is outside?"

Because she hadn't been able to breathe. Not with her chest so tight, her stomach churning with guilt. Every time she got close to Tori or Nora, she struggled to hold on to her secret. To not blurt out everything that had happened. To tell them the very real possibility that their mother was dead.

Thank God her father wasn't due back from sea for a few more days. It would've been worse, so much worse, if he were here.

"Tori and I had a slight…disagreement…this morning." She wiped the butter from her fingers with his napkin. "I thought we both could use some space."

"I wondered why Tori was acting so weird. I figured it was because Greg brought his new girlfriend."

Greg Mott and Tori had been high school sweethearts and when Tori found herself pregnant during the middle of their senior year, he'd stepped up and did the right thing. He was a good guy. Decent. Respectable and responsible. And a wonderful father to Layne's nephew.

But he hadn't been enough for Tori.

"If Tori didn't want him seeing other women," Layne said, "maybe she shouldn't have divorced him."

"Well, yeah, but still it can't be easy seeing the guy you were married to snuggling up with someone new." Anthony wiped his mouth with the napkin. "Or to have Brandon being so into her. Especially when he's been giving Tori such a hard time."

Layne shrugged. "He's a preteen. Plus he's pissed at his mom for tearing his family apart."

"Not that you're judging her much."

She shrugged that off. Maybe she was acting sanctimonious. And judgmental. But while she loved Tori, she couldn't sit by silently while her sister made so many mistakes.

Besides, she didn't know how to fix this rift between them, one that went deeper than what happened at the station this morning. They'd always clashed. Tori was too reckless. Too focused on her own wants and needs.

Too much like Valerie.

The kitchen door opened and Erin, Anthony's older sister, stuck her head inside. "Hey, you two, come on. Brandon's getting ready to open his presents."

"Coming," Layne called as she and Anthony both stood. They walked into the tiny kitchen. "I'll be out in a minute," she told him. "I want to get a drink first."

She waited until after he left to get a glass from an upper cabinet. Filling it with water from the sink, she stared out the window overlooking Tori's patio. Except for her dad, all the people she cared about most were out there, smiling, talking, laughing.

At the head of the picnic table Brandon tore into a brightly wrapped present. He had his father's light brown hair and quick grin, his mother's guarded eyes and, unfortunately for Tori, the Sullivan stubbornness.

Tori, in a pair of tight jeans and a T-shirt the color of daffodils, took pictures off to the side. Nora stood to the right of Tori, her wavy blond hair pulled back, making her look even younger than twenty-six. She talked with Uncle Ken, their father's brother and Nora's mentor and a senior partner at the law firm where she'd recently started working.

Under the large oak tree, Aunt Astor and Erin shared a laugh. Both women were coolly blonde, completely beautiful and classy and still seemed right at home at a small family birthday party held in a backyard roughly the size of their inground swimming pool. Astor touched her daughter's cheek, her love for her clear on her face.

An image of a smiling Valerie flared to life in Layne's mind, a memory from Layne's own twelfth birthday. Layne had just opened the gift from her parents—tiny blue diamond stud earrings so stunning they'd taken her breath away.

Valerie had encouraged her to put them in right away, had even held Layne's hair back while she did so. Then she'd taken Layne's face in her hands, smiled and kissed both Layne's cheeks before pressing her own cheek against her daughter's. Layne had shut her eyes, breathed in her mother's sweet perfume.

And in that one perfect moment, Layne had loved her. More than anyone or anything.

Happy birthday, baby girl.

Tears clogging her throat, Layne lightly touched her right ear, her fingers skimming over the naked lobe.

Curling her fingers, she lowered her hand, pushing the memory from her mind as she exhaled slowly until it felt as if her lungs were empty.

Outside, Brandon whooped loudly. Layne shook her head, focused on her nephew as he yanked a New England Patriots jersey over his head. He ran around the table to give Colleen Gibbs, Greg's plain but very sweet girlfriend, a hug. Greg's parents exchanged a fond glance at each other over their grandson's head.

Witnessing the cozy scene from her spot at the edge of the patio, Tori appeared ready to leap across the table and challenge Colleen to a no-holds-barred cage match.

Luckily Celeste Vitello, Tori's boss at the café and their father's longtime girlfriend, put a comforting hand on Tori's arm. Celeste, a trim and athletic fifty-year-old, had brown, wildly curly hair styled in a short bob that showed off her long neck and made her large, warm brown eyes appear even bigger.

Celeste spoke close to Tori's ear and Tori's glower faded, replaced by a small, reluctant smile. She nodded, responded to Celeste then gestured for Colleen and Brandon to pose for a picture while Celeste slipped away to gather the wrapping paper Brandon had tossed on the ground.

Possible crisis, or at the very least one of Tori's tantrums, averted.

As if sensing her gaze, Celeste raised her head. Their eyes met and she lifted a hand. In greeting? Or perhaps as a sign for Layne to join them.

Layne returned the wave but then held up her forefinger. She needed that minute, that time to get the horrible dream out of her head. To clear the memory of it clinging to her consciousness.

She finished her water, refilled the glass and had it halfway to her mouth when she heard a car door slam. Several heads turned toward the driveway, most showing nothing more than mild curiosity.

And then Police Chief Ross Taylor strode into view, the setting sun glinting off his shiny badge, his mouth set in a serious line.

Shit.

She put the glass on the edge of the sink where it tottered precariously before falling in. It shattered, water and glass shards sprayed her bare arms and hands. She ignored it all.

She pressed a hand against her churning stomach. Inhaled deeply, held it for the count of five. The time had come. Whirling on her bare heel, she walked outside and prepared herself to face the truth.

ROSS CROSSED THE NEATLY trimmed lawn toward the covered patio. Navy blue and red balloons, tied to each of the table legs, bobbed in the evening breeze. Brightly wrapped presents were piled high in front of a boy in an oversize Patriots' jersey, his brown hair sticking up, the braces on his teeth flashing when he smiled.

A chocolate frosted cake—one of those round, two-layered ones like his mom used to make for his and Heather's birthdays—sat on the far end of the table surrounded by paper plates, forks and napkins.

He scanned the faces of the partiers gathered around the table and the few scattered around the yard, still close enough to watch the kid open his gifts. He recognized a couple—Tori Mott, of course, and Ken Sullivan, a prominent lawyer and a former county district attorney.

But he didn't see Layne. Meade had told him she was attending her nephew's party tonight so why wasn't she out here with her family?

"Evening," he said as he approached the group. "I apologize for—"

The back door swung open, hitting the outside of the house with a bang. Ross blinked, glad his dark sunglasses hid the betraying motion. But he couldn't help it. Sullivan stood in the doorway like an Amazonian princess ready to battle to protect her domain.

Her white shorts ended well above her knees giving him a never-before-seen view of her tanned, toned legs. An image that would no doubt show up in the very vivid, very steamy dreams he'd been having about her. Her green, long-sleeved top clung to her breasts, showed the well-defined muscles of her arms. Worst of all, her hair was down, the dark strands sliding over her shoulders as she hurried down the wooden steps.

He forgot, for the barest of moments, that she'd tried to hide that the necklace found at the scene had possibly belonged to her mother. That she was an officer under his command. She had him thinking thoughts better left alone. Wanting something he had no right to covet.

He released a slow breath from between his teeth.

"I'll be right back," she told Tori before crossing to him. "Chief. How about we talk over here where it's… quieter?"

It wasn't a question—more like a command. But

he heard the slight unease, saw the nerves in her hazel eyes. Sympathy stirred. Damn. He didn't want to feel for her, but he did.

He gestured back the way he came. "After you."

She brushed past him. He followed her down the driveway, passing a line of parked vehicles—including a new red Jeep and a glossy black Lexus. Her feet were bare, long and narrow with pink paint on her toes. Her arms swung with purpose. At the end of the driveway, behind the Lexus, she stopped and crossed her arms as she waited for him.

"You found out the identity of the body," she said without preamble. "Is it my mother?"

He hesitated. She held herself stiffly, her chin lifted as if she was bracing for bad news. But really, how could you ever be prepared for this?

"Just tell me," she said, linking her hands together in front of her at her waist. "Please," she said, sounding as if she'd rather choke on the word than spit it out. "Please," she repeated, softer. More sincere. "I need to know."

"Captain…Layne," he corrected without thinking, not missing the surprise on her face as he said her name, the sound of it odd coming out of his mouth. "The dental records prove the body we found was Valerie Sullivan."

She swayed.

He reached out, took a hold of her arms. She seemed delicate despite the play of muscles under his fingers. And she smelled good—light and fresh and feminine. He ground his back teeth together.

"You need to sit down," he said curtly, "before you fall down."

She shook him off. "I'm fine."

She wasn't, but he stepped back anyway. "I'm sorry for your loss."

"I realize you've done this hundreds of times—"

"This?"

She waved her hands in the air. "Death notifications. And while that may be part of your normal spiel, you don't need to bother with it this time. I don't need your professional sympathy."

"You're right," he said so coldly, his breath should've fogged in the summer air. "It is part of my normal spiel to offer my condolences when I have to inform someone that their loved one has died. But that doesn't make those words, or the sympathy behind them, any less genuine."

She pulled both hands through her hair, held it back from her face. "I didn't mean… I'm just saying I'm not a victim here. I don't want to be a victim. Or treated like one."

How could he argue—or get angry—over that? "Fair enough."

"Cause of death?" she asked, slumped back against the passenger-side door of the Lexus as if her legs wouldn't fully support her. But though her eyes were huge in her pale face, they were clear. Determined. Her voice strong.

"Forensic anthropologist found contusions on the skull indicating a sharp blow to the head."

"Skull fracture?"

"That's the most probable answer right now. He's going to go over the remains again tomorrow, make sure he didn't miss anything."

"Okay. Okay," she repeated as if to herself, pushing away from the car to pace along the sidewalk. The sun was slowly sinking behind the trees at her back, haloing her in soft light. "What about Dale York? Have you found him?"

"Working on that. In the meantime, we'll talk to any remaining family he may have in the area—"

"His son." A car went by, beeped. She waved without even looking at it. "Griffin York. He went to school with Tori, owns a garage over on Willard Ave. Griffin's mom is still in town, too. I think she's remarried though…." She tapped her thumb knuckle against her mouth. "What is his name? They live over in Valley Brook Court. Johnson or Johnston or—"

"We'll find her," Ross said, lifting his hand to touch her arm in support. Except touching her, when his body reacted to her the way it did, was such a bad idea, he curled his fingers and lowered it again. "The MPPD will do everything in its power to find out what happened to your mother. To find who did this."

"I know you will. And I…" Her mouth flattened. "Oh, for the love of God," she muttered.

He turned to follow her gaze. A shapely blonde walked toward them, her ponytail swinging behind her. "Hi," she said. "I don't mean to interrupt—"

"Then why are you?" Layne asked.

The blonde merely smiled. "Because Tori, Erin and I did rock, paper, scissors to determine who would come over here and I lost. Two out of three," she told Ross. "Should've went with rock that last shoot—" she shrugged "—but what are you gonna do?"

Layne pressed her fingers against her temple. "What do you want?"

"I came over to see if you've invited Chief Taylor to stay for cake and ice cream."

"No," Layne bit out. "This isn't a social call."

"I'd apologize for her," the blonde told Ross, "but I'm

sure you've already figured out that it'd be a waste of my time. I'm Nora Sullivan, by the way." She offered her hand. "Layne's favorite sister."

She glared at Nora. "You've been demoted to second place. Look, I'll be over as soon as I'm done."

"I can take a hint. Nice meeting you, Chief Taylor," Nora said pleasantly before walking away. She must've gotten all the cheerful genes in her family along with her fair complexion and sunny blond hair.

"As you can see," Layne said, "your timing sucks."

"I'm sorry to interrupt your nephew's birthday," he said, "but this can't wait."

She nodded. Blew out a heavy breath. "You're right." Two words he'd never thought he'd hear from her.

Ross took off his sunglasses, hung them on his shirt. The party burst into a round of Happy Birthday and Layne watched as they sang, her expression unreadable. Tori carried the cake, candles burning brightly in the encroaching twilight, over and set it in front of the boy. Song finished, he leaned over, blew out the candles. His family clapped.

"I need to tell my sisters," Layne murmured, still staring at the family scene. "And my dad."

"Is that him?" Ross asked, nodding toward a stocky man talking with Ken Sullivan at the edge of the patio.

"That's Christopher Mott, Tori's father-in-law. Tori's ex-father-in-law. My dad's not here."

"He's not at his grandson's birthday party?"

Her mouth turned down. "That's pretty much what I meant by he's not here." Finally she faced him. "He's on the *Guiding Light*. And before you ask, let me add that the *Guiding Light* is a fishing vessel."

Ross took his notepad from his shirt pocket and

wrote down *Guiding Light*. "He's out on a boat? When will he get back?"

"Hard to say for certain, but if the good weather holds, they should dock either late Sunday night or early Monday morning."

"I was hoping to speak with him sooner than that," he said, earning himself one of her *you-do-not-belong-here* stares.

"You have a lot to learn about Mystic Point, don't you?"

"That's what they tell me," he managed, sick and tired of people saying he shouldn't be here because he didn't know the names of every single person who waved or said *hello* to him. Because he hadn't gone to school with his coworkers, still needed his GPS to help him find addresses and didn't understand even the basics about the fishing business—Mystic Point's largest industry.

That he never should've been hired instead of a local. Instead of Layne.

"There's not much we can do to get him here any faster," she said. "Just be glad they caught their quota and are already on their way back."

"My father was right," he heard himself say. Then, because her dark eyebrows drew together in question, had to continue, "I should have watched a couple of seasons of *Deadliest Catch* before taking this job."

Her lips twitched. "It's not exactly the same since they're off the coast of Alaska but it's pretty close," she said, watching her sister serve cake. "I'd rather wait until everyone's gone but since you'll be tagging along—"

"Excuse me?"

"I want you there when I tell my sisters. You have

more information about the case than I do plus you're going to want to question us…all of us…and I'd rather do it tonight instead of dragging my sisters down to the police station at a future date."

"And here, after what happened with that necklace, I was worried I'd have to fight you every step of the way."

Even in the fading light, he had no problem detecting the blush that rose up her neck, colored her cheeks. "I told you, that was mistake. A misunderstanding. I can guarantee you'll have my—and my family's—full cooperation during your investigation."

"Going to be like open books, is that it?"

"Why wouldn't we be? We have nothing to hide."

He thought of how incompetent he felt trying to raise his niece. Of his attraction to Layne and how he hated that he couldn't control it. "That's where you're wrong," he said huskily. "Everyone has something to hide."

LAYNE'S HEART TRIPPED as his musky scent reached her, his voice rubbing against her nerve endings, all gravelly and intense and erotic as hell.

She sucked in an unsteady breath and walked toward the patio before Taylor could read something in her face, some truth she'd rather not give away. Would rather not even acknowledge herself.

Her thoughts were jumbled. Her emotions tumbling one into another into another. Surely she couldn't be blamed for a momentary loss of control.

"Brandon," Tori said when Layne passed the bumper of Anthony's new Jeep, "there's Aunt Layne."

He lifted his head from his food. "Yeah. There she is."

Tori's eyes narrowed to slits at his disrespectful tone. "Don't you have something to say to her?"

He shrugged. Scooped in a huge bite of cookies-and-cream-flavored ice cream.

Colleen touched his arm. "Brandon," she said, her light admonishment clear. Brandon got to his feet and walked toward Layne.

Leaving Tori glowering, as if she wouldn't mind shoving both Brandon and Colleen off a very high cliff.

Her nephew stood before Layne. Tall like his mother, he was still very much a little boy with his round face and the speck of chocolate frosting on his upper lip. "Mom wants me to thank you for the video game."

Yep. Little kid and acting like a grade-A brat.

"Does she?" Layne asked. "In that case, maybe I should return the game and get a present for her instead." His eyes widened as that sunk in. "Seeing as how she's the one who appreciates it."

"Sorry." He gave her a one-armed hug around her waist. "Thanks for the game, Aunt Layne. I love it."

"Better." She squeezed him against her side for a moment. "Seems to me," she said close to his ear, "you have a lot to be grateful for."

He tipped his head up and looked at her curiously.

"Like this party," she said, pretending not to notice how his thin shoulders stiffened. "Your mom not only put up all the decorations, she also made your favorite dinner and chocolate cake."

He glanced over at Tori. "I guess."

She patted his back, sent him on his way. Dragging his feet, he went around the table to his mother where he spoke so softly, she had to lean toward him to hear. But then she hugged him, an embrace he returned if not enthusiastically, at least sincerely. Tori sent Layne a small, grateful smile over Brandon's head.

That's what she did, Layne thought as she shifted

her weight from one foot to the other. She fixed things. Took care of her family. It was a responsibility she'd never questioned, never regretted taking on. She couldn't regret it now.

"Hey, Aunt Layne," Brandon called, wriggling out of his mother's arms and picking up the game Layne had bought him. "Wanna play?"

"Actually I need to talk to your mom and Aunt Nora first." She felt her sisters' gazes on her. Questioning. "How about you spend the night sometime next week? I'll gladly kick your—"

"Careful," Tori warned.

"—butt then."

Brandon snorted. "Yeah, right. You are so going down."

"In your dreams. But hey, if it makes you feel better to think that, go ahead." She put her hands into her front pockets then took them out again. "Nora? Tori? Let's go inside."

"What's up?" Nora asked the same time Tori said, "Kind of busy here hosting my son's birthday." Tori handed a plate of cake to Anthony who added a huge scoop of vanilla ice cream. "Can't it wait?"

"If it could've waited," Layne said in what she considered a highly reasonable tone, well aware of Chief Taylor watching her, "I wouldn't have asked you to come inside now, would I?"

"I'll take over," Celeste said, taking the cake knife from Tori—probably a good idea since Tori's expression said she'd rather use it to stab Layne in the heart. Celeste gave Tori a light hip bump. "Go on. It's fine."

Tori gave an ill-natured shrug then went into the house followed by Nora. At the top of the back steps, Layne wavered, the door open, the handle in her hand.

"You want me to tell them?" Taylor asked lowly from behind her, his solid chest brushing against her back. It cost her, more than it should, not to lean into him, not to let him take over.

But this was her family. Her responsibility. She shook her head and walked inside.

"Is this about Dad?" Nora asked as soon as the door shut behind Taylor. "Is he all right?"

"No. No, Dad's fine." Crap. She should've realized that would've been their first thought. Everyone in town knew the risks commercial fishermen took every time they went out to sea, that it was one of the most dangerous professions out there.

"Whatever it is, it better be important," Tori said, putting the lasagna Anthony must have left on the table back in the refrigerator, "because now Little Miss Sunshine is out there making points with my in-laws—"

"Ex-in-laws," Nora and Layne both said.

"Swooping in, inserting herself into my family—" She waved her hands in the air. "Acting like she's nothing but sweetness and light—"

"Colleen is sweetness and light," Nora said. "She's nice. And Brandon really seems to like her."

"Thank you," Tori said icily. "That makes me feel a whole lot better."

"Enough," Layne snapped, drawing her sisters' attention. And their silence. "Listen, I...I think we should all sit down first."

Without giving them a chance to agree—or, more probable, argue—she went into the living room. Waited in front of the TV while her sisters sat on the couch and Taylor took up sentinel in the doorway, his hands linked behind his back, his feet wide.

"You're really scaring me," Nora said. "What is it? What's wrong?"

"Yeah, quit with the dramatic buildup and tell us," Tori said, sitting on the edge of the couch. But the way she laid a hand on Nora's knee, in support and comfort, belied the edge to her voice.

A lump formed in Layne's throat, making it difficult to swallow. Impossible to speak.

Her sisters were a unit. Always had been. While she preferred to stay on the fringe. It was safer. Easier to maintain control and her objectivity that way.

Don't get too close, not to anyone, and it won't hurt when they leave you.

And everyone left eventually.

She opened her mouth but no sound came out. Swallowing, she glanced at Taylor, equally relieved and irritated when he stepped forward.

"Mrs. Mott," he said, bumping up that irritation, "Miss Sullivan, there's been—"

"No." Layne pressed her lips together then cleared her throat. "I can do it."

She was a cop. A professional. And this, while not just another death notification, was still her job. She didn't need him to do it for her.

"As you might already know, human remains were found at the quarry early this morning," she said, proud of how detached she sounded. Like she didn't care.

She didn't want to care.

"Those remains have been identified," she continued. Her eyes going from one sister's face to the other, she let her guard down enough to feel a sense of loss. Of sadness and regret. "It's Mom."

CHAPTER SEVEN

"OH, GOD," NORA BREATHED, clutching the hand Tori still had on her knee. She slowly shook her head. "Oh, God, oh, God, oh, God."

"Are you sure it's not a mistake?" Tori asked, her eyes stark. "Mom left Mystic Point."

"We thought she'd left," Layne agreed. "But obviously we were wrong."

Taylor crossed to stand beside her, as if letting her know he had her back. She wanted to snarl at him, tell him she didn't need his support. Didn't want to admit that having him there actually helped.

It helped a lot.

"I'm afraid there's no mistake," he said. "We were able to identify the remains using dental records."

"Wait, wait, wait," Nora said, holding up her free hand. "This doesn't make any sense. We all thought Mom left town with Dale York," she told Layne. "So why would you check her dental records? Why would the police even consider that those remains could be hers?"

She felt Taylor's gaze on her but he kept silent. Giving her the chance to explain. Better yet, not telling her sisters how she'd tried to keep that necklace a secret.

"A necklace was found at the scene," she admitted. "It's Mom's."

Nora, always too perceptive for her own good—

or anyone else's—narrowed her eyes. "When did you see it?"

"At the scene. When Chief Taylor gave it to me to take to Processing."

Nora's head snapped back as if she'd been slapped.

Tori on the other hand, leaped to her feet, looked ready to rip out Layne's throat. "You saw the necklace this morning? You knew there was a possibility it could be Mom and you didn't say anything?" She pressed both hands against her head as if stopping her brain from simply exploding. "What the hell is wrong with you?"

Guilt nudged her, hard and insistent. "I didn't want to say anything until we had a positive ID."

"Do you even hear yourself? It's always about what you want." Tori's mouth twisted in disgust. "You have to control everything."

"What good would it have done if I'd told you? I had no proof."

"Could you stop being a cop for one minute? She's our mother." Tori's arms were rigid, her face flushed. "She *was* our mother. You should have told us."

"I did what I thought was best." That was all she'd ever done. And she'd be damned if she'd apologize for it.

"There's no sense arguing about it now," Nora said, her eyes wet, the tip of her nose pink. She took a hold of one of Tori's fisted hands. "Please. Not now."

After a moment, Tori linked her fingers through Nora's and sat back down. "How did it happen?" she asked Taylor. "Was she murdered?"

He stepped forward. "We don't have an official cause of death—"

"But you have a theory." This from Nora.

"We have reason to suspect your mother was the

victim of a homicide," he said. "There was a noticeable skull fracture consistent with being hit with a large, heavy object."

Nora used her fingers to wipe away the tears that slid down her cheeks.

Slumping back against the couch, Tori met Layne's eyes. "Do you think Dale did it?"

"Yes," Layne said emphatically.

"We don't have all the facts yet," Ross cautioned, giving Layne a warning look. "The Mystic Point Police Department is going to be investigating all the possibilities."

But Tori, never one to be satisfied, brushed that aside. "Dale York was an abusive son of a bitch. Everyone in town knew he was bad news and to stay away from him—"

"Everyone but Mom," Layne pointed out.

Tori's mouth pinched. She turned her body toward the chief, shutting Layne out. "What other possibilities could there be?" she asked Taylor.

"We're searching for Mr. York," Taylor said, the perfect example of a cop giving a nonanswer. "But I wouldn't be doing my job if I didn't look into any and all possible scenarios concerning—"

The kitchen door slammed shut followed by the sound of someone—from the sound of his pounding footsteps, a male, one-hundred-ten-pound someone with too-big feet—running through the kitchen. A moment later Brandon appeared. He didn't even pause at the sight of them in the room, at the tension in the air.

"Dad said I could spend the night at his house," he said, skirting around Taylor and heading toward the stairs in the foyer. "I'm gonna pack and—"

"You're not spending the night at your father's," Tori said, her tone brooking no argument. "Not tonight."

Brandon, always more than happy to argue with his mother lately, spun around. "Why not? He said I could."

"Well, I'm saying you can't. You're supposed to be here tonight. You'll be with your dad the rest of the weekend starting tomorrow."

"It's my birthday. I want to stay at Dad's."

And he took off up the stairs, his feet slapping on the treads.

Tori stared at his retreating back for a moment. "I have to go talk to Greg. Straighten this out."

Before she took a full step, Layne blocked her escape. "We're not done."

"I realize this is difficult," Taylor said in his unruffled way, as if he could infuse the situation with his calm. "And a really bad time, but I'd like to ask you all some questions—"

"Difficult?" Tori repeated with a short laugh. "Yes, I guess you could say that. And it is a bad time. Which is why I'm not doing this now." She scowled at Layne. "Don't make me move you," she said darkly.

Layne almost dared her to do just that but having Taylor there stopped her. Too bad. A battle with her sister would give her something else to focus on, a much needed distraction from her whirling thoughts, the way her lungs felt constricted, as if she'd never take another full breath.

"We need to give Chief Taylor as much information as possible as quickly as possible so he can do his job," she said using her best impassive, I-know-so-much-better-than-you, cop voice. "This is important, Tori."

"You think I don't know that? But right now I have other matters to tend to."

"Just let him go with Greg," Layne said. "What is the big deal?"

Tori's shoulders snapped back hard enough to dislocate a vertebrae. "The big deal is that he should be home on his birthday. Especially tonight. His grandmother was murdered. He needs to be told and he needs to hear it from me, not—" she waved her hand in the air "—read it in the paper or from Greg. He needs to be with me." Her voice thickened. "I want him with me."

"Tori's right," Nora said, as always taking Tori's side over Layne's. "We need time to process what's happened, time to tell the rest of our family what's going on. We'll come down to the station whenever it's convenient for Chief Taylor and answer any questions he might have. With our attorney present."

"You don't need an attorney present," Taylor said. "None of you are under arrest."

"You don't have to tell her that," Layne said. "She is an attorney. Therefore, if she's present, we'll have an attorney present, as well."

But Nora, God bless her, with her soft beauty and sunny disposition could be as stubborn as her sisters. More so when she felt she had something to prove, and if it had the added benefit of grating on Layne's last nerve? All the better. "I'd still like Uncle Kenny there in an official capacity."

Brandon stomped down the stairs, a bulging backpack tossed over his shoulder.

"Brandon!" Tori yelled as he hurried past Taylor. "You'd better not even think about—"

Once again the back door slammed.

Tori pushed past Layne, bumping into her shoulder hard enough to have Layne stepping back to keep her balance. It took every ounce of willpower she possessed not to tackle Tori and grind her gorgeous face into the carpet. A moment later, the door shut again, the bang this time even louder.

"Maybe we should schedule a meeting for tomorrow morning at my office?" Taylor asked, drawing a business card from his back pocket and handing it to Nora. "That way we can get through it without any interruptions."

"No." Layne pressed her lips together. Okay, that had sounded militant at best. Panicked at worst.

What a mess. She'd wanted Chief Taylor to stay, to be here when she told Tori and Nora so he could get started on his investigation. The sooner they answered his questions, the sooner Taylor could concentrate on finding Dale York, on bringing him to justice for what he did to her mother.

She wanted to be through with it all. To contact her father so they could start making plans to lay her mother's remains to rest. Then they could all finally move on and put Valerie where she belonged.

In the past and out of their minds. For good.

"Let's give her a few minutes to deal with Brandon," Layne said, inwardly cringing at the desperation in her tone, "then we'll all sit down—"

"I told you, this isn't happening tonight," Nora insisted, her arms crossed, her expression clearly stating nothing short of a bulldozer could get her to change her position. "So, unless you plan on arresting me—"

"Who's being the drama queen now?" Layne asked in exasperation.

Nora's eyes about popped out of her head. "Drama queen? Our mother is dead. And you're acting like it doesn't even matter." Her voice rose, her hands fisted, reminding Layne that for all of her youngest sister's charms, she'd always been capable of throwing one hell of a tantrum. "How can you be so…so unfeeling? So heartless?"

Layne went hot, then cold. It didn't matter that her boss watched this little familial exchange or that part of her wondered—worried—that Nora was right. Anger clouded her thoughts, made it impossible to look inside herself for some deeper inner meaning. A meaning she was afraid to discover.

"How dare you?" she asked but the words came out barely above a whisper. She cleared her throat. "How dare you judge me? I'm not the one who left."

"Mom didn't leave." But although Nora stood her ground, she sounded uncertain. "She was killed."

"She left first. What happened afterward doesn't change the fact that she chose Dale over her husband. Over us." Her hands were shaking, her breathing rapid. "It's not unfeeling or heartless to do my job and help Chief Taylor get some answers about what happened to her that night. But I won't pretend to mourn a woman who almost ripped our family apart. Not when she's been dead to me for the past eighteen years."

LAYNE'S VOICE, ROSS NOTED, like her expression, was hard. Bitter. But her lower lip trembled.

Nora, on the other hand, had tears falling freely, her arms wrapped around her middle. "Whatever she did, whatever her mistakes, she was still our mother. It's only right to mourn her now. To feel sadness. Regret."

Layne's hazel eyes flashed. "She didn't deserve my sympathy when she was alive. I'm sure as hell not going to give it to her now." When she stepped closer to her sister, he moved as well, making sure to be within easy reach in case he had to hold her back from doing bodily harm to the baby-faced blonde. "And how I do, or do not, react or act, and my feelings are none of your goddamn business."

She stalked out, her long legs eating up the distance to the front door in a matter of moments. Unlike her nephew and sister, when she shut the door, she did so with the barest of sounds.

Leaving him alone with her now openly weeping sister.

Nora, her head down, her long ponytail brushing her shoulder, sniffed, her body shaking. In his line of work, he dealt with more than his fair share of tears. There were plenty of times when he'd been a shoulder to lean on, a steady presence in a time of complete upheaval in someone's life. He'd commiserated and consoled, counseled and, at times, got information about a case by letting someone whose guard was down talk about their loved one.

Gaining trust and listening were all in a day's work. But part of being a detective, of what he liked to think made him good at his job, was knowing when to press forward for that information and when to ease back.

It was definitely easing back time. Nora Sullivan wouldn't give him anything valuable. Not tonight. And she didn't need him to help her through her shock and grief. She needed the people out back—Tori and her aunt and uncle.

And, perhaps, most of all, she needed Layne.

"I'll see myself out," he said.

She lifted her head, her face tear-streaked. "Oh, no." She sounded horrified, as if he'd said he'd decided to bunk down there and planned on taking a bubble bath in her sister's tub before calling it a night. Wiping her face with her sleeve, she sucked in a deep breath. Seemed calmer after she exhaled. "I'll walk you out."

At the door, he paused. "Again, I'm very sorry for your loss." She nodded and he stepped out onto the porch. "Good night."

The door shut behind him. But he didn't take the few steps necessary to cross the small porch. Just stood there, his hands loose by his sides, as the night surrounded him. Stars dotted the sky; the air was warm and sticky, heavy with humidity and the cloying scent from the large, flowering bush hiding half the porch from view of the road.

He did a few slow neck rolls but the tension pinching his shoulders remained. The weight of expectations, of what he had to do pressed down on him. He was dealing with a crime that happened eighteen years ago, a crime they hadn't even known about until today. Unless someone came forward as a witness—or to confess—he was going to have one hell of a time finding enough evidence not only to arrest someone, but for a conviction.

Something moved to his right, made a creaking sound. Squinting, he noticed a slight figure on a long wooden swing. Layne sat forward, her elbows on her knees, the light throwing shadows across her features.

But he didn't miss how her gaze flicked to his hand hovering over his gun then back up to his eyes.

"Easy there, Quick Draw," she said sounding weary, "it's just me."

He flexed and straightened his fingers. "Sorry. Habit."

She hummed, a soft, contemplative sound. "My fault. I shouldn't have startled a cop. We're a jumpy breed."

"I prefer to think of it as being alert."

"I'm sure you do." The swing creaked as she sat

back. His sight adjusted to the dark enough to see her tip her head up to look at him. "Sorry about dragging you into our sibling misery."

"Do you mean sibling rivalry?"

She thought that over for a moment. "No, I'm pretty sure it's just pure misery at this point." She grimaced. "Guess it's my day for making a fool out of myself in front of you, huh?"

He stepped closer, the movement blocking the light. He shifted to the side. "That a habit? Making a fool out of yourself?"

Her lips twitched in self-depreciating humor. "Not sure it's a habit yet. But today wasn't the first time and it probably won't be the last."

"Warning heeded."

She brought her legs up, set her feet on the swing and laid her head on her bent knees, much the same way Jess had done last night. Layne's hair swung forward, covering her face like a silk curtain.

His palms itched to reach out and brush her hair back, to let the strands slide through his fingers. To see if it was as soft as it looked.

He swallowed hard. Linked his hands behind his back.

"You probably have to get going," she said, glancing up at him, her head still on her knees.

He did. He needed to get home, check on Jess, see if he could make a dent in the paperwork that went along with running a small-town police station. He shouldn't be out here in the near-dark. Not with her. Shouldn't want to mend the rift between her and her family.

It wasn't up to him to fix this.

But, if it'd been Meade or Campbell or any other male officer under his command, he wouldn't be having any of those thoughts. Would have no problem helping them through a difficult time, all while maintaining his professional distance.

He was making his attraction to Layne bigger than it was, more important than it had any right to be, and that pinched his pride. And his ego.

He glanced toward his parked car. "I'm not in any hurry."

Relief crossed her face. She set her bare feet on the wooden floor and scooted over on the swing. Making room for him. He clenched his teeth until his jaw ached. And then he stepped forward. What else could he do? She seemed so alone. And she obviously needed someone. Needed him. He couldn't leave her. Not yet.

He sat and the swing moved, arcing backward. As soon as it settled he realized he'd made a mistake. A big one. Their arms brushed, their thighs touched. Her warmth and fresh scent wrapped around him like the night itself. It was too dark. Too intimate. Too tempting.

He shifted until the arm of the swing dug into his side, until a good three inches of space separated them.

"Was I wrong?" she asked with a soft exhalation. "Not to tell them about the necklace, about my suspicions earlier?"

Getting in the middle of a family argument wasn't his first choice of activities for the evening. "I couldn't say."

He felt her watching him. Kept his own eyes straight ahead. "Can't?" she asked. "Or won't?"

"How about don't want to?"

She laughed, a small burst of sound, and he couldn't stop himself from turning toward her. "Good answer. No wonder you're the chief."

And I'm not.

The words, left unspoken, were there, though. In every conversation they had, every time they butted heads. She resented him taking what she perceived—rightly or wrongly so—as her position. He resented how she challenged his authority. And that he thought of her.

Dreamed of her.

"I think," he said slowly, "that if I was in your shoes, I would've done the same thing."

Her eyebrows winged up. "Except not speaking up about the necklace sooner."

"Except that. You let your personal feelings get the best of you in that situation. Which proves emotions have no place in a police investigation."

"Another of those no-shades-of-gray areas?"

He lifted a shoulder. "Emotions can cloud a person's judgment, make them lose perspective. Which is why you can't be involved, in any way, in this investigation. And no matter how many times you try to deny it—to me, to your sisters, even to yourself—this isn't another case. Not to you."

"Ah, but I don't have to deal with such untidy things such as emotions," she said, her light tone not hiding the hurt in her voice. "Haven't you heard? I'm heartless."

"Everybody reacts to news like this in their own way. Grieves in their time."

"That's just it. I don't want to grieve my mother. I'm not even sure if I can. I don't…" She tucked her hair behind her ear, kept her gaze on her lap. "My mother is dead and I don't feel anything," she said so quietly, he had to strain to hear her. "I'm…numb."

She wasn't but she was in denial. He'd seen it plenty of times in his career, had experienced it himself with his sister when he hadn't wanted to admit how bad her addiction had gotten. But he'd witnessed how Layne had fought to hold herself together when he told her they'd identified the remains. She wasn't ready to deal with whatever was going on inside her, wasn't strong enough to deal with it yet.

"Jess didn't cry," he heard himself saying, "when her mom—my sister—was sent away."

"Sent away? As in…*sent away,* sent away?"

He nodded. "She's had some…legal problems that finally came to a head this past winter. We were all in the courtroom—me, my parents, Jess—and when the judge handed down the sentence, Mom and Dad both broke down. Heather, too." He stabbed a hand through his hair remembering how powerless he'd felt. How guilty having let Heather spiral so far out of control. "But Jess…she just sat there. Completely blank, like none of it affected her."

"Seems to me," Layne said, compassion lacing her tone, "it affected her the most."

"Exactly." The sound of canned laughter from a television show floated through an open window from the house next door, the sound incongruous with his memories. "I couldn't understand it. Here's a kid who cries at the drop of a hat. When she's frustrated or angry or, as you noticed last night, drunk, the waterworks start. But she didn't shed one tear that day. Or, as far as I know, one yet over her mom."

"So," Layne said, dragging the word out, "you're saying I'm acting like a teenager?"

"I'm saying there's no timeline for a situation like this, or what Jess went through. And Jess will mourn what happened to her mother when she's ready."

Silence. He glanced at Layne to make sure she hadn't stopped breathing. She was staring at him, her brow furrowed, but then, as if wiped clean, her expression cleared.

"Wow," she said, bending one leg and tugging it under the other, causing the swing to sway. "I never would've pegged you for a Dr. Phil fan."

"I'm a man of varied and eclectic taste in television shows," he assured her solemnly.

"All sarcastic comments aside—"

"Is that even possible for you?"

"—I appreciate you coming out here to tell me first about Mom."

"You're a colleague," he pointed out, not wanting her—not wanting anyone—to think he'd given her special treatment because she was a woman. Because he was attracted to her. "I would've done the same for any of the other officers in my squad."

She smiled…a soft, sad smile that made his breath catch. "I'm sure you would. But you didn't do it for someone else, you did it for me—despite our…personality conflict."

He opened his mouth to brush it off, to downplay it but she leaned toward him, the material of her top pulling taut against her breasts, and the words dried in his throat.

"And," she continued, laying her hand on his knee, "I wanted to thank you."

His muscles contracted under her fingers, her warmth seeped through the material to heat his skin. He couldn't stop himself from looking at that hand, then at her face. Couldn't stop his gaze from settling on her mouth for two heavy beats of his heart.

Her lips parted on a soft inhale and he jerked his gaze up. Her eyes darkened even as her fingers tightened on his leg. The night air seemed to still. To thicken with awareness and need.

An awareness that was out of bounds. A need he couldn't fill.

He stood. Took a step back. "I'd do it for anyone who worked for me."

"Yeah, you already said that."

So he had. He thrust his hands into his front pockets. "Good night, Captain."

"Tori was right," Layne called when Ross was halfway down the front walk. "You're not nearly the asshole I said you were."

Lifting a hand in acknowledgment he kept walking. Only when he was safely in his car a block away did he let himself grin.

You're not nearly the asshole I said you were.

Coming from Layne, that was high praise indeed.

CHAPTER EIGHT

ON ANY GIVEN DAY, the Ludlow Street Café's kitchen was busy. But on a weekend morning when tourists and locals alike waited in a line that wound around the block? Chaos. Utter and complete chaos.

And Layne was right smack-dab in the middle of it. Cutting home fries, no less.

She hated cutting home fries.

"You don't have to do that," Celeste told Layne. She set an order under the warming lights on the window that opened into an alcove between the kitchen and dining room. A wide, black headband held her curly hair from her face and food and grease stained the white apron covering her black capri pants and T-shirt. She tapped the bell twice—the cheerful *ding, ding* getting on Layne's last nerve. "Sandy. Pick up," Celeste called then turned back to her workstation.

Layne scooped cut potatoes into a bowl. "I don't mind pitching in. Seems you need it since Tori isn't here."

Plus, keeping her hands busy, her mind occupied by being surrounded by so much noise and all these people didn't give her much chance to think, to worry and chew over the decisions she'd made. To wonder what she should've done differently.

To relive that charged moment between her and Chief Taylor last night.

She fumbled the large chef's knife, almost cutting off the tips of a few fingers.

"Careful," Celeste admonished gently, adding chopped peppers, onions and mushrooms to a veggie-lover's omelet. "You shouldn't be here. You should be with your sisters."

Layne's throat closed. They didn't want her.

"I'll see them at the station in—" she checked the large Coke clock on the wall "—just over an hour."

"That's not what I meant."

"They're still angry with me," she said with a casual shrug. "So some space will do us good."

Which was why she'd chosen to go back to her own house last night instead of spending the night at Tori's as Nora had.

Sprinkling a generous amount of shredded cheese onto the omelet, Celeste glanced at her. "And some-times, too much space creates a bigger rift."

True. But it was easier to be alone. Safer.

Less chance of getting hurt. Or, as she so often seemed to do, hurting others.

"Tori and Nora need you now," Celeste said, her dark eyes serious, her tone somber. "And, I think, you need them. You don't have to do everything on your own," she added quietly, giving Layne's forearm a quick squeeze before folding the omelet. "You're not alone in this. You're never alone. But you need to learn to let people in, let them help you. That's what family is for."

Her jaw tight, her eyes burning, Layne could only nod. Keeping her gaze down, she carefully cut yet an-other parboiled potato as Celeste transferred the omelet onto a plate, added home fries and toast and carried it to the window.

Layne set aside the knife. Yes, that was what family

was for. And Layne had always been there for hers. Had always done what was best for them and put them first. She didn't know how to let them do the same for her.

Didn't trust them to be there when she needed them.

Picking up the knife again, Layne laid another potato on the wooden cutting board and split it in half with one, swift swing.

Coming here had not been the best idea she'd ever had. All she'd wanted was some noise, and possibly a mindless task to keep her busy until she had to go to the station. Instead she got one of Celeste's thoughtful and yes, damn it, correct assessments of what was currently wrong with her life.

She could've stayed home. But she hadn't been able to spend one more minute in her big, rambling house, her only company the lovable, dopey mutt she'd adopted from the shelter a few months back. But Bobby O—a lab-rottie mix with more heart than brains—wasn't much of a talker. On the other hand, there were no judgments from Bobby. No recriminations or hurt feelings.

As long as she fed him, rubbed his stomach each night and played Frisbee with him until it felt like her arm was going to fall off, she had his unconditional love.

If only all her relationships could be that easy.

"I wish I could be there with you girls this morning," Celeste said when she returned. "I don't like the idea of the three of you going there alone."

"How can we be alone if we're there together? And we're going to the police station," Layne pointed out, "which also happens to be where I work. Not a third world country overrun with terrorists."

Celeste set her hands on her nonexistent hips—the

woman was so thin, she disappeared when she turned sideways. "I worry. You're my girls."

Layne sighed and slid off her stool and wrapped her arm around the older woman's shoulders. "I know you do."

"Maybe I should go anyway. Joe can cover—"

"No, he can't."

No one, not even Joe Bernhardi, the cook who'd been with the café since Celeste opened it sixteen years ago, could handle a Saturday breakfast rush on his own. Usually it took Celeste, Joe and Tori—who pitched in on cooking duty one day of the weekend—to make it through.

"We'll be fine," Layne continued. "And we'll tell you everything as soon as we're done."

Sniffing, Celeste nodded. Started working on an order of raspberry/cream cheese stuffed French toast. "I know you will. It's…it's still such a shock. It's stupid. She's been gone all these years but…I still can't believe Valerie is…dead." The last came out just above a whisper.

They'd all agreed last night not to say anything about Valerie's death to anyone outside the family until Tim got home. "It's going to take some time to get used to," Layne said.

Though even she could admit the thought of Valerie not being out there, somewhere, living and breathing and wreaking havoc on others' lives, caused a pang— a small one—in her chest.

"Tim seemed to take it well." Celeste dipped two thick slices of homemade bread into egg batter. "Don't you think?"

"As well as can be expected," she said carefully, not seeing any point in telling Celeste that when Layne had initially told her father last night, he'd sobbed like his heart was breaking. Breaking. Over the woman who'd cheated on him. Lied to him. Left him.

Not what his current girlfriend needed to hear. No matter that, at one time, Celeste had loved Valerie, too. The two women had been the best of friends since high school, had worked together at the Yacht Pub, a bar on the docks.

And how two such different females had created such a strong bond was beyond Layne.

"Well, I for one will— Jessica," she said to someone behind Layne. "Right on time."

Layne raised her eyebrows at the sight of Taylor's niece standing inside the swinging doors. With her pale hair all shiny and wavy, the dark makeup on her eyes and her lips a glossy pink, she could've passed for at least eighteen.

Throw in those shorty-mcshort-shorts she wore and the deep V-neck of her clingy, white top showing some grown-up-size cleavage and Layne bumped that up to twenty-one. Twenty-two if you saw her from a distance.

The kid's expression turned wary when she spotted Layne. "Hi," Jess mumbled.

"What's going on?" Layne asked Celeste.

"Jessica is my new waitress." Celeste flipped the bread on the grill then sent Jessica a wink. "She had a very good reference."

"That so?" Layne asked. She checked the time. "And you asked her to be here at eight forty? Strange time to start work, isn't it?"

Jessica lifted her chin, her eyes defiant. "I had to walk. I didn't think it would take as long as it did."

"Your uncle couldn't give you a ride?" Layne asked.

The kid's mouth flattened, just like Ross's did when he got irritated. "He wasn't home."

"That's fine," Celeste said, waving her arms as if erasing the time, Layne's comments and the girl's tardiness. "Come on in, honey, before you get smacked in the rear."

Jessica's mouth popped open. "You're going to spank me for being a few minutes late?"

Celeste shook her head. "Wha—"

"The door," Layne said, fighting laughter. She cleared her throat. "You're going to get hit by the door if you don't move."

The kid's face flamed red. "Oh," she said, stepping forward.

"I'm afraid we're swamped at the moment," Celeste told Jessica. "Usually I ask one of the waitresses to take new hires around, show them where everything is and let them get comfortable before I toss them to the wolves, so to speak, but we're shorthanded this morning."

"I'll do it," Layne offered.

Celeste smeared sweetened cream cheese onto a slice of toasted bread, topped it with raspberry sauce and the second slice of bread. "Do you two know each other?"

Layne noticed Jess's shoulders stiffen, as if waiting for a blow. Or for Layne to tell Celeste all about her new hire's drunken debauchery from two nights ago.

"Not really," Layne said, holding the kid's gaze. "But we have met."

"You don't mind showing her around?" Celeste asked. "What about your appointment?"

"I have plenty of time."

"I'm not sure… It's been a long time since you worked here."

"Has anything changed?"

Dusting powdered sugar over the toast, Celeste's lips twitched. "We did get a new fryer back in '05."

"Well, there you go," Layne said. "Changes galore."

"Why fix something if it's not broken? And the system here works."

"It does. All of which I'll explain to Jessica."

"Thanks. It would help if she could get her paperwork filled out and you could at least show her around. Everything you'll need is in the file cabinet under New Hires. When you're done with Layne," Celeste told Jess, "come on back here and we'll give you a crash course in what your duties will be."

Jessica shrugged. "Sure. Whatever."

"Pleasant little thing," Layne said to Celeste under her breath. "She'll be a huge hit with the patrons."

"If I recall, you were one of my most popular waitresses. And no one's ever accused you of being pleasant."

"True. And on that note…" She faced Jess. "Come on. We'll start in the office, go over a few laws and regulations."

Jess followed Layne out of the kitchen, down the back hallway and into Celeste's office. The cherry desk that had been Celeste's grandfather's when he captained a ship dominated the small room. Two narrow windows let in morning sunlight, framed articles about the café hung on the walls along with a portrait of Tim and Celeste taken a few years back and Layne and her sisters' high school graduation photos.

"Take a seat," Layne said, gesturing to the chair in front of the desk. She crossed to the squat, metal filing cabinet. "So, does your uncle know you're here?"

"I told you, he wasn't home when I woke up."

"But you left him a note?"

Scowling, Jess slid down in her seat. "He didn't leave me one."

So, that was it, huh? Jess obviously thought there was a double standard there and resented having to follow rules her uncle was exempt from.

Then again, maybe she was just pissed—and hurt— that her uncle didn't care about her feelings enough to tell her where he was going.

Or, Layne mused, maybe Ross didn't think of his niece often enough at all.

"Let's try it this way." Having found the folder she wanted, Layne closed the cabinet drawer, tossed the file onto the desk. "And this is one of those multiple choice questions where your choices are yes or no. Does your uncle know you're starting work here?"

"He—"

"Yes? Or no?"

"Yes," the kid ground out.

"Good." She opened the file, pulled out a sheaf of papers and handed them to Jess. "Fill these out. When you're done we'll take a little tour."

Layne sat in Celeste's chair while Jess went to work on filling out tax forms. She couldn't help but wonder what the deal was between Ross and his niece. Thanks to his little pep talk last night, she knew why Jess lived with him but she still had little sense of their relationship other than it was strained. Had that always been the case? Or had Jess's recent circumstances put her and her uncle at odds?

She was curious. With a bit of nosiness tossed in for good measure. Which was crazy. Not to mention hypocritical since Layne had hated when her family had been the subject of other people's curiosity.

Thanks to her mother, they'd spent more than a year as the hot topic of local gossip, had endured more than their fair share of rumors. There'd been talk—there was always talk in a small town. But that didn't make it right.

Didn't make it hurt any less to be discussed and judged and whispered about.

So, no, Ross's issues with his niece were none of her concern and certainly not her problem.

And when the hell had she started thinking of him as Ross?

Pressing her forefingers against her eyes, she leaned back. She never should have touched him last night. What had started off as a casual, no-thought gesture had morphed into some crazy, summer-night-induced heated moment.

He'd wanted to kiss her. She'd seen the desire in his eyes. His need. For a moment she'd forgotten where she was, who she was. Who they were—chief and assistant chief—and what they had to remain to each other.

Worse, much worse was how much she'd wanted to kiss him, too.

Being a good cop means being able to keep your personal life and professional one separate.

Good advice. Layne had a feeling she'd better heed it.

JESS GAVE THE LAST COMPLETED form to the cop from the other night—the one with the Angelina Jolie body and badass attitude. The one Uncle Ross had made drive Jess home, who'd ended up having to help her into the house and up the stairs to her room because she'd been too drunk to make it there on her own.

Jess gnawed on the inside of her cheek. Good thing

she didn't care what anyone thought of her or she'd be humiliated right about now.

"Come on," the cop said as she walked toward the door. "I'll show you around, introduce you to everyone and give you the basics."

Jess followed her back into the hallway. She'd told Jess to call her Layne—yeah, like that would happen. Bad enough she had to live with the top cop of this stupid town, she wasn't about to be on a first-name basis with this one.

"Cleaning supply closet," the cop said as they passed a closed door. "Employee bathroom," she continued of the tiny room with the toilet and sink.

She veered off to the right and entered a decent-size room. There was a square table, several chairs, a TV on the counter and row of small lockers—like the ones the school here used for gym class—against the wall.

"This is the break room/locker room. Celeste will give you a locker where you can store your stuff— purse, cash…" She shrugged. "Whatever. There's no smoking at all in the building so if you feel the need to light up—"

"I don't smoke."

"No skin off my nose whether you do or don't. They're your lungs. But if you do, do it outside."

Jess narrowed her eyes. What kind of game was this chick playing? She'd sworn to uphold the law and all that crap. Of course she cared whether some teenager smoked or not. She probably staked out convenience stores wearing a stupid hat and sunglasses so she could bust some clerk for selling tobacco to an underage kid.

"I don't smoke," Jess repeated, not because it mattered to her what some small-town cop thought of her.

She just didn't like people judging her. That's all. "It's stupid."

"Agreed."

And…that was it. She didn't go on, didn't mention how Jess hadn't seemed to think drinking until she puked and having sex with some guy out in the middle of the woods was stupid, so why not go ahead and suck on a nicotine stick?

She didn't act like Jess expected her to.

Who could blame Jess for not trusting her?

"Put your hair back," Layne said, "and we'll go over a few things in the dining room before I take you back into the kitchen."

Lifting a hand to her head, Jess frowned. "Put it back? Do you know how long it took me to get it this way?" It'd taken her the better part of an hour to curl it, spray it and curl it again so it looked like the waves were easy and effortless. "It's perfect."

Layne—okay, so maybe Jess would use her first name, but only in her head—nodded, her own dark, silky hair pulled back into a French braid that reached the middle of her back. "Yeah, it's pretty. However, anyone with hair shoulder-length or longer must wear it pulled back when working with or near food. So… pull it back."

Damn. "I don't have any hair bands," she lied, as there were a few, along with half a dozen bobby pins, scattered at the bottom of her bag.

"In that case, we'll have to hunt you up a pretty little hairnet."

Jess blanched.

Layne laughed. "I'm kidding. Just pull it up. It'll be fine."

She played with the strap of her bag. "I…" What

the hell? She'd always believed it better to stick to the bulk of the truth. Made it easier to make up stories. "There's this guy…"

Layne's eyebrows shot up. "Nate?"

Fidgeting, Jess stared at the floor. "No. Just…a guy I met. He said he might stop by the restaurant today." And she was an idiot, telling some stranger about Anthony. An even bigger one for spending so much time and energy getting ready for him. He probably wouldn't even show, despite what he'd said last night when he'd called her.

Why would a guy like him—rich, charming and gorgeous—waste time chasing after her?

"Never mind. It's no big," Jess said, digging through her bag until she found a neon pink hair band. Bending forward, she gathered her hair at the top of her head, wrapped the band around it and straightened.

Layne covered her mouth with her hand. Snorted out a laugh.

"What?" Not seeing any appropriately reflective surfaces, she crossed the hall to the bathroom. She shut her eyes with a groan at her reflection in the mirror, but the memory remained.

Her hair, so stiff with hair spray it could poke an eye out, stuck out at odd angles from the band. Opening her eyes, she took the band out, combed her fingers through her hair again and smoothed it back into the band, but it did no good.

She looked like a reject from a Lady Gaga video.

Layne stepped into the room, her reflection joining Jess's in the mirror. "It's not that bad."

"I thought cops weren't allowed to lie."

"I think that's priests."

"It doesn't matter," Jess murmured, refusing to let

herself feel disappointed over some guy she barely even knew. Besides, Anthony should like her for who she is, not her looks.

She rolled her eyes at her reflection. What a colossally dumb thing to think. Her looks were all she had going for herself. Boys paid attention to her because she had a pretty face, big boobs and had recently begun giving them what they wanted.

Facing Layne, Jess cocked her hip and silently dared her to make another comment about her hair. "You ready?"

Layne searched her face. Jess smirked. So, the lady cop wanted to try to figure her out, huh? Good luck with that.

After a long moment, Layne muttered, "Oh, for the love of… Take the band out."

"You just told me to put it in."

Layne didn't even blink at her bitchiness. "And now I'm telling you to take it out." When Jess didn't move, Layne made a hurry-up gesture with her hand. "Come on, come on. I don't have all morning."

Jess reached back, pulled the band off. Grown-ups. They were so weird. And bossy.

"Tip your head to the left a bit," Layne said.

"Why?"

"Because I'm going to braid your hair."

Jess leaped back. "That is super creepy."

"It's unusual, I'll give you that. But the door is open and you can scream at any time you feel uncomfortable."

"Uh…you mean like now?"

"I guarantee you I can make it a whole lot better than the Frankenstein ponytail you had. Plus, when you take out the braid, your hair will still be wavy. What's the problem?"

Problem? Nothing much except that she hadn't had anyone else touch her hair in years. Her mom used to. When Jess had been little, she'd sit on her mom's lap while Heather pulled a brush through her waist-length hair. Her mom would brush it and brush it, her touch so gentle as she ran her hand down the long strands, her voice soothing as she told Jess about her plans. Her dreams.

That was what love felt like. When her mother got out the brush and patted her knee, Jess knew where she belonged. That she was wanted.

Until getting high became the most important thing in Heather's life. More important than those big plans she'd had. More important than her daughter. And Jess had learned to take care of herself.

Layne was a cop. Sure, she'd seemed kind of cool when she'd stood up to Uncle Ross at the quarry that night but that didn't mean Jess could trust her.

"The offer's expiring in ten seconds," Layne said. "Ten…nine…"

"Okay, okay." Jess faced the mirror, tipped her head to the side. "God. Are you always this impatient?"

"Only when I have things to do. So…yeah. Pretty much all the time."

Jess held her breath, her shoulders tense but there was no painful tugging. No pulling. Layne's fingers were gentle and cool as she tucked the hair below Jess's right temple behind her ear, then separated a small, upper section into three parts and started braiding.

It was kind of…nice. So nice that for a few minutes, Jess let herself enjoy having someone do something for her without wanting anything in return.

"Is that lady…the owner…is she your mother?" she asked when Layne had reached the end of the braid.

"Hand me that hair band, would you?" Layne asked. Jess did so and Layne wrapped it around the end of her hair. "That lady's name," she continued, "is Celeste and no. She's my father's girlfriend."

Switching sides, Layne started a second braid.

"Are you going to tell her…Celeste…about the other night?" Jess blurted. Only because she didn't want to get in trouble her first day on the job. Not because she felt bad about getting busted. Or was embarrassed by what she'd done.

Layne gently nudged Jess's head up. "What do you think I am? Some kind of narc?"

"I'm pretty sure narc spelled backward is *C-O-P*."

"Do you want me to tell Celeste?"

"I don't care if you do," she said, sounding defensive and bratty even to her own ears. "I'd just like to know."

Nothing good ever came out of a surprise.

"Like being prepared for the worst, huh?" Layne asked in a soft, compassionate tone that made Jess's stomach feel funny.

"Something like that," she muttered.

Layne stayed quiet for so long, Jess didn't think she was going to answer.

"There's no legal reason Celeste needs to hear about the other night," Layne finally said. "So why would I tell her?"

Because that's what cops did. They ruined things. She couldn't count how many times the police had been called to whatever crappy apartment she and her mom had been living in at the time. Though they all said they wanted to help, it always ended the same way.

Her mom in handcuffs in the back of the police car

or, on two very scary instances, loaded on a gurney into the back of an ambulance. And after they took Heather away a social worker with bad hair and even worse shoes would haul Jess to some foster home. A couple of times her grandparents had come to get her, had taken her in until her mom got out. Got clean long enough for the courts to order Jess back in her custody.

And every time, her grandparents let her go. Just like that. As if letting her go was easy. As if they couldn't wait to get rid of her. Which was how she got stuck with Uncle Ross.

"There," Layne said, stepping back. "You're all set."

Watching her reflection, Jess reached up, touched her hair. Instead of parting it down the middle and braiding both sides back like a little kid would wear, Layne had kept Jess's side part. She'd plaited the thinner section of hair on the left straight back on the side of her head while the braid on the right went across the top of her forehead before angling down toward her right ear.

With her hair away from her face, Jess's eyes seemed bigger. Darker. Older. Her cheeks thinner. She looked sophisticated, like a movie star on the red carpet.

"You only used one hair band," Jess said. "It'll fall out."

"I combined the braids in the back. It'll be fine." Layne stepped out into the hall. "You coming?"

Nodding, she touched her hair one more time then reluctantly followed Layne, her thank-you stuck in her throat. She thought of asking her to show her how she'd done it but then, as quickly as the idea formed, she brushed it aside. She didn't ask for help. Not with anything. If you asked for something, it gave people the opportunity to say no.

"Customer bathrooms," Layne said, gesturing to

the doors to their right. "And through here is the dining room."

Jess followed Layne into the large, noisy room. Her pulse quickened. Maybe this wasn't such a good idea. Tasting lip gloss, she realized she was gnawing on her lower lip and forced herself to stop but nerves jumped in her stomach. Had her rethinking the brilliant plan to earn enough money to run away.

It was packed. Each table, every booth along the wall—all filled. The noise level off the charts. Babies cried, kids yelled, people talked and laughed. Waitresses took orders or cleared tables, silverware clanging and crashing as they tossed it into big plastic bins, the sharp crack of dishes being stacked.

Maybe this wasn't exactly the best place for someone who couldn't stand most people on her best day. And Jess didn't have many good days. Just standing there, realizing she'd have to talk to people, take their orders, schlep their food and then—she grimaced—clean up after them made her break out in a cold sweat.

"Drink station," Layne said, gesturing to her left. There were water pitchers, a coffeemaker with three pots and a soda fountain machine. "Bottled water, juice and milk—chocolate or regular—are under here," she continued, giving the cupboard below the counter a tap. "Milkshakes are made in the back as are the fresh lemonades. You'll learn how to make those later.

"You'll be assigned a section of the room," Layne continued as they wound their way around tables. She waved at a family in a booth but didn't even slow, forcing Jess to practically jog to keep up with her long-legged self. "For the first few days, one of the other waitresses will work with you, show you the ropes, but I'll give you quick rundown now to give you a heads-up."

They stepped into a short hallway between the dining room and kitchen. There were wooden high chairs and plastic booster seats stacked off to the side and a station with paper placemats, clean silverware wrapped in paper napkins as well as salt and pepper shakers.

"Weekends are pretty busy so customers have to wait to be seated," Layne said, flipping her long, dark braid over her shoulder. "Celeste will put the waitresses on a rotating schedule throughout the day as to who is to man the front of the restaurant. When it's your turn, all you have to do is take people's names, how many are in their party and write it down. When one of the waitresses clears their table, they'll let you know so you can send in the next group."

The door from the dining room swung open. A waitress, a year or two older than Jess with curly red hair and a gorgeous, milky complexion, walked into the small space.

"Hey, Layne," she said. "How's it going?"

"Good. Keira, this is Jess Taylor. She's starting here today. Jess, Keira Thacker."

"Hi." Keira's smile had her adorably freckled nose crinkling. Adorably. "Nice to meet you."

"You, too."

Keira stepped up to the window. She had on black pants, sneakers and a short-sleeved, white T-shirt. Jess tugged at the hem of her shorts. "Two specials," Keira called into the kitchen, "one with home fries, one with two eggs, over easy. Both with eight-grain toast." She picked up plates from under the warming lights, stacking two on her arm and then sashayed her way out the door again. "See ya."

She left as an older waitress with an ample chest and loud laugh who Layne introduced as Sharon came in.

"Come on," Layne said, pushing open the kitchen door while Sharon talked to someone in the kitchen through the window. "I'll introduce you around."

Twenty minutes later, Jess's head was spinning.

She'd met the kitchen staff—Joe, who helped Celeste cook. With his shaved head and tattoos, he could've belonged in the gang on *Sons of Anarchy* instead of flipping pancakes at a busy café. George, who did prep work like chopping vegetables, was tall and thin with a scruffy moustache and an ill-advised soul patch. And Robbie and Luke, two high schoolers who washed dishes.

Neither one of them would meet her eyes, although Luke did gawk at her boobs until Layne loudly cleared her throat.

After introductions, Layne had listed all of Jess's duties: taking drink orders first, then food orders, checking on customers to make sure their meals are satisfactory, that their drinks are filled, clearing her tables and resetting her tables. She'd then explained how the kitchen ran, how orders were to be delivered and picked up.

And all the while Jess watched as the waitresses called in orders to the kitchen, delivered food, hauled dirty dishes to the dish room, dealt with kids running around underfoot, pacified grumpy customers and generally worked their asses off.

So much for thinking this job would be easy.

God, she hoped she didn't mess it up.

"And that's about it," Layne said, as they finished up back in the kitchen.

"You still here?" Celeste asked, frowning at Layne. "You're going to be late."

Layne's expression darkened. "The station is a three-minute drive from here. I'm fine."

"You're going to work?" Jess asked, taking in Layne's dark jeans and short-sleeved top the color of cranberries. "You change into your cop suit at the station?"

Uncle Ross didn't. He got dressed at the house. Some days she thought he slept in that thing—badge and gun included.

"I usually do change into my uniform at the station. But I'm not working today." Her mouth turned down for a moment but then she grinned. Jess didn't buy it for a minute. "I'm meeting your uncle at nine."

Oh. Well, that explained the strained smile. "Yeah, I figured he was working when I couldn't find him at the house."

Not that she'd searched particularly hard.

"Jess?" Celeste said, scooping bacon onto a plate with a metal spatula. "Since Layne gave you the nickel tour, we'll go ahead and start your training. I've paired you up with Keira."

The nerves in her stomach spiked. "What do I do?"

"You've met Keira, right?" At Jess's nod, Celeste continued, "Just stick with her. Go where she goes and watch how she does everything. She'll take the orders today. Tomorrow, you'll still be working with her but she'll be there as backup in case you need help."

"Okay." She walked to the door and stopped, keeping enough distance so if someone came in, she wouldn't get a broken nose.

"Your feet frozen to the floor?"

Jess glanced up to see Layne watching her. "I thought you were leaving."

"I am. Thought I'd say goodbye first. Since we've bonded and all."

"Right. Bye."

"It's all right if you're nervous."

"I'm not." But her palms were damp. Her throat dry. And Layne studied her as if she could see right past all her lies, past the walls she'd tried so hard to build these past few years, into her soul.

That sucked.

See? You really couldn't trust cops. They were all the same. Either they were trying to bust you or they thought they could save you. But she didn't need saving. She needed to be left alone.

"I'm fine," she said firmly. More determined. She was fine. Would be no matter what. "Thanks for the braid," she said then went out to start making money so she could get the hell out of Mystic Point.

"I'M SORRY," NORA TOLD LAYNE, sounding more annoyed than apologetic, "but I'd still feel better if Uncle Kenny was here. Anytime a citizen is questioned by the police, they should have an attorney present."

And here we go, Ross thought, helping himself to one of the cups of take-out coffee Layne had brought when she'd arrived a few minutes ago. Taking his seat behind his desk, he took off the lid, sipped and settled in for what promised to be a long day.

Layne, leaning against the bookcase, her long, jean-encased legs crossed at the ankles, sent a beseeching glance to the heavens. But when she spoke to her sister, she was all calm and patience. "Uncle Ken himself told you that wasn't necessary. The MPPD isn't the Gestapo,

Nora. Chief Taylor just wants to get some background information. Or don't you want him to investigate what happened to Mom?"

"What I want," she said through barely moving lips, her hands clutching the chair arms, "is for Dale York to pay for what he did."

Ross sipped his coffee to hide a flare of surprise. Who would've thought sunny Nora would have a vengeful streak? Good reminder not to make judgments before all the facts were gathered.

"Exactly," Layne said, straightening. "We all want the same thing here. To find out what happened to Mom and bring the person who hurt her to justice. So let's stop arguing—"

"I must've walked into an alternate dimension," Tori said as she sauntered in, her high heels clicking against the scuffed linoleum. "I thought I heard Layne say she didn't want to argue."

"You're late," Layne said.

Tori shrugged then sat in the chair next to Nora. "So arrest me."

"Now that we're all here," Ross said when Layne opened her mouth, no doubt to spew some toxic comment at her sister, "we can begin. But before we start, I'd like to lay out the ground rules."

"What kind of ground rules?" Layne asked.

He couldn't do much more than glance at her without being reminded of what it had felt like to sit in the dark with her the night before. How her hand had felt on his leg. How badly he'd wanted to sink his hands into that glorious mass of hair, press his mouth against hers and take what he needed from her.

How perilously close he'd come to doing just that.

So when he answered her, he did so while gazing

somewhere above her head. "The kind that will allow me to get through this meeting with as few interruptions as possible. First rule. As the officer in charge of this investigation, I will be asking the questions. And I won't need any help or input with those questions."

Tori sneered at Layne. "He's telling you to stay out of it."

Layne's scowl darkened, whether due to his edict or Tori, he couldn't tell. "Thanks," she said. "I got that all on my own."

"Second rule," he said, moving his attention to Tori. "No provoking each other."

Tori flipped her hair back, the move more defensive than seductive. "I'm not sure I'm following you," she said in a throaty purr.

"Then let me make it crystal clear for you." He kept his voice low, his tone mild. Professional. "No antagonizing remarks to each other. If what you have to say isn't directly related to the questions I ask or otherwise pertinent to this investigation, keep it to yourself."

"In other words, you want me to do a Thumper," Tori said. When he looked at her inquiringly, she continued. "If I don't have something nice to say…"

"Exactly. Third rule. In order to find the truth, I'm going to have to dig into Valerie Sullivan's past. Ask some questions that are personal in nature. I'm not here to judge your mother," he told them. "And while some of the questions may be difficult to hear and even harder to answer, it's important that you answer truthfully."

Nora blew out a breath, nodded slowly.

"Good." He leaned back far enough to open the top drawer. "Do any of you have any objections to my recording this conversation?"

"No," Nora said while both Layne and Tori shook their heads.

Setting the tape recorder in the middle of his desk, Ross pressed Record. He stated his name, rank and the date, along with the names of each woman present and the case they were discussing.

"Would you like to sit down?" he asked Layne.

She glanced at the empty chair next to Tori then planted her feet wide. "I'm good."

Not his business, he thought, pulling out a legal pad so he could keep his own notes about the conversation and the women's reactions. If she wanted to stay separated from her sisters that wasn't his problem. He needed to focus on finding the facts about what happened the night Valerie Sullivan disappeared. Hopefully those facts would lead him to a killer.

He couldn't do his job, couldn't do it as well as they needed him to, if he let personal feelings interfere.

"Where were you the night your mother disappeared?" he asked.

As if by silent agreement, Layne spoke first. "Home."

"We were all home," Tori said while Nora nodded.

"So you saw Valerie?" he asked. "Spoke to her?"

"She tucked me in," Nora said, her fingers twisted together in her lap. In a steel-gray pantsuit, her hair pulled back in a severe bun, she appeared every inch the attorney. But she still looked like a kid just out of high school. "That probably doesn't seem important," she told him, "and it wouldn't be if it'd been a normal occurrence…" She pressed her lips together and swallowed hard.

He waited but she remained silent. "It wasn't a normal occurrence?" he asked.

"No. She usually worked nights," she added quickly,

as if worried about painting Valerie in a less-than-flattering light. "But that night she came into my room and read me a story. Then she told me she loved me and hugged me." Her mouth wobbled. "I can still smell her perfume."

Ross checked the notes he'd made earlier. "You were how old...eight?" She nodded. "Do you remember what time you went to bed that night?"

She looked at Layne.

"Eight-thirty," Layne said, turning the cup in her hands round and round. "It was a school night so her bedtime was eight-thirty."

He wrote that down, made a note to question Layne on how she remembered the time later. "Do you remember your mother seeming upset or anxious that night?"

Nora shook her head at the same time Tori said, "She was...revved up...like she was nervous but that those nerves were from excitement. Anticipation."

"Did that seem unusual to you?"

"Not at the time. Mom was often keyed up. Always... on. Like *life of the party, look at me!* on. No matter where we were or what the situation, she had to be the center of attention. She craved the spotlight and she didn't care who she had to push aside to make sure she was the one shining."

Nora made a sound of distress. Or maybe, Ross thought, seeing her eyes flash, one of anger.

"I'm sorry," Tori said, patting Nora's arm. "I loved her, too. I did. But she wasn't perfect."

"She was beautiful," Layne said quietly, staring at the floor. She lifted her head. "She was so beautiful people used to stare, no matter where we were, what we were doing, they couldn't help but notice her because of that beauty. But what they didn't know, what only those of us close to her knew was that she was also clever. Creative. And when you had her attention, her full attention, it was like…God, it was like standing in a block of sunlight. Warm. Glowing." Layne met his eyes and in hers he saw longing and the grief she'd just last night denied feeling. "It was as if you were the single most important thing in the world to her."

Inhaling a shaky breath, she stepped over to stand behind the empty chair. "But more often than not," she continued, "Mom didn't give attention. She stole it. She was selfish and did whatever it took to get what she wanted. And if she was denied, she pouted like a three-year-old until whoever was holding out on her gave in. Valerie Sullivan was charming and witty and manipulative and so very, very imperfect. But for all her faults, despite everything she did and the people she hurt, she was still our mother."

Nora, holding Tori's hand, cried softly while Tori reached out across the chair with her free hand. Without hesitation, Layne clasped it, twined her fingers with her sister's. They faced him. A unit. One made all the stronger by the bond they shared and perhaps, because of their differences.

"She was our mother," Layne repeated, her voice strong, her eyes dry. "And she didn't deserve what happened to her. Find out. Find out the truth so we can give her justice."

CHAPTER NINE

HELL. NO PRESSURE there or anything.

"I can promise you I'll do my best," Ross said, realizing how badly they needed to be reassured that he'd fix this for them. But he couldn't lie, couldn't give them false hope. "Unfortunately there are no guarantees when it comes to any criminal investigation."

Especially one that happened eighteen years ago, one with no evidence, no eyewitnesses and the likeliest suspect nowhere to be found.

All of which Layne damned well knew but she wasn't reacting as a cop. She was reacting, thinking and feeling, like a daughter who'd just found out her mother had been murdered.

"The more information I have," he said, picking up his pencil, "the better. So let's get back to what happened. Mrs. Mott, you said your mother acted nervous that night? Edgy?"

Layne let go of Tori and laid both her hands on the back of the empty chair.

"The last time I saw Mom," Tori said, "spoke to her, was that night. The night she left. I was in my room listening to music and doing homework when she came in looking ready to take on the world. She was all dolled up, which wasn't unusual, either."

"Mom didn't step outside of the house without her hair and makeup done," Layne put in, her own hair a simple braid, her face clean. "And she changed her clothes at least twice a day."

"Right. So, she comes in, practically bouncing around the room." Tori tucked her hair behind her ear—the movement, the way her mouth turned down— reminding him of Layne. "I tried to ignore her. I was studying for a big history test—"

"Never your strongest subject," Layne murmured, but not unkindly.

"True," Tori agreed, her lips twitching. "But I was determined to kick butt on that test no matter what."

She and Layne shared a smile, one that showed their history and the bond between them as clearly as when they'd held hands.

"Did your mother help you study?" Ross asked.

This time, Tori aimed that killer grin his way. "Mom wasn't big on educational pursuits. But if you ever needed someone to do your hair or nails—"

"Or help you plan the best Halloween party ever," Layne interjected.

"Or teach you how to paint a mural on your bedroom ceiling," Nora added.

"She was the perfect person for the job," Tori said. "For any of those jobs. But homework? She had no desire to spend her time going over spelling words or multiplication tables. When she came into my room and turned up the music, I snapped at her to turn it down. To leave me alone."

"Did she?" Ross asked.

"No. She cranked it up even louder, pulled me to my feet and started dancing. She told me there were times when we needed to do what we wanted instead of what we should do or some such crap. So we danced."

"Mom was hard to resist," Layne told Ross. "Especially when she put on the charm."

Tori either didn't hear the hard edge to her sister's voice or chose to ignore it. "We danced until we were both breathless and laughing. When I collapsed onto the bed, she sat on the edge, brushed my hair back and told me she loved me. Then she kissed my forehead and walked out of my room and out of my life forever."

How hard that must have been for Valerie's daughters, being left by their mother. Her choosing a life without them.

"What time was this?" Ross asked.

"It must've been right after she put Nora to bed," Tori said. "Early. Maybe eight-forty-five?"

Nora shifted, scooted forward on her seat. "I remember hearing them. Hearing the music and their laughter as I lay in bed. It was unusual but comforting. But it didn't last long so I'd say no later than nine."

"That sounds about right. Hard to say for certain, though," Tori said apologetically.

"Just do the best you can," he said, writing down the events and their best guess as to the time. "It was a long time ago and some events—and the timeline— might not be as clear. Now, you say she left your room around nine...did you speak to her again after that? Do you know if she left the house at that time?"

"I didn't talk to her again ever. But no, she didn't leave the house right away. She was still there a few hours later."

"How can you be sure of that?"

"I'm sure," Tori said slowly, "because I..." She flicked a glance up at Layne. "I heard her around eleven."

Layne moved to sit in the chair, her expression unreadable.

"You heard Valerie moving around inside the house?" Ross asked. "You heard her voice? Was she talking to someone?"

Dropping her gaze to the top of his desk, Tori fidgeted then stopped when she raised her head and saw him watching her. "I heard her voice."

"It's okay," Layne told her. But when she faced Ross, her eyes were wary. And so sad it felt as if someone had kicked him in the chest. "She heard Mom yelling. Half the block probably heard Mom yelling that night. Along with me screaming right back."

"You and your mother had an argument?" he asked.

Crossing her legs, she smiled sadly. "An argument? No. We had a fight. A heated one—as our fights usually were."

"And what was this…heated fight…about?" he asked.

"It started because she was wearing my skirt."

"Your skirt?" he asked, not bothering to hide his disbelief. "Really?"

"Chief Taylor," Nora said, her tone frosty, her fierce demeanor as intimidating as a fluffy kitten with her back up, "are you accusing my sister of lying?"

He leaned back, noted Layne's smirk, Tori's scorching glare. Guess the Sullivan sisters could say anything they wanted to and about each other, could hiss and scratch at each other, but if anyone else so much as looked at one of them the wrong way, there'd be hell to pay.

Good thing he didn't have a problem covering his debts.

"What gave you that idea?" he asked smoothly be-

fore meeting Layne's eyes. "Did your mother often borrow your clothes?"

"More often than any thirty-two-year-old mother of
three should." But her dispassionate tone couldn't hide
the way her jaw tensed. "When I caught her wearing my
brand-new denim miniskirt—the one I'd bought with
my own money—I got pissed. Went off on her about
how she couldn't borrow my clothes without asking,
that I didn't want her in my room at all unless I was
in there…" She waved a hand, as if flicking away the
rest of what happened that night. "Trust me, the whole
conversation went downhill from there."

Trust me.

His fingers tightened on the pencil before he deliberately, carefully set it down. She was a colleague. A
trusted officer in his department. She had a stellar reputation, a strong work ethic and the respect of her peers.

Trust me.

He wanted to. Damn it, he wanted to believe every
word that came out of her mouth, wanted to ignore
the instincts screaming at him that she held something
back. That she was lying to him—like she'd lied about
the necklace.

He wanted to put her first, before the facts, before
his instincts. Before the job.

Trust me.

He couldn't.

He picked up the pencil again. "What happened
then?"

"When she refused to change I said a few…choice
words…" Layne swallowed visibly. But when she spoke
again, her voice was steady. "Words that were not ap-
propriate for a fourteen-year-old to say to anyone, let
alone her mother. Then I went to bed. I was lying there

still fuming when I heard the front door shut about fifteen minutes later. I looked out my window and saw Mom drive away."

"You're certain she was driving?"

"Positive. My bedroom was at the front of the house, which faces the driveway and the street. I saw her clearly. She was driving. She was alone," Layne added, anticipating his next question.

And yes, he'd been about to ask just that.

Layne knew what questions to ask, what information he wanted. Which could mean nothing more than she was a good cop. A smart one. That she offered the facts as they'd happened eighteen years ago, that she wanted to help him find the truth.

Or it could mean she knew exactly how to manipulate those facts to her advantage.

"What was your parents' marriage like?" he asked.

Nora stared at her lap; Tori checked the ends of her hair as if bored with the whole conversation while Layne studied him as if trying to see inside his brain—when more than anything he wanted her out of his head, out of his thoughts and dreams.

"Did your parents argue often?" he asked, his tone gruff. Impatient. And he couldn't do a damn thing about it. "Was there abuse?"

"No," Layne said quickly. "No abuse." She exchanged a long look with each of her sisters then shifted slightly in her seat to face him head-on. "Mom and Dad's relationship was…well…I guess imbalanced would be the best way to describe it. Mom needed a lot of attention and Dad was more than happy to give it to her."

Tori snorted. "Attention. Clothes. Money. Jewelry. Didn't matter if we could afford it or not, if Mom wanted something, he made sure she got it. Even if that meant he had to work upward of ninety hours a week, be away from home for weeks at a time, to make it happen."

"Sounds like your father was very devoted to his wife. Is that why he never filed for divorce?"

"You checked into our dad's background?" Tori asked. She looked at Layne. "Can he do that?"

"I checked into Valerie Sullivan's background," he clarified.

"It's a matter for public record," Nora said, speaking over him. "As to why he never filed for divorce, I'm afraid that's a question none of us can answer without a great deal of supposition."

Ross hitched a hip onto the corner of his desk. "Very well, counselor. How about this one, then—were you all aware that your father never filed for divorce from your mother?"

She fidgeted. "I don't see what this has to do with—"

"We knew," Layne said. "We all knew."

"You don't sound too happy about it," he said.

She flipped the end of her braid over her shoulder, almost hitting Tori in the face in the process. "I'm not happy that he's been in a relationship with another woman—a decent, caring woman who loves him—for almost ten years, has lived with her for the past five and yet he won't fully commit to her."

"You mean—" He slid the notebook over, scanned his handwriting. "Celeste Vitello?" Layne nodded. "Miss Vitello didn't mind that your father was married to another woman?"

"This whole line of questioning is irrelevant," Nora said sharply. "Because, as we all now know, our father wasn't still married all these years. He was a widower."

"Or maybe your father knew that all along." Ross watched Layne carefully, searching for a sign, any sign that would tell him, once and for all that his suspicions were wrong. That she didn't know more than she was saying. That she wasn't hiding something from him.

"Maybe your father never filed for divorce," he continued, "because he knew he didn't need one to be free of his wife."

IT TOOK ALL OF LAYNE'S self-control not to let any of the emotions churning inside her—frustration, anger, fear—show on her face.

Nora, however, didn't have Layne's self-restraint.

After a moment of stunned silence, Nora leaped to her feet. "My father didn't kill my mother." Her voice shook, her eyes flashed with indignation. "He'd never hurt her. Never. He loved her."

Nora sounded so certain. As if the words were true simply because she wanted them to be.

"Unfortunately," Ross said in what Layne had come to recognize as his professional tone—authoritative, patient and sympathetic enough to make her teeth ache, "love isn't always a deterrent against acts of violence."

Tori leaned forward, gripping the chair's arms as if holding herself back from taking a flying leap at Ross. "He had no reason—"

"If he loved her that much, finding out she was unfaithful could have pushed him to the edge."

Layne's breath caught, became trapped in her chest. As if she was trapped, between the past and the present. Between the choices she made eighteen years ago, what she did then and what she needed to do now to protect those she loved.

"Dad didn't even know about the affair," Tori said

hotly. "No one did. Not until Mom left and Dale's vehicle was found abandoned at the quarry. Only then did it come out that they'd been seeing each other."

And in the seconds after her sister spoke Layne made another choice. The choice to keep the truth to herself.

It was the right thing to do, she assured herself as she swallowed the sick feeling rising in her throat. Because it didn't matter, wasn't important to the investigation.

"Dad wasn't even in Mystic Point the night Mom disappeared," Layne pointed out, thanking God that she didn't have to wonder, didn't have to worry if what she'd done as a scared, angry kid had played an even bigger role in her mother being killed. "He was hundreds of miles away working aboard the *Wooden Nickel*. They didn't get back to port until the next afternoon."

Ross stood but didn't pace—like Layne would've done if she'd had the opportunity. If it wouldn't make her seem nervous to him and her sisters.

The man sure was contained. He made a note— probably writing down the name of the ship her father had been on—then moved to the front of the desk. "Did your father spend a lot of time out to sea?"

"He's on water more than he's on land," Layne said, making sure to give none of her thoughts, her feelings away on the subject. Certainly nothing that would make it seem as if she'd hated how often her father left them. How much she'd wished they'd been enough to keep him home. But Tim Sullivan had two great loves in his life: Valerie and the sea. There'd never been room for anything or anyone else.

Not even his daughters.

"Could your father have hired someone to murder your mother?" Ross asked.

"That's it," Nora said as she got to her feet. "We're leaving."

Tori got to her feet, her movements jerky as she yanked her purse onto her shoulder. Layne didn't move.

"Relax," she told them, earning two glares. "Nora, Chief Taylor is only doing his job." A job that included asking hard questions and dealing with their familial drama. Not that Ross seemed affected by any of it. "In a case like this, we often check into the husband and the people closest to the victim first."

"So now we're all suspects?" Tori asked, as usual taking what Layne said and twisting it until everything was messed up. Standing hip-to-hip, her sisters stared at her, a show of unity against a common enemy. Their older sister. "We all know who did this," Tori continued, now facing Ross. "I don't understand why the police are wasting time with these questions when they should be searching for Dale York."

"Mr. York is being sought for questioning. But it's too early in the investigation to narrow our focus on one suspect." He didn't snap, didn't seem the slightest bit offended her sisters were taking their grief and fear out on him. "I realize these questions are difficult—"

"Difficult?" Nora repeated, reaching a pitch only dogs should hear. "Our mother is dead and instead of finding Dale York, you're trying to pin her murder on our father."

"Oh, for God's sake," Layne grumbled as she rose to face her sisters. "No one is accusing anyone of anything. Chief Taylor wouldn't be doing his job if he didn't ask tough questions. We need to calm down and answer him to the best of our ability. We can do this. We can get through it like we got through Mom leaving. Together."

But when Layne held out her hands, Tori narrowed

her eyes then slowly, deliberately, turned away. Nora shook her head, kept her own hands on her hips.

Her throat burning, her pulse drumming in her ears, Layne lowered her arms.

"If you have any more questions you want to ask us," Nora said to Ross, "you can do so in the presence of our attorney."

They left, walking out while Layne watched. Leaving her to deal with this on her own.

Neither one of them looked back.

She heard Ross move, felt him come up behind her. "Are you—"

"Don't," she said wearily, facing him only to have her heart jolt in her chest at him being so close. She took a step back and bumped into her chair.

"Don't?" he asked lowly, his gaze intense on her.

"Don't ask if I'm okay," she clarified. "Because I am. I'm fine."

Or, at least she would be if he'd give her some space, enough room where she could breathe without inhaling the musky scent of his cologne. Where she couldn't feel the warmth emanating from his body. Far enough that she wasn't tempted to lean into him, just a little.

"Good to know," he said. "But I was going to ask if you're able to answer a few more questions for me?"

Yeah, she thought with an inward sigh, she was an idiot. Going all feminine, practically melting because he was solid and handsome, strong and steady and honorable. While for the first time in her life she felt weak and unsure of herself. Her stomach sank. And as deceitful as her mother.

"Sure," Layne said, praying he couldn't detect any of her worry, her guilt, on her face. "I'll do whatever I can to help."

He gestured for her to retake her seat but she shook her head. Walked back to the bookcase where she'd left her coffee. She picked it up, sipped and grimaced. Cold. Damn. And she could really use a shot of caffeine.

"Do you think," Ross said, hitching a hip onto the corner of his desk, "that it's possible your father hired someone to kill your mother?"

She set her cup back down, her eyes never wavering from his. "Getting back into the ring with a one-two punch, huh?"

"As you pointed out to your sisters, I'm doing my job."

Right. But that didn't mean she had to like it. "No. I don't think my father would ever do anything to hurt my mother."

"Then I guess it's back to my earlier question—if your father really thought your mother was still alive all these years, why didn't he file for divorce?"

"Well, as Nora mentioned, I can't tell you what's in my father's head—"

"You're a cop. A good one. You must have a theory."

A burst of pleasure at his offhand compliment flew through her, almost made her forget what they were discussing. Almost. "My theory," she said, "is that he always hoped she'd come back."

"Even after all these years? And after he'd moved in, moved on with his life, with another woman?"

"He loved her," she said simply, despite there being nothing simple about the situation. And certainly nothing fair about it. Valerie had lied and cheated and left Tim for another man and yet Layne had no doubt that if things had been different, if instead of discovering Valerie's remains her mother had showed up very much alive and wanting Tim back, he'd have opened his arms to her.

Just as he had in Layne's dream.

Leaving Celeste, the woman who'd loved him, who'd always been there for him and his daughters, with nothing.

"Dad was never the same after Mom left," she continued, rubbing her palms down the front of her jeans. "Not really. It was as if something inside of him... broke."

And nothing, and no one, could help him heal. Not Celeste. Not his daughters.

So Layne had stopped trying. Had learned not to give her love to someone who couldn't, who wouldn't, return it. She'd learned what happened when a person loved too much. They lost themselves.

Ross straightened. "What can you tell me about Dale York?" he asked as he went behind his desk.

The relief at not discussing her family anymore made her shoulders sag. "He was a small-time crook. Had a record, mostly petty stuff but there were a couple of B and E and assault charges against him."

Bent over his desk as he wrote on the legal pad, Ross lifted his head. "You seem to know a lot about him."

"It's a small town. Pretty much everyone's life is on display."

"Do you think that's what your sisters are worried about? Your family's privacy being invaded?"

"Possibly." Probably. Especially Nora who'd been too young to understand what had happened, what people were saying about them. How their personal business had been discussed, their family judged. "Mostly I think it's...well...it's not easy being on this side of an investigation. Actually it sucks."

"Neither you nor anyone in your family is under investigation," he pointed out calmly.

She ran her finger down the spine of a hardbound copy of *Massachusetts Driving Laws*. "Funny, but it doesn't feel that way."

"That was never my intention."

She glanced up at him. He sounded sincere, but could she trust him when she no longer even trusted herself? "I know. You wouldn't play games like that."

The corners of his mouth quirked in a completely unexpected, totally sexy, grin. The first real smile she'd seen from him. She finished her cold coffee in an effort to ease her suddenly dry throat.

"You don't think I'd do whatever I had to in order to get to the truth?" he asked with a lazy inflection that made his Boston accent even more pronounced. "To make an arrest?"

There were cops who used lies or intimidation or who twisted the law to suit their purposes. Who weren't above bending the rules or resorting to trickery to get what they wanted. Evidence. A confession. Their questions answered.

There's right and there's wrong.

"I think you'd go up to that line, maybe even straddle it. But cross it?" She shook her head, tossed her empty cup into the trash. "Not a chance."

He'd been nothing but honest with her. Fair. More so than she deserved after she'd kept her knowledge about the necklace from him. At the very least she owed him the truth.

Enough of it to keep him from suspecting she was hiding the rest away.

"Look," she said, taking the two steps needed so that she stood at the back corner of his desk. Closer to him. "In the interest of full disclosure, I need to tell you something. I wasn't...completely honest about what happened between me and Mom the night she disappeared."

"Let me guess," he said, crossing his arms. The muscles of his forearms flexed. "You didn't fight over a skirt."

She jerked her gaze from the sight of his biceps straining his uniform sleeve to his face. "Oh, no, we fought over that skirt. At least, that's what it started out about, but it escalated from there. I didn't want to say anything in front of my sisters because I didn't...I don't...want them to know how bad it was."

A lump formed in her throat. She tried to clear it away but it stuck there, right there, as if she needed reminding of what she'd done that night, what she'd said.

Ross trailed his fingertips over the back of her hand, the touch so soft, so brief, she would've thought she'd imagined it if not for the sharp prickles of awareness shooting up her arm.

"Tell me about the fight," he said, his hands now behind his back, his expression clear.

Inhaling deeply, she let herself be taken back to that night. To the truth.

"I was in my room reading when I heard several thumps on the stairs, like someone had fallen. I checked on both Nora and Tori but they were sleeping so I went downstairs. I stepped into the kitchen as Mom came in through the back door. I didn't even ask her what she was doing. As soon as I saw her wearing that skirt, I lost it."

She became aware of a soft whirr, glanced down and saw the tape player still recording. As it should be. It, more than anything, reminded her of where she was, what she was about to do.

Ross moved over to stand in front of her. Though there was a respectable distance between them, she leaned back, pressed against his desk. The hard metal edge of it dug into her thighs but she didn't move, afraid if she so much as shifted her weight, she'd brush against him.

"You argued with your mother," he prodded.

"I yelled at her," Layne said, unwilling to let what happened between her and her mother that night be classified as anything as civilized as an argument. "But it wasn't just about the skirt. It was her. It was eleven o'clock at night and instead of being in bed, instead of staying home like a good mother should, she was sneaking out of the house."

"Did she do that often? Leave the house late at night?"

"When she wasn't working? Sure," she said, sounding as if it didn't matter. "I didn't even realize it until one night when I was at a sleepover at a friend's house and Tori called me, frantic because Mom wasn't home. I guess Nora had had a bad dream and when she couldn't find me or Mom, she woke up Tori. Mom had left them alone. A ten-year-old and a six-year-old. She knew I wasn't there and she still left."

And Layne had never gone on another sleepover.

"I was tired of her doing whatever she wanted whenever she wanted," Layne told Ross. "Acting like she didn't have any responsibilities, as if what she wanted was more important than her kids. We were screaming at each other, me telling her to stop dressing like a teenager, to grow up and be the mother we needed. Her telling me I had no right to speak to her that way, that no matter if I agreed with her decisions or not, she still deserved my respect…"

Her breathing hitched, her words trailed off as her throat closed. Slumping back against the desk, Layne curled her fingers around the edge. Ross watched her, waiting patiently. Hard to believe a few days ago she'd sneered at his ability to remain imperturbable in all situations. Now she envied it.

"And as she's telling me how I need to respect her for no other reason than because she gave birth to me, I…I noticed the suitcase by the door. The one she'd obviously come inside for when I first saw her."

"You're sure the suitcase was hers? That she'd planned on leaving?"

"I asked her. I asked her if she was going somewhere, when she'd be back. She told me she and Dad were having some problems and she needed a break from being his wife. And our mother."

She'd been lying, of course. And Layne had known it, had known Valerie was going to be with Dale. That she'd chosen him over her family.

But she couldn't tell Ross that. Not without him wanting to dig deeper into her story. Not without giving the rest of her secrets away.

"She told me when I was older, I'd understand." Layne lifted a shoulder. "I'm older and I still don't get how she could walk away from us."

"Did she mention where she was going? If she planned on coming back?"

"She said she was staying with a friend for a few days."

"You never told anyone about this? Never told your father or your sisters?"

"No. Because if I admitted that I knew Mom was

leaving, I'd have to tell them the rest. That I didn't try to stop her. That I told her I was glad she was leaving. And I hoped she never came back."

CHAPTER TEN

ROSS REACHED OVER and shut off the recorder then shifted to the side to put some distance between him and Layne. Before he did something stupid like touch her again. He rubbed the tips of his tingling fingers against his thumb. Inwardly cursed himself for giving in to his instincts to soothe her. To take away her pain.

"Do you think anything you could've said would've stopped her?" he asked, glad he sounded as professional as always.

"I'm not sure." Layne hugged her arms around herself and walked to one of the small windows behind his desk overlooking the alleyway. "But I let her leave. And now she's dead."

Ross stopped himself from pointing out that Valerie had been dead for eighteen years, because he knew to Layne and her family, it was as if the murder had just happened. "It's not your fault."

"Yeah. I know that." But her voice shook, and it took all he had to stay where he was. To not close the distance between them and pull her into his arms.

"Do you?" he asked and she dropped her gaze. "You were a kid. It wasn't up to you to stop her from leaving. She made that choice."

"I kept telling myself that. After she left I must've stood in the kitchen, right in the spot where she'd left me, at least two hours, waiting for her to change her mind. To come home. I had it all worked out in my head. How she'd come in, tell me she was wrong, that she was going to change and finally become the kind of mother my sisters and I deserved." Laughing softly, Layne shook her head. "God, what a fantasy. When she never came home, I wondered…what if? What if I'd tried to stop her? Maybe she wouldn't have left. Not that night."

He couldn't help but step closer, so close he could smell her light scent, could see the flecks of gold in her whiskey-colored eyes. The flare of surprise in them when he skimmed his fingers up her arm to her elbow and back down to her wrist. Let his hand linger there.

"What happened to her wasn't your fault," he said.

She swallowed but didn't step back, didn't pull away from his touch though part of him wished she would. "I should've asked her to stay. Maybe if I had, she'd still be alive."

If she'd simply been the daughter of a murder victim, a civilian, he'd treat her with kid gloves. Would help her back to the chair, try to gently convince her she was wrong. He'd be thoughtful. Kind. But that wasn't what Layne, with her smart mouth and her loyalty to her sisters and her tendency to want to control everything, needed.

She needed a swift kick in the ass.

"That's a load of bullshit," he said, more than mildly pleased when her eyes narrowed. "Unless you've changed your mind about being treated like a victim after all?"

Stepping back, her mouth opened. Shut. Opened again. "Don't they give cops in Boston police sensitivity training? Or maybe you skipped that day."

Her tone was snippy, her shoulders stiff and she

looked at him as if contemplating the chances of her being able to toss him out the second-story window.

Much better.

"I was there," he assured her. "But I hadn't realized I'd need to convince you not to blame yourself for something that was out of your control."

"I could've stopped her. I could have—"

"Could have what? Tied her to a chair? What good would that have done? She was an adult, she wanted to leave and there was nothing you could've done to stop her. And you're too smart, too good of a cop, to think otherwise."

He almost squirmed under her long, intense stare. Him. A veteran homicide detective and now a police chief.

No doubt about it. He was in hell and Layne Sullivan was the devil in charge.

"You're right," she finally said. "Which really ticks me off, by the way."

"Glad I could help."

"That's another thing. It did help. Which, aside from being weird, makes me wonder how you seem to know what to say to make me feel better. Can't say I like it much."

"That makes two of us." He considered turning the recorder back on for his next question but figured he had so much off the record, he might as well keep going. "The night your mother left, did she happen to mention which friend she was going to stay with?"

"Celeste Vitello."

He paused in the act of spelling the name. "Your father's current girlfriend?"

"Celeste and Mom were friends, best friends. They also worked together at the Yacht Pub."

"That the bar on the docks? The one with the front half of a boat sticking out of the second floor?"

"It's more of a rowboat." She smirked, cocking one hip to the side in the way that made him want to grab her waist and yank her against him. "I'm having a hard time picturing you hanging out with the Yacht Pub's clientele."

"I answered a public disturbance call there my first week in town."

"Ah. That makes more sense. Though if you ever do want a drink, most of the department prefers T.J.'s Bar and Grill over on Barber Street."

"Including you?" he couldn't stop himself from asking.

Her smirk changed, morphed into a sharp grin. "Hanging out in bars was my mother's idea of a good time. Not mine."

He glanced through the notes he'd made earlier. He hadn't realized Celeste had a history with the Sullivans so the only notation about her was that she currently resided with Tim Sullivan on Northcott Ave. "Does Miss Vitello still work at the bar?"

Layne picked up the stapler on his desk. Turned it in her hands. "Seriously?"

"Is this a joking matter?

"No, it's just...Celeste owns the Ludlow Street Café." When he looked at her blankly she added, "The restaurant Jess started working at today."

"Is everyone in Mystic Point somehow linked to everyone else?"

"Small town," she said, as if that explained it all. She set the stapler back down. "Which reminds me, I saw Jess when she showed up for work this morning."

"I'm sorry."

"What for?"

"For whatever she said that was offensive or rude, or did that was illegal or immoral."

Layne laughed, the sound husky and low and so damned sexy he considered lifting the stapler to his temple and putting a dozen or so staples into his head. Except that wouldn't put him out of his misery. So he moved the stapler to the right, spinning it so it lined up once again with the edge of the desk.

"She wasn't that bad," Layne said.

"You're kidding."

Her smile slid away. "Maybe part of the problem is that you expect the worst from her. She's living down to your expectations."

His shoulders tensed, indignation making his face feel stiff. "I expect the worst from her," he said evenly despite the urge to growl, "because over the past six months, her behavior has been nothing but worst."

"I'm not saying she's up for the Teenager of the Year crown but it sounds like she's been through a lot. It must be hard on her, coming to a new town, being away from everyone and everything she knows." Layne shrugged. "You might want to cut her some slack."

Damn it, he didn't need to be reminded he was screwing everything up. That he was incapable of dealing with a slip of a girl with a penchant for trouble, an acerbic tongue and her mother's somber eyes.

"Thank you for your invaluable input, Captain," he said coolly, not missing the way her lips thinned at his use of her rank instead of her name, "but I'm not really comfortable discussing my personal life with you."

Hurt flashed across her face but vanished so quickly he wondered if he imagined it. Especially when her expression darkened. "Forgot for a moment there are rules," she said, walking to the bookcase where she'd left her large purse. "We wouldn't want to get too close to that line separating personal from professional."

He was already at that line, he thought as he watched her pick up her bag, sling the strap over her shoulder. He'd dug into her family's past, into their lives, in an effort to unearth a truth that had been buried for eighteen years. But that was different. That was his job.

Wanting to know Layne better, wanting her to trust him with whatever secrets she kept hidden? That had nothing to do with his investigation or his position as police chief and everything to do with him just wanting her.

He had to maintain a certain distance between them.

"Celeste is at the café most days from morning until after six or so," Layne said, already heading for the door. "I'll tell her you'll be contacting her."

He should thank her. Should tell her he appreciated her cooperation during this difficult time. More than that, he felt honored she'd opened up to him, that she'd told him the secret she'd kept for so long, something she hadn't shared with anyone.

He should keep his mouth shut and let her leave.

She was two steps away from the door when he heard himself say, "She's an addict."

For a second, he didn't think Layne would stop. Thought she'd keep going as if he hadn't spoken. When she faced him, he couldn't decide if he was disappointed or relieved.

"What?" she asked, her chin lifted in challenge.

"My sister…Jessica's mom…she's an addict. She started using in high school, got clean for a while when she was pregnant but went back to using when Jess was around a year old." He thrust his hands into his pockets. "That's also when she left Boston. Took off to Nashville to sing backup for some guy she'd hooked up with at the hotel where she worked. She was there six months or so then, when that guy moved on, she found another one, followed him to another city—Memphis, I think. The pattern repeated—different men, different cities and states—until a year ago when she ran out of money and boyfriends and came home."

"Where was Jess during all of this?"

"With Heather. Mom and Dad tried to get custody of her but until a few years ago, Heather was still able to function enough to hold menial jobs and make sure Jess was taken care of. At least, enough to satisfy the courts that she'd be better off with her mother than her grandparents." He paced behind his desk, feeling edgy and angry and helpless to do anything to rid himself of the emotions roiling through him. "Ten months ago Heather was arrested for possession with intent to sell. Since it wasn't her first offense, she got the maximum sentence and Jess went to live with my parents. When she started acting up, it was too much for Mom and Dad to handle so I stepped in, told them I'd take her."

"They didn't want her."

The words, spoken just above a whisper, seemed to echo in the room. Shades of Layne's own past.

He stopped, forced himself to remain still and face her. "They wanted her. Or, at least, I think they wanted to want her. But when her behavior became reminiscent of Heather's at that age, they weren't willing to go through that same nightmare again."

Hadn't had the energy, the resolve or, Ross suspected, the desire to do so. Not even for their granddaughter. It'd been easier for them before Heather and Jess returned to Boston. Easier to pretend there was nothing they could do to for Jess. But when push came to shove, his parents hadn't stood up, hadn't done what was right.

They'd left it up to him.

"So you gave up your life in Boston, your career there, for Jess?" Layne asked.

"For both of us." He liked to think he was a good guy but he wasn't a damned saint. "I'd been debating getting out of the Boston P.D. for over a year."

He'd been tired of the departmental politics and being passed over for promotions. Plus he'd seen how difficult it was for his fellow officers to maintain stable personal lives when dealing with shift work and horrific crimes. But more than that, he'd quickly been approaching burnout, had worried that when he reached that point, there'd be no turning back.

Layne raised her eyebrows. "And moving to Mystic Point gave you an opportunity to make your dream of being a small-town police chief come true?"

"It gave me the opportunity to continue doing what I love to do, what I hope makes a difference in people's lives while bringing Jess someplace where she could have a fresh start."

"Why tell me all of this?" she asked, her tone laced with suspicion. "Why break your own rule about not mixing your private life with your work one?"

Because she intrigued him with her brusqueness and sense of humor and responsibility to her family. Attracted him with her intelligence and long legs and reluctant grin. Because for the first time he found himself wanting to share a piece of himself—no matter how small—with someone else.

And he couldn't admit any of that. "I told you," he said, letting her in on as much of the truth as he could, "because I wanted you to know."

LAYNE'S CHEST GREW TIGHT and she realized she was holding her breath. Exhaling on a soft whoosh, she regarded Ross warily. "You were probably right. About keeping this—" she gestured between them "—separate."

He rocked back on his heels. "Undoubtedly."

"I don't want you breaking any of your rules for me," she blurted.

She was flustered. Nervous. He made her nervous. What was up with that?

"I'll keep that in mind," he said, giving her no clue as to what he really thought. "Before you leave, there's one more thing—"

"Really?" she asked, her lips twitching despite her best efforts. "You're using the Columbo line on me?"

"It just came out," he admitted, somewhat disconcertedly. Good to know there were times when even cool, controlled Chief Taylor spoke without thinking. Though she doubted it happened often.

"Why was Tori so determined to do well on her history test?" he asked.

That was the last thing she'd expected him to ask. Layne set her right hand on her hip. "Why?"

"Is there a reason you don't want to answer the question?"

"Other than it's a stupid question?" And because answering it would be breaking his rule again. Except this time, it'd be her sharing a piece of herself when she preferred to keep all her pieces inside, all safely hidden away. "No. No reason. I told Tori if she got a B minus or above on the test, she could borrow anything out of my closet for an entire week."

"B minus, huh? Not just a passing grade?"

"She was capable of A's but she didn't apply herself." Still didn't but that wasn't Layne's problem anymore. "She ended up with a B plus and wore every outfit in my closet at least once."

"And Nora?"

"Nora aced history. Nora aced all her classes. She didn't need to be bribed to study."

"She mentioned that your mother wasn't around to tuck her in at night, and I can't help but wonder who did." He walked around to the front of his desk, and she hoped he didn't come any closer. Hoped almost as desperately that he would. "Who took care of your sisters, Layne? Who gave them a bedtime and helped with their homework and read to them before they went to sleep?"

She switched her purse from her left shoulder to her right. "What does that have to do with Mom's murder?"

"Not a thing."

He wanted her to share a part of herself that wasn't about the case or their jobs.

"I did," she said, somehow sounding defensive and proud at the same time. Which pretty much summed up how she felt about her childhood. "I took care of them."

She'd always take care of them.

"Who took care of you?"

The question, asked so gently, had tears threatening. She ducked her head for the count of five until she gained control.

Confident he wouldn't detect anything she didn't want him to see, she met his eyes. "I'm more than capable of taking care of myself. Was there anything else, Chief?"

His lips flattened but then he schooled his expression. "Any confirmation of when your father will return? I'd like to set up a time to speak with him as soon as possible."

"If the current weather predictions hold, he should be home by Sunday."

"Please have him contact me at his earliest convenience," Ross said.

"Sure. Look, I know I'm supposed to report back to work Tuesday night—" thanks to her not being scheduled Monday, her forced mini-vacation was a day longer than he'd decreed "—but I need it off." When he looked surprised, she hurried on, "I can switch with someone, take an earlier shift but we're scheduling Mom's memorial service for that evening." Or, at least they would, once they met with the funeral director later today.

"I haven't double-checked, but don't MPPD officers get a week off for bereavement?"

"I don't want a week off." She didn't need it. "I just want Tuesday."

He studied her for so long, her face grew hot. "You don't want a full week? Fine. But in addition to Tuesday I want you to take Wednesday, too."

She drummed her fingers on her thigh. "But I don't want—"

"I'm not asking you what you want, Captain."

"Is this more punishment for not telling you about the necklace?"

He pinched the bridge of his nose as if she got on his last nerve when he was the one pushing her buttons. "It's not a punishment at all," he said, dropping his hand. "It's a few days off for you to spend with your family during a difficult time."

How was she supposed to argue with that logic?

"Fine," she managed to say through her clenched teeth. "I'll report back to duty Thursday night." It couldn't come soon enough for her.

She walked out before he could try to get inside her head again. Before he could do or say something that made her forget why her pulse shouldn't race when she looked at him, why her mouth shouldn't get dry when he got too close.

Why she had to protect her secrets. And her heart.

"MOONLIGHTING?" ROSS ASKED Layne two days later, coming up behind her as she cleared a table at the Ludlow Street Café.

Reaching for a plastic cup with melting ice cubes and a chewed plastic straw, she stilled for the barest of seconds then flicked him a glance over her shoulder. "I'm filling time until my boss lets me come back to work."

Damn if he hadn't missed the sound of her smart mouth.

She added the glass to a large, plastic tub then crumpled the paper placemats and tossed them into the tub, as well. Stepping back as she sprayed some sort of cleaning solution that burned his nose, he couldn't help but let his gaze drop to her ass. Her dark jeans cupped her curves, her entire body swayed as she wiped the table.

Sweat broke out along his nape. Desire settled hot and heavy in his gut, made him itchy with want. Restless with need. He jerked his eyes up. All the booths were full, a few tables sat empty but seeing as how two cars had pulled into the parking lot after him, he doubted they'd stay that way. There were two waitresses—no, make that three, he amended as a young redhead came out a door on the other side of the room. The other two were older, one heavy with a permanent smile, the other barely topping five feet with the same curly hairstyle his grandmother had.

Three waitresses. But no Jess.

Straightening, Layne's rear brushed against his thigh and his mind blanked, just…emptied of all thought. "Any news on my mom's case?" she asked.

How was he supposed to think when she was so close? He eased back, put some much needed distance between them. "Dale York's ex-wife and son are coming in to the station tomorrow to speak with me. But so far, I've been unable to ascertain Mr. York's current whereabouts."

Frustration ate at him. No, he had no clue where York was, where he'd been during the past eighteen years or if he was even still alive. It was as if the man simply ceased to be the night he left Mystic Point.

"Good luck with that interview." Layne picked up the basin and held it under her arm. "I don't know much about the ex-wife but Griffin York isn't exactly known around town for having a sparkling personality and civic-minded mentality."

"What is he known for?" Though, from checking into the younger York's background and seeing the sealed juvie record, Ross could guess.

"He's a loner. A badass with a chip on his shoulder about his past and upbringing, especially when it comes to his old man."

"I'll keep that in mind. Thanks. Have you seen Jess? I thought she was working tonight."

"She's here. Probably in the kitch—no, there she is," Layne said, inclining her head toward the swinging door the redhead had come through.

Only this time, Jess came out, a coffeepot in one

hand, a small bowl in the other. She headed to a booth in the corner, set the bowl down and filled the couples' coffee cups before saying something to them and hurrying back to the kitchen.

"What the hell is she wearing?" he muttered.

"Yeah. That skirt is short," Layne said lightly. "Let's hope she doesn't bend over. She might cause a riot."

"Short? I can see her ass." Noticing three guys in a booth on the other side of the room checking Jess out, Ross curled his fingers into fists. "Everyone can see her ass."

"Not quite, but it's close, I'll give you that. I think she borrowed it from Keira. Which is good news. I think they're becoming friends," she said, nodding at the redhead.

No wonder the skirt was so short, so tight on Jess. His niece had five inches and at least fifteen pounds on the redhead. "I'd rather she be friends with girls her own size. Ones who wore longer skirts."

"I'm pretty sure the *Little House on the Prairie* look is out of fashion with the kids these days." Had he really thought he'd missed that sardonic tone? He must be out of his mind. "Are you eating here, or did you stop by to check on your niece and critique her clothes?"

"Any reason I can't do all three?"

"Not that I can think of." She hitched the bin higher. "Take a seat. This is one of Jess's booths so she'll be your server."

She walked away. Purposely not watching her go, Ross sat in the booth on the side facing the door. A minute later, Layne returned with a new place setting.

"You work here often?"

"Keeping tabs on me, Chief?" she asked, laying

down a paper placemat. She added silverware wrapped in a paper napkin and a coffee cup and saucer.

"I'm interested." In her. In what she did, what she thought, what went on in that clever head of hers. Way more so than he should be. "I'm interested what all of my officers do when they're away from the station."

She laughed. "Really? And what do you know about what any of us does with our free time?"

He moved the silverware so it lined up with the edge of the placemat. "Campbell races dirt bikes. Meade spends most weekends watching his grandkids' sporting events. Forbes builds furniture, tables mostly but he'll also do special designs if the price is right. And Donna somehow finds time to volunteer at her church, organizes a monthly food drive and babysits her daughter's infant three nights a week." He told himself the skepticism in her gaze didn't bother him. "I know my people, Captain."

"Maybe." Today a thick band held her hair away from her face, but instead of the long fall of it trailing down her back in a tail or braid, she'd pinned it up in a messy bun. "Or maybe you're just a really good detective. There's a difference between conversing with someone, asking questions and paying attention to what they say, and overhearing bits and pieces of conversation or seeing the magazines they read in the break room."

"Guess I'm not the only good detective here," he said, fighting his irritation, his embarrassment that she'd pegged him so easily. He wasn't about to feel guilty because he didn't buddy up to his officers. He wasn't their pal. He was their boss. Her boss. There was a protocol he had to stick to. "You do realize you're to inform your superior officer if you have a second job."

"I'm not working here. I'm helping out while Celeste, Tori and Nora drove down to pick up Dad."

Layne had left a message for him yesterday that her father's return to Mystic Point would be delayed due to the *Guiding Light* having some sort of mechanical problem. The ship had docked in Marblehead late last night.

"Are you spying on me?" Jess asked as she approached the booth, her gaze apprehensive, her makeup too heavy for a girl her age.

"If he is," Layne said, before he could respond, "he's doing a crappy job at it." She scrunched up her nose at him. "Maybe next time you could wear a disguise. I'm thinking a fedora and a fake mustache. What do you think?" she asked Jess.

Jess rolled her eyes. "I think you get creepier with each passing day."

"Oh, ha-ha. And you keep getting wittier. Now, are you going to wait on him or should I give his table— and the big tip I'm sure he's going to leave—to Patty?"

Jess slammed a laminated menu down in front of him as Layne walked away. "Our specials today," she said flatly, "are chicken and biscuits, blackened tilapia and stuffed pork chops. Soup of the day is fish chowder." She held up her order pad. "Do you want a drink?"

"You must rake in the tips with that attitude."

"Why are you here?" she asked though not as harshly as usual. She sounded more curious. Nervous. "Were you and Layne talking about me?"

He was there because the house had been too quiet. Too still.

"I'm hungry," he said, opening the menu. "It's one of those annoying biological oddities that happens to me several times a day. And no, the assistant chief and I were not discussing you." Other than her clothing choices but since he doubted that's what Jess meant, he'd keep that to himself. "Why? What did you do?"

"Nothing. God. I just don't like you checking up on me."

"It's my job to check up on you. But if you didn't get into so much trouble," he pointed out reasonably, "I wouldn't have to do it."

Her lower lip stuck out making her look younger than fifteen despite the revealing clothes and makeup. Shit. He'd hurt her feelings. Again. He wasn't any good at this.

"Hey," he said, reaching for her hand, "I didn't—"

"Do you want a drink or not?" she asked stepping back.

He sighed. "Coffee. Black."

She left but came back thirty seconds later to pour him a cup of coffee. "I'll be back in a few minutes to take your order."

And she went off again. This time taking with her the attention of the three guys in the far booth. They were in their early twenties with scruffy beards. They talked too loud, laughed too much. Two of them, the one with the short, dark hair and the blond, had on bright, designer Polo shirts. The third, stockier than his buddies, wore a plain white T-shirt, his brown hair pulled back into a low ponytail.

He hadn't seen them around town before—not that he recognized many of the faces he encountered each day but he was getting better at spotting tourists among the locals. And those three fit the bill. He glowered at them. Not that they noticed. They were too busy tracking his underage niece as she worked. He started out of the booth, ready to get his Taser from his patrol car when common sense took control. He couldn't go around electroshocking every guy who looked at Jess. That would be a full-time job.

Settling back into his seat, he shoved the menu aside and sipped his coffee. Across the room, Layne cleared another table while she talked to Jess. Ross tapped his fingers on the table. He hadn't realized Layne would be here or he would've stayed home. Bad enough he couldn't get her out of his head, he'd hoped he wouldn't come face-to-face with her at least until she returned to work Thursday.

Had hoped the hold she had over him would go away by then.

Jess's hands gestured in clear agitation as she talked. After letting his niece run out of steam—or words— Layne spoke and Jess smiled. She actually smiled. And when Layne squeezed her hand, Jess didn't jerk away. She said something that made Layne laugh before she picked up the bin of dirty dishes and walked through the swinging door.

He clenched his jaw. He didn't need them getting chummy. Didn't want any more lines blurred. He needed to keep Layne completely separate from his personal life. What was it about this town where every aspect of people's lives intertwined?

Jess went over to the guys' table. The dark-haired one grinned and leaned forward. Whatever he said caused Jess's polite smile to strain at the edges as she picked up an empty plate. The guy grabbed her hand and she shook her head as she tugged in an effort to get free but he held firm.

Ross was out of the booth and halfway across the room before he even realized he'd moved.

Luckily he regained enough control to keep his expression clear, his tone low when he reached the table. "Let go of her," he said. "Now."

Looking way too cocky, the kid slowly released Jess. "Who's this guy?" he asked Jess, his accent giving him away. Jersey, or maybe Philadelphia, but definitely not from around here. "Your dad?"

Add in the expensive watches two of them wore, the designer clothes and the air of entitlement and Ross amended his initial view of them to wealthy tourists. Ones with more free time than they needed, more money than they could spend and the sense that everything they wanted could be theirs for a price. Including Jess.

"He is not my dad," Jess ground out, her face red.

"Guess I should introduce myself," Ross said, pulling his badge out of his front pocket. He opened it, feeling no little amount of satisfaction when all three members of the scruffy beard brigade straightened in their seats. "I see you've already met my niece, Jessica." He held the dark-haired kid's gaze. "My fifteen-year-old niece."

The kid blanched, shrank farther into his seat, pointedly keeping his eyes—and his hands—off Jess.

And Ross's job here was done.

He put his badge away. "Enjoy the rest of your evening."

He was halfway to his booth, thinking he'd try the fish chowder followed by the stuffed pork chops, when Jess caught up with him.

"What is your deal?" she asked harshly, glaring at him as if she'd like him to catch fire on the spot so she could watch him burn.

"No deal." An elderly couple at the table next to them

stared. Ross nodded at them then took a hold of Jess's arm and escorted her to the far corner. He didn't want a scene in Mystic Point's most popular restaurant. Not when he was trying to establish himself, and his authority, in town. When he stopped under the sign pointing down a hallway to the restrooms, she wrenched away from him.

"I don't think that kid should put his hands on you," he said, not understanding how that made him the bad guy.

"That's not up to you to decide," she snapped, drawing several eyes their way.

That's where she had it wrong. She wasn't responsible enough or mature enough to decide for herself. As she'd made perfectly clear time and time again with her bad behavior.

Maybe part of the problem is that you expect the worst from her.

"I was protecting you."

That was his job. To keep her safe. Healthy. To keep her from making the same mistakes as her mother.

Her eyes about popped out of her head. "Protecting me from what? He was just flirting a little. I've got news for you, he's not the first guy to try to pick me up, and I doubt he'll be the last."

"That's the problem," Ross growled. "Maybe if you didn't dress that way—"

"Dress what way?" she asked, her tone whisper-soft, her eyes narrowed to slits.

Even he knew better than to answer that.

Thank God Layne arrived and he didn't have to. She looked from him to Jess and back to him. "I'm not sure I should be asking this but…what's going on?"

"Oh, not much," Jess said, a defiant expression on her face despite the fact that her eyes were wet. "Except that Uncle Ross thinks I'm a slut."

CHAPTER ELEVEN

LAYNE'S MOUTH DROPPED OPEN. Well, she had to give Jess credit—the kid sure made one hell of an unforgettable statement. One loud enough, shocking enough, to have the attention of everyone in the restaurant.

Just, Layne was sure, as Jess had intended.

What better way to stick it to her uncle than to embarrass him in front of a roomful of people? And Ross, God bless him, was falling for it as fast and hard as if he'd walked off a cliff. The landing was probably going to be just as painful.

He stood stiffly, a muscle working in his jaw. "That's not what I said." He met Layne's eyes. "I wouldn't say that."

Maybe not. But he didn't actually try to deny he'd thought it.

And if Layne noticed she'd bet Jess did, too.

"Let's go out back," Layne said, using the tone she employed when dealing with domestic disturbances, bar fights and the inebriated. Attentive and authoritative with a healthy dose of I-have-a-gun-and-badge-and-I-will-cuff-you-and-toss-your-sorry-ass-into-a-holding-cell-if-you-don't-do-as-I-say. "We'll get this straightened out."

"I'm not going anywhere with him," Jess insisted. "Not after he humiliated me that way."

"Humiliated?" Ross asked, sounding as if this whole

situation had been blown out of proportion, as if his niece had nothing to be upset about. As if he didn't care that he'd upset her. "If you ask me, you're being overdramatic."

Layne sighed and scratched the side of her nose. The man was a dunce.

Jess, her face red, her eyes glimmering with tears and anger, stepped forward. Next to Ross, she seemed small and slight and so very young, Layne's heart ached for her. Especially when she looked so embarrassed. And hurt.

"I didn't ask you to butt in," Jess said, jabbing a finger at his chest, stopping shy of making contact. "I don't need your help. I don't need you at all. I can handle myself just fine. And I could've handled those guys, too."

"Like you handled that Nate kid the other night?" he snapped.

Layne inhaled sharply then glanced at Jess. The poor kid looked crushed. The color drained from her face and she sort of curled into herself, her arms hugging her waist, her shoulders hunched as if protecting herself from a physical blow.

Or another emotional one from her uncle.

Swearing softly, his face sickly pale, Ross dragged his hand across his mouth, as if erasing what he'd said. "Jess, I'm sorry. I didn't mean—"

"Go to hell," she said, her voice breaking. She rushed past him and down the hall toward the bathroom. A moment later, the door slammed shut.

Ross followed her. By the time Layne caught up to him, he had his fist raised, ready to pound on the bathroom door.

Layne took a hold of his wrist. "Not a good idea," she said, tugging him down the hall.

He must've been more upset about what happened with Jess than Layne realized because he let her pull him past the break room door before digging in his heels. He went absolutely still, looked at her hand on his arm. When he lifted his gaze to her face, she almost burst into flames from the heat in his eyes. "I need to talk to her."

"Yeah, you do," she agreed, "but right now you need to give her some space. And, I think you need to cool off a bit. Now, you can either come with me until you've both had enough time to calm down—"

"Or?" he asked quietly, as if daring her to continue. His muscles tensed under her fingers.

She smiled thinly and let go of him. "Or you can leave. And if you won't do so of your free will, I'll be more than happy to have someone from the MPPD escort you off the premises. Your choice."

He glanced at the closed bathroom door then back to Layne. "I'll wait."

"In here," she said, gesturing to Celeste's office. She followed him inside, flipped on the overhead light and shut the door. Leaning back against it, she crossed her arms and watched as cool, controlled and contained Chief Taylor paced the small confines of the room like a caged animal. Even though tension radiated from him, he moved with natural grace. Like a big cat, all sleek and predatory and dangerous.

Sexy.

Her mouth went dry, her face got hot. He must've sensed her watching him because he stopped and whirled on her.

"You don't need to stand guard," he bit out. "I'm fine."

"God, but you're stubborn," she said, tossing her

hands in the air. "You drove your niece to tears. Is that what you call fine? Or maybe that's your brilliant plan. To totally squash her spirit so she won't have the spine to cause you any trouble."

"I didn't mean it the way it came out." His voice was level, his eyes hooded. "She should know that."

"Well, I'm sure that'll make it all better. You didn't mean to insult her, hurt her feelings and make her feel like a piece of crap so, really, what right does she have to be upset?"

He stalked toward her and anticipation, hot and sexual, settled in the pit of her stomach.

"I don't want or need you involving yourself in my personal life," he told her, not stopping until he was so close, she had to tip her head up to meet his eyes. "In fact, I'd rather you and Jessica didn't form any sort of...relationship."

She gaped at him. "That has got to be one of the dumbest things I've ever heard. Why shouldn't I be friendly with Jess? She's smart and sarcastic and she makes me laugh. Maybe you'd do better to stop criticizing her all the time, finding fault with her and start finding positive things in her to appreciate."

"That's exactly why I don't want you around Jess. I don't need your help or your advice when it comes to how I'm raising my niece. I can handle her without your input."

She rolled her eyes. "You don't handle kids, especially teenagers. She isn't an officer under your command, someone you can expect to obey without thought or question. You can't control everything."

Something shifted in his eyes, darkening them from gray to a deep pewter. The air she breathed heated, was tinged with his scent.

"You think I don't know that?" he asked in a low rumble that seemed to abrade her skin. Goose bumps rose on her bare arms. He shifted ever so closer. She pressed back, plastered herself against the door. "If I could control everything, my fifteen-year-old niece wouldn't get drunk or have sex with some kid she just met out in the middle of the woods. She wouldn't blame me for what happened to her mother, wouldn't hate me for bringing her here."

Layne couldn't move as he bent his knees slightly so they were eye to eye, mouth to mouth. "If I had more control," he said roughly, "I wouldn't think about you as much as I do. I wouldn't want you."

Oh, God.

Her heart pounded. Her breathing quickened. Swallowing hard, she tried to regain her equilibrium but she felt off balance. Like a boat bobbing in the ocean. "I… You… What?"

Pure male satisfaction entered his eyes, but it did nothing to soften the harsh lines of his face, the tightness of his jaw. "What's the matter, Captain? No smartass comment? No witty refrain?"

He wanted her to be witty? To think? Not possible. Her brain had shut down. A low buzzing filled her ears. She wanted to bolt, was afraid to stay where she was, trapped between the door and his solid body. But she feared moving even more, of doing anything that would shatter this moment and bring her back to reality.

"Tell me to back off," he murmured as he slowly, ever so slowly, leaned in. "Tell me you don't want this." His coffee-scented breath washed over her mouth. Her lips parted. "That you don't want me."

"I should," she said, barely recognizing the rasping voice as her own. Holding his gaze, keeping her butt, her shoulders settled against the door, she stretched her neck until her lips were a hairbreadth from his. "But I've never been much of a liar," she whispered.

She sensed his surprise, his slight hesitation, and then he pressed his mouth against hers.

He lifted his arms, settled his palms against the door on either side of her ears, keeping enough space between their bodies that they didn't touch. His lips were warm. Firm. His kiss hot and hard enough to knock her head against the door with a soft thud.

Her focus narrowed until the only thought she had was of him, her only need for him. Her mind, so clouded moments before with doubts and fears, cleared. She knew exactly what she wanted, exactly why she'd told him the truth. It was so she could experience Ross's kiss, just once, so she'd feel his lips moving over hers.

He tasted of coffee and mint and when he growled in the back of his throat and deepened the kiss, she was helpless to do anything other than open for him.

Ross swept his tongue into Layne's mouth. His want for her, the insatiable need he'd tried to deny for so long should've dissipated or, at the very least, lessened. Instead it grew more demanding with each passing second.

She moaned, low and throaty, into his mouth and he curled his fingers, his nails scraping against the door. It was a dream. A nightmare. One he never wanted to end. He was kissing Layne Sullivan.

And she was kissing him back.

He got lost in her…her taste and scent, the feel of her lips against his. So lost he didn't realize she'd moved, had lifted her hand until he felt the brush of her fingers against his cheek. Her touch like an electric shock, one that brought him to his senses.

He leaped back, kept his eyes on hers while he dragged in a ragged breath. Her cheeks were flushed, her lips swollen and red. Her chest rose and fell rapidly. Christ but she was beautiful. Sexy and alluring. And if he wasn't careful, she could become his greatest weakness.

He stabbed a hand through his hair. She was an officer under his command. He'd risked his career and his reputation, had broken his own moral code for a few minutes with her.

And dear, sweet God it took every ounce of self-control he possessed not to kiss her again.

He cleared his throat. "I apologize," he said stiffly. Not knowing what to do with his hands, he tucked them behind his back. "What just happened was completely my fault. I take full responsibility and understand if you want to file sexual misconduct charges against me."

She straightened slowly, her eyes slumberous as she held his gaze. But then she blinked and they cleared, seemed to focus. Exhaling heavily, she hooked her thumbs in her front pockets. "You can put your sword away. I'm not interested in having you fall on it. Seems to me there are two of us here and I'm responsible for my own actions. And, in case it escaped your attention," she said in that dry tone that both irritated and appealed to him, "I wasn't exactly fighting you off."

Tell me to back off.

She hadn't, though part of him had prayed like hell she would. But he didn't delude himself into thinking this was her fault. No, the blame lay squarely with him. He'd let his frustration over the situation with Jess, his anger at himself for what he'd said to his niece, and his attraction to Layne drive him to make a bad decision.

But that didn't mean he had to repeat that mistake. Ever.

"I don't want you to feel uncomfortable at work," he said.

She raised her eyebrows. "Do you plan on making advances toward me at the station?"

The idea simply appalled him. "No."

"Are you going to offer me promotions, better shifts, higher profile cases and/or other perks in exchange for sexual favors?"

"Where are you going with this?"

"Of course you're not," she said, answering her own question. She shrugged. "I say we chalk it up to curiosity on both our parts and move on."

She was right. But it did little to assuage his guilt. Or lessen how much he wanted her. "If you're sure that's what you want…"

"It is."

What choice did he have except to take her at her word? But that didn't mean he had it in him to hang around there any longer than necessary. He'd already snapped at his niece and kissed an officer under his command. Who knew what other boneheaded move he might make if he didn't get out of there?

"Under the circumstances—" which included, but weren't limited to him being an asshole and making Jess cry, "—I think it might be best if I waited for Jess at home."

"I think you're right," Layne said, mimicking his grave tone. "If she needs a ride, I can drop her off. Unless that makes you uncomfortable."

Hell, yes, it made him uncomfortable. And if he admitted it, it would also make him sound like an idiot. One who was losing his grip so he kept casting wildly about for anything that would help him keep things under his control.

"That's fine. I appreciate it." This time, when he approached her, Layne moved out of his way. Smart move. For both their sakes. His hand on the doorknob, he paused. Kept his gaze ahead as he said, "Tell Jess…"

Tell her I'm sorry.

Except, the only thing worse than being a bastard was not having the balls to admit it. He'd apologize to her himself. "Just tell her I'll see her at home."

He stepped out into the hall…saw the door to the restroom was still closed. And as he walked down the long hallway, away from Layne, away from Jess, he wondered if he hadn't made two of the biggest mistakes of his life tonight.

"IT'S RIGHT THERE," Jess told Anthony, pointing to her house from the passenger side of his Jeep. "Second one on the right."

Anthony pulled over at the curb. Shutting off the ignition, he leaned forward and peered at her place through the windshield. "Doesn't look like anyone's home."

No kidding. The windows were dark but the porch light was on, its soft glow not doing much to dispel the shadows. The driveway was empty.

A lump formed in her throat. She swallowed it. "No. I guess not."

After the horrible things Uncle Ross had said to her at the café, you'd think the least he could do was stick around. Beg for her forgiveness.

Not that she planned on forgiving him. Not anytime soon, at least.

But he still should've apologized, she thought, fiddling with her seat belt strap. He should've been there when she'd finally come out of the bathroom, her eyes dry, her makeup repaired so no one would be able to tell she'd been crying.

That he'd made her cry.

Oh, no. He'd been gone. Had told Layne to bring her home when her shift was done. He couldn't even be bothered to stick around long enough to make sure she got home safely. Couldn't be bothered with her at all.

Bastard.

So she'd told Layne that Keira had already offered to drop her off. Then she'd called Anthony.

And he'd come.

She unhooked her seat belt and swiveled to face him. The moon shone through his window, highlighted his golden hair, the stubble on his cheeks, the strong line of his jaw. He was so handsome. And funny. And really sweet, the way he'd called her every night since they met. How he sent her funny texts throughout the day.

The way he always asked her out—for dinner or coffee or a movie—during their nightly chats. How he didn't get angry when she declined.

She'd been testing him. Making him work to prove he really wanted to be with her. That she was worth some effort.

And despite all her games and the fact that they hadn't even kissed yet, he was there now.

He hadn't given up on her.

"I really appreciate you picking me up," she told him, trying for a low-pitched, sexy tone but wincing when she just sounded stupid. Thank goodness it was dark enough he couldn't tell if she turned red. She cleared her throat. "I didn't mean to take you away from your friends."

"You heard them, huh?"

She bent her left leg and tucked it up under her. "Heard them call you whipped? Yes."

His grin flashed. "They're just jealous because beautiful women aren't calling them."

He thought she was beautiful? God, she could just melt in a puddle at this guy's feet. "Does that mean I'm not the only girl calling you?"

"The only one I want to call."

She laughed. "Good answer."

He was full of them. Always seemed to say the right thing or at least, what she wanted to hear. Because he really was as good of a guy as she thought? Or was he just a really good actor?

She was starting not to care. And, God, but that scared the hell out of her. Because it meant she was playing this game when she didn't know the score, didn't know the rules. But maybe, just maybe, he'd be worth the risk.

Maybe this time she'd be the winner.

He sat back, stretched his arm across the top of the seat. "I'm glad you called me." he said quietly. the tips of his fingers grazing the side of her neck.

Her breath caught, a shiver of delight gripped her. "Me, too."

A car drove toward them, the headlights illuminating the interior of the Jeep, and in that flash of light, she clearly saw her future. Her immediate future.

He was going to kiss her.

And she was going to let him.

He edged closer, his hand sliding to the back of her

neck, his fingers in her hair. Her eyes drifted shut, anticipation built, made her heart pound. His lips brushed against hers once. Twice. She braced herself, her hands clutching the seat as she prepared for him to act like the other guys she'd kissed. Desperate as they shoved their tongues into her mouth, their kisses sloppy and wet. Clumsy with their groping, their sweaty hands diving under her shirt to get at her boobs.

But when his lips touched hers again they were dry. Sure. His hand remained at her head, the other on the seat next to her thigh. He deepened the kiss slowly, his mouth moving over hers so softly, so sweetly, tears pricked her eyes.

Raising her hand, she touched his cheek, skimmed the tips of her fingers across the rough stubble. Kept touching him even when he leaned back slightly. She opened her eyes, met his gaze, returned his smile.

He pressed another quick kiss to her mouth then sat back. "I'll walk you to the door."

Before she could gather enough of her scattered brain cells to tell him not to bother, he was out of the Jeep and rounding the front bumper. Reaching for her bag on the floor, she straightened as he opened her door. Held out his hand to help her get down.

Held her hand as they walked up the driveway, his palm dry and warm, his fingers interlaced with hers.

And how sad was it that she couldn't remember a time, ever, when a guy had held her hand? Had kissed her without wanting to go further? Had simply liked being with her?

At the front door she reluctantly tugged her hand away so she could dig for her key.

"You okay being alone here at night?" he asked.

Inserting her key into the lock, she glanced up at

him. Shrugged. "I'm used to it. My uncle works odd hours."

Like all the time.

Anthony looked into the crescent-shaped window at the top of the door. "You want me to go in with you? Make sure everything's all right?"

She stiffened. Was that some sort of ploy to get into her house? Her bed? Her pants? Had she been wrong about him?

Nibbling on the inside of her lower lip, she studied him. He seemed sincere enough. As if his only concern was her safety. As if he wanted to take care of her.

Yeah, right. No one had ever taken care of her. Like she'd told her uncle, she didn't need anyone to do so. There was only one person she could count on. Herself.

So maybe it wouldn't be such a bad thing if Anthony did want more. Maybe she was setting herself up for a huge disappointment hoping so hard that he was different. Could be better for her to prove to herself right here, right now, that he wasn't.

Before she did something completely stupid. Like fall for him.

She could make up some excuse, pretend she was afraid to go inside alone, that she needed him to check things. She could take him upstairs into her room, have sex with him in the bed Uncle Ross had bought her.

What better way to prove to her uncle that he couldn't control her, that she didn't give a flying damn about what he thought of her?

But the truth was…she didn't want to. She wanted to keep pretending, for as long as possible, that Anthony liked her. Could grow to care about her. Maybe even love her one day.

"I'll be fine," she said, turning the key. "We have

a pretty good alarm system. My uncle…he's sort of a freak about personal safety. But thanks."

Anthony nodded. "Just make sure you lock the door as soon as you get inside."

"I will." She took the key out, curled her fingers around it so the sharp edges dug into her palm. "Thanks again for the ride."

He ducked his head, gave her another of those sweet kisses, his lips clinging to hers for a breathless moment. "Have dinner with me," he said, his voice a low rumble.

How could she keep resisting him, keep holding him at arm's length when he kissed her that way? "When?"

"Tomorrow," he said quickly.

"I'm working. But I…I have Saturday night off."

He smiled, his face lighting up like he'd found Emma Watson under his Christmas tree wearing nothing but her Harry Potter robe. "Perfect." He trailed his hand down her arm, squeezed her hand before stepping back. "I'll pick you up at six. Good night."

"'Night," she said, then opened the door. After shutting it, she plugged in the code for the alarm system, leaned back against the door with a sigh.

"Lock the door," Anthony called.

Because he cared about her. Wanted her to be safe.

She twisted the lock, pressed her ear against the door so she could hear him walk away then ran to the living room window, stood to the side and peeked out as he drove away.

Saturday.

She giggled, the sound seeming odd coming from her as she wasn't much for giggles. Or even laughter. But it felt good. Right. Like her and Anthony.

Saturday.

Giddy…happy…she smiled and did a hip swaying

dance right there in the dark living room next to her uncle's god-awful coffee table. Saturday. She had a feeling it was going to be her best birthday ever.

CHAPTER TWELVE

IN LIFE, VALERIE SULLIVAN had been nothing short of stunning.

Surrounded by the cloying scent of flowers, the air-conditioning doing little to stir the heavy, warm air inside Galileo's Funeral Home, Ross stuck his hands into his front pockets and studied the large, framed photograph. Her hair, a dark mahogany, fell past her shoulders, heavy and straight as a curtain. Her lush mouth curved as she sent a seductive smile at whoever had taken the picture. Her eyes, a rich, golden-brown, held intelligence and humor.

And secrets.

Layne looked like her. Tori, too. Both favored their mother, this woman who'd needed so much more than her family had been able to give her. Who'd left her husband and daughters to be with a man who, from all accounts, was abusive. Violent.

Had she met her death at that man's hands? Or was there someone else out there, someone other than Dale York who'd had motive to want her dead? Who'd taken the opportunity to see that reason through?

He was a good cop, a damned thorough one. But even he couldn't guarantee that they'd ever know the truth about what happened to her.

"She was beautiful," a man said as he joined Ross.

He couldn't take his eyes off that picture. "Yes."

But not as beautiful as her daughter. Not as strong or as capable or as giving as Layne. She'd given up her childhood to care for her sisters, to give them as much normalcy as possible. Even now, beneath her gruff exterior and snide remarks, she couldn't hide her humor, the affection she felt for her family. She guarded her heart, yes, but at least she had the capacity to love.

He wasn't sure the same could have been said for her mother.

"—think she is?" Tori was asking Nora as they entered the small foyer.

"She was just trying to help," Nora said quietly. She shut the door to the room marked Chapel then held Tori's hand and started tugging her toward Ross. "There's no reason to jump down the poor woman's throat. God, Brandon's probably scarred for life now."

Tori tossed her hair, her combative expression a perfect match for her aggressive stride and the I'm-ready-to-kick-some-ass glint in her eyes. "She shouldn't even be here. She didn't even know Mom and she's sure as hell not friends with any of us."

Nora exchanged a long look with the man behind Ross before speaking. "Colleen came for Brandon. I'd think you'd be glad she cares that much about him."

Crossing her arms, Tori sneered, looking so much like Layne, Ross did a double take. "It just pisses me off that so many people are here when half of them wouldn't have even given Mom the time of day when she was alive."

"They came for Dad," Nora said, as patient as a kindergarten teacher. "For Celeste and for all of us."

"Yeah?" She nodded at Ross. "What's his excuse?"

"Mrs. Mott," he said evenly then met Nora's eyes. "Miss Sullivan. My condolences on your loss."

"Thank you," Tori said in the same tone one would use when thanking a poisonous snake for curling up in a kitchen cabinet. "Don't let us keep you."

"Tori," the man to Ross's right said with enough warning and authority in that word that Ross immediately figured out his identity.

"Mr. Sullivan," he said, offering the older man his hand. "I'm Chief of Police Ross Taylor. I'm very sorry for your loss."

"Appreciate that." Tim Sullivan was tall with gray hair, blue eyes, a heavily lined face and a firm handshake. He wore a wrinkled white dress shirt, black slacks and had a dried spot of blood on his cheek where he'd cut himself shaving. "You'll have to excuse my daughter. It's been a difficult evening."

"I can apologize for myself, Dad," she said in exasperation.

"Then I suggest you get to it."

She huffed out a breath but then, as she'd done at the station that day when she'd argued with Layne, her persona shifted, more subtle than her sex-kitten routine—more than likely due to her father being there—but still somehow seductive. Manipulative. And blatantly false.

"Dad's right," she said, her voice huskier now, "it's been a rough night. But that's no excuse for me to take it out on you, Chief Taylor."

"Someday you really have to teach me how to do that," Nora said.

Tori patted her sister's cheek. "It's just for us big girls. Now," she continued, shocking the hell out of Ross by linking her arm with his, pressing up against his side, "why don't I just escort Chief Taylor into the Chapel for the service? It'll be starting soon."

He untangled himself from her before she could drag

him away. "That won't be necessary. I don't want to intrude on your privacy. I just came to express my condolences."

"And to see our father," Nora said.

That should have been his reason, he realized, but it didn't top his list.

Seeing Layne did. And while he could lie to others and say he was there in his role as her superior officer, he couldn't lie to himself. He'd come to be with her, to be there for her during her mother's memorial service.

But no one, not even Layne—maybe especially not Layne—had to know that.

"Actually that is part of the reason I'm here," he told Nora before facing Tim. "I was hoping we could set up a time for you to come down to the station at your earliest convenience."

"I can be there tomorrow morning."

"Nine o'clock?" Ross asked.

Tim nodded, studying Ross in a way that told him the older man had something on his mind. "Girls, I'd like a minute alone with Chief Taylor. Could you excuse us?"

Nora stepped forward. "I don't think that's a good idea. Let me just get Uncle Ken—"

"I'd rather you find your sister," Tim said mildly. "Tell her the service is starting soon."

"But, Dad—"

"Nora." He squeezed her arm. "Please find your sister."

"Come on, baby girl," Tori said, taking Nora's hand. "He'll be fine. He has nothing to hide."

"Sometimes that doesn't matter," Nora muttered sounding like most of the defense attorneys Ross had known. But she let Tori lead her down the hallway toward a smaller viewing room.

"I didn't kill my wife," Tim said as soon as his daughters were out of earshot.

Ross noted Tim's steady gaze, his relaxed features. "I know you didn't, sir."

He knew because his instincts told him to trust the older man and the truth he saw in Tim's eyes. But more than that he knew because he'd done his job: he had checked out Tim's alibi for the night in question. Tim Sullivan had been miles out to sea, a story that was corroborated by a half dozen crew members of the *Wooden Nickel* along with the ship's log.

Nor did Ross think Tim had hired someone to kill Valerie. Not when close to every dollar he made was easily accounted for with his bank, payroll and tax records.

"But I'd still like to ask you some questions," he continued. "Maybe get some information that will help us piece together what happened that night."

He nodded. "I'll do whatever I can to help. I just…" His lips thinned making him look suddenly older. "I just didn't want my girls to think for a moment that I could've done anything to hurt their mother. I loved her," he said so simply, so heartfelt, Ross had no choice but to believe him. "She was everything to me."

Mom needed a lot of attention and Dad was more than happy to give it to her.

"Sir, were you aware of your wife's affair with Dale York?"

"Not until after she left. I wish I had known," he said softly, staring off into space. "I wish I'd had the chance to fight for her."

"And if you'd have lost that fight?"

Tim blinked as if being pulled back to the present. "Have you ever been married?"

Ross fought the urge to squirm. He hated being on the other side of the questions. "No, sir."

"Ever been in love?"

For some reason, Layne's face flashed through his mind, how she'd felt, how she'd tasted when he'd kissed her yesterday. He scowled. "I don't see what that—"

"When you love someone, as I loved my Valerie, their happiness means more than your own and you'll do anything, anything to ensure that happiness. Even if it means letting them go."

"I'm going to kill her!"

Ross looked over Tim's head to see Tori heading toward them, once again steaming mad, Nora looking worried as she scurried after her.

"I mean it," Tori said, her cheeks red. "And I don't care if she does carry a gun and knows how to put a prisoner in a choke hold. She is a dead woman."

Shit. He knew a woman who fit that description exactly.

He looked down the hall. Empty.

"Don't bother, she's not there," Nora said, reading his thoughts.

"Layne's gone."

INSIDE THE YACHT PUB, the nautical theme of its name and exterior was continued with framed photos of fishing boats, yachts, sailboats and their crews. A huge stuffed swordfish hung above the bar, a pink, ruffled bra dangling from its nose. The steering wheel from an old tugboat leaned precariously against the wall between the restrooms and above the small dance floor, a large, green fishing net had been strung with tiny, white lights.

The tops of the booths and tables were chipped and scratched with more than one bearing the initials of lovers encased in a heart and favorite cusswords. The wood floor was warped and dull with age.

But the chairs were new, the leather stools recently recovered and, Layne thought as she sipped her beer at the bar, the drinks were cold. Best of all? Everyone there kept to themselves.

Wiping the pad of her forefinger through the condensation on her bottle, she set an elbow on the bar. Over the past ten years, the Yacht Pub had changed owners three times, had gone from dive bar, to dance club and back to dive bar again—albeit one with twinkling lights and a brand-new pool table.

On the bar, her cell phone vibrated. She checked the incoming number. Her dad. Again. She shut it off.

"Turn the Page"—the original, Bob Seger version—played from the jukebox in the corner. A group of fishermen, their faces lined from spending so much of their lives on the sea, sat down the bar from her. Two younger men in T-shirts and jeans occupied a booth while a middle-aged couple cuddled together at a table in the corner near the dartboard.

More people than she'd expected for a Tuesday but not enough to send her back out into the night. Not nearly enough to send her back to the funeral home where she'd snuck out two hours earlier, leaving her family without a word.

She'd had to leave. It'd felt as if the walls were closing in, the air itself suffocating her. She was restless. Keyed up. It felt like there was a hard ball in the pit of her stomach. Each breath was painful, a reminder that she was alive. And that she was the exact same age as her mother had been when she'd died.

"Buy you a drink?" a male voice asked.

Layne turned and met a pair of light blue eyes. "My mother always warned me not to let strangers buy me drinks," she said. A lie, of course, as Valerie hadn't been much on giving advice. Though she had shown by example that if someone wanted to give you something, you should always take it.

"That's easy enough to fix." He held out his hand. "Hunter Foster."

"Layne Sullivan."

His handshake was warm, firm. His auburn hair wavy, his smile easy. He was attractive and, if she read him right, interested. He was probably a nice guy. A safe guy. Someone she could hook up with tonight, spend a few mindless hours with if she so desired. There were no ties between them to get tangled. And if ever she needed a distraction, it was tonight.

But she couldn't work up the slightest bit of enthusiasm.

Not when Ross's face kept slipping into her head. Not when she'd spent a sleepless night reliving that kiss.

"Thanks," she told Hunter, lifting her half-full bottle. "But it seems I already have a drink."

"If you change your mind—"

"I won't." And, taking a long sip, she turned her back on him, unable to work up much guilt for her rudeness.

She wrapped a strand of hair around her finger. Tugged. Then let it go. This may have been a mistake. Coming here, being in the place her mom had worked, where—in all likelihood—she'd started her affair with Dale York, was a bad decision. But she hadn't wanted to go home. There were too many memories there. And she hadn't wanted to be in that big, empty house all by herself.

Not tonight.

The door opened and she swiveled slightly as Griffin York strolled in looking like some sort of bad-boy fantasy in his work boots, faded jeans and a black T-shirt that clung to his flat stomach and broad shoulders. His dark hair was tousled and stubble covered his cheeks and chin.

His features were sharp, chiseled. His nose straight, his mouth full above that slight indent in his chin. It was a face that could make angels weep with joy, one that could tempt mere mortal women to sin.

It was his father's face.

And, like Dale York, Griffin couldn't be trusted.

He saw her, of course. His glittering gaze raked over her slowly, from the top of her head to the pointy toes of her high heels and back up again. She fought the urge to tug at the hem of her skirt when he lingered at the few inches of bare skin exposed above her knees, making her feel as if her clothes—modest enough for a funeral—were somehow alluring. His lip curling, he touched two fingers to his forehead in a mock salute before sitting at the far end of the bar, his back to her.

Bitterness burned in her stomach, her pulse kicked up.

She slid off the stool, letting her anger and frustration push her to the other side of the bar.

"Hanging out at the Yacht Pub," she said, standing at his shoulder, one hip cocked, her toes aching in her high heels. "Like father…like son."

He paused in the act of raising his beer to his lips, the hesitation so slight, if she hadn't been watching carefully, she would've missed it. "What can I do for you, Officer Sullivan?" he asked, his tone mild, his eyes straight ahead.

"It's Assistant Chief Sullivan," she snapped before pressing her lips together.

They weren't any closer to finding Dale, no closer to bringing her mother's killer to justice. It was as if he'd simply vanished into thin air all those years ago. Ross had called her earlier and told her, very briefly, that he'd interviewed Griffin and his mother and both had claimed not to have heard from Dale since his disappearance eighteen years ago.

Ross had promised her he wouldn't stop searching. But she had to face the truth. They may never find the man. He'd never pay for what he'd done.

She couldn't accept that.

"Where is he?" she demanded of Griffin.

Still not looking at her, he sipped his beer. "Who?"

"Don't play games with me. Tell me where your father is so he can be arrested for murdering my mother."

She'd always kept her distance from Griffin in the past. They shared a history—sort of. A terrible one. And while she knew better than to blame a child for the sins of the parent, that hadn't stopped her from giving Griffin a wide berth all these years. Would have even if her mother hadn't left her husband, her daughters, for his father.

She recognized trouble when she saw it and she saw it now sitting in front of her, calmly drinking a beer. Her entire life she'd avoided trouble, had spent more than her fair share of time getting others out of trouble. But tonight she felt like diving into it, letting it overcome her good sense, her sense of self-preservation.

Griffin lowered the bottle, turned enough to give her

a smirk. "I have no idea where he is. Guess you'll have to put that badge and handy dandy detective license to good use and find him yourself."

And he went back to drinking his beer.

"Want to know what I think?" she asked, wedging herself between him and the empty stool to his right.

"Nope."

She crowded closer. "I think you're lying. I think you know exactly where that bastard is."

He raised one dark eyebrow, let his gaze drop to the deep V of her shirt where she'd left the top two buttons undone. He smiled, a sharp, killer grin that must've brought dozens of women to their knees. But when his green eyes met hers, they were flat. Cold.

"I don't give a rat's ass what you think," he said almost conversationally.

Fury—at him, at the situation—had her hands curling, her vision turning red. He lifted his beer and she grabbed his arm, jerking the bottle. Beer foamed, splattered over his arm, her hand, dripped down the neck of the bottle.

"Tell me where he is." Her voice shook—with anger, she told herself. Not because she was having some sort of emotional breakdown. Her nails dug into his arm. "Tell me."

"Police brutality," Griffin murmured.

"Is there a problem here?"

Layne glanced at the bartender, a petite, bleached blonde in her twenties who'd spent more than her fair share of time in the tanning booth.

"No," Layne said tightly, "no problem."

The bartender's narrowed gaze zeroed in on Layne's hold of Griffin's arm then up to his face. "She bothering you? Should I call the police?"

Layne tossed his arm down, put her hands behind her back to hide their unsteadiness. "I am the police." Except she didn't have her badge, didn't have any ID on her at all. "This man is wanted in connection with a murder investigation."

Griffin wiped his hand down his wet arm. "Now you just sound desperate."

"Do you know what the penalty is for aiding and abetting a felon? Not to mention obstruction of justice and hindering an ongoing investigation."

Maybe she did sound desperate. Desperate and frantic and heading quickly to hysterical. The worst part, the most frightening?

She didn't care.

"This is all fascinating, especially those charges you've dreamed up, but I didn't come in here to be harassed by Mystic Point's finest. I came to have a couple of beers and to get laid. So unless you're buying the next round and you plan on volunteering for the second half of that equation, we're through here."

A primal scream rose in her throat. She swallowed it. Held her head high, her shoulders back as she went back to her stool and got her cell phone. Forced herself not to rush as she passed by him on her way to the door.

"If you change your mind about that lay," he called, "let me know."

She faltered and inwardly cursed herself for giving him even that slight satisfaction.

Outside, she walked around the back corner of the bar, leaned against the building and gulped in air. The briny scent of the ocean filled her lungs but it still felt as if she couldn't breathe properly. She couldn't remember ever feeling this way before. As if she hung off the edge of a precipice, her grip slipping, her feet trying to find purchase.

Chewing her lower lip, she went over her options but there wasn't really a choice. She knew what she wanted. And with one last look at the drop awaiting her, she dialed a familiar number.

And prepared to take a fall.

No sooner had Ross pulled into a space in the Yacht Pub's small parking lot, when he spotted Layne walking toward him, caught in the headlights of his truck.

His heart stopped. His chest tightened.

Her hair was down, the ends of it lifting in a breeze that also had the ruffled collar of her white shirt fluttering against the pale skin of her throat. The shirt was tucked into a narrow black skirt that ended above her knees. Her legs were bare, her feet encased in a pair of pointy-toed high heels.

She pulled on the passenger-side door handle but he'd been too absorbed in watching her, he hadn't unlocked it yet. He quickly disengaged the lock and she pulled again, opening the door.

She regarded him seriously, her eyes hidden in the shadows of the night. "I didn't think you'd come," she said in her husky voice.

"Yes, you did. Or else you wouldn't have called me."

She smiled, a small, extremely satisfied, completely feminine smile. His stomach pitched, the sensation reminding him of riding a roller coaster. The fear and excitement of not knowing what was coming next, of being out of control. Then she tugged on her skirt, hitching it up over her smooth thighs so she could climb in beside him and he started to think maybe not knowing wasn't such a bad thing.

Maybe just this once, he could live in the moment instead of trying to control what happened next.

He switched on the dome light as she shut the door. "Are you okay?" he asked.

She exhaled a soft laugh. "Not really, no."

He studied her. She'd done something to her eyes to make them all smoky and mysterious. Her lips were a bold, shiny red. She stole his breath. She tempted him beyond measure, beyond good sense.

But her eyes were clear and focused. And while her voice was wobbly, she didn't slur her words, hadn't stumbled when she'd walked up to his truck.

"You're not drunk?" His words were a question. And an accusation.

She buckled her seat belt. "I never said I was."

No, he thought, his eyes narrowed, she hadn't. But why else would she have called him?

"It's almost midnight," he pointed out. "And you called and asked me to pick you up at a bar."

Which he'd done without thought. Without hesitation. Something he'd have to think about later when her scent wasn't clouding his thoughts.

"I know. Seeing as how I only had half a beer, and the phone call you're referencing happened not fifteen minutes ago, I remember it clearly." She pushed her hair off her shoulder. "Can we go?"

He put the truck in Park and stretched his right arm along the back of the seat. Close enough to brush his fingertips across her shoulder, to feel the softness of her hair. He curled his fingers. "Layne, what's going on?"

She didn't answer, was quiet for so long, he didn't think she would. How long should he sit there, pushing her with his patience, his silent insistence that she open up to him?

He wanted her to trust him.

He was a fool.

Sliding his arm off the seat, he took a hold of the gearshift when her voice stopped him.

"We had my mother's memorial service tonight."

"I know," he said. "I was there."

"You were?"

He nodded. "I got there just before the service was to start," he said, leaving out his conversation with her father. That would have to wait for another day. "Was still there when your sisters discovered you'd jumped ship. Did something happen to make you run?"

"Nope. It was all very...ordinary. Mundane, even. People came, offered their condolences." Her voice was level, her gaze straight ahead. But he still had the feeling she was slowly coming apart at the seams. "And as I glanced around at our family, our friends, at the tears in their eyes, the grief on their faces and I...I suddenly couldn't breathe. So I excused myself to use the restroom except I walked right past it. The next thing I knew I was outside the funeral home and I just kept walking..." She shrugged, met his eyes. "I ended up here. Where my mom worked. Where she met the man she planned on leaving her husband for, the place where they probably planned their escape."

He studied her. She was in such denial, was in so much pain, but it wasn't up to him to ease that hurt, to get her to face her feelings or acknowledge how much she was hurting over her mother's death. But he wanted to. He could admit that to himself, as long as he remembered there were boundaries he shouldn't cross.

He shifted into Drive when the door to the bar opened and a dark-haired man stepped out.

"That's Griffin York," he said.

"Yep."

Suspicions started forming in his head as he watched Griffin swing onto a Harley and roar off into the night. "Did something happen between you two?"

"We had a discussion," she said, a shrug in her voice. But she wrapped the delicate silver chain she wore around her finger only to unwind it and then repeat the entire process.

An ache formed behind his right eye. "Did this discussion involve aspects of your mother's case? A case, I might remind you, that you are not to have any involvement in, whatsoever."

"All I did was ask him where his father is."

"Did I hallucinate that phone call this afternoon? The one where I specifically told you that I'd interviewed Griffin and his mother and both claimed not to know anything about Dale's current whereabouts?"

She dropped the chain. "I didn't believe it."

Ross wasn't sure he believed it, either. But then, he tended not to trust many people associated with a murder investigation. It was his job to be suspicious of everyone, to question their motives, their every word. To sift through the emotions of others, to find the facts.

His job. Not hers. Not in this instance.

"Tell me you didn't do anything that could jeopardize my investigation," he said flatly. "That you didn't go all rogue cop on him."

"Relax. Your investigation is safe. As is Griffin. You saw him walk out of there, didn't you?"

"Which only means you didn't cause any bodily harm."

"Oh, I wanted to," she assured him solemnly. "I wanted to hurt him. To make him pay for what his father did. God, all my life I've tried to live down being

Valerie Sullivan's daughter, of looking so much like her, and I go off on some guy because he just happened to have the bad luck of being fathered by Dale York." She frowned thoughtfully. "Plus, I just didn't like him much. But that was all on him. He's kind of an ass."

He snorted out a laugh. "I got that impression, too." And he wasn't going to think about how relieved he was that she hadn't liked York with his permanent sneer and dark good looks. "You were right about Griffin—he's got a chip on his shoulder and he wasn't too eager to answer questions about his past, but I think that had more to do with a general resentment toward law enforcement rather than a need to protect his father."

"I lost it," she admitted, rubbing her hands down the front of her skirt, drawing his attention once again to her long legs. "Completely lost control and any hold I had on my judgment. Just for a minute but it was enough to make me realize I needed to get out of there, fast. So I…I called you."

Him. Not one of her sisters or her father. Not Meade or Campbell or one of her fellow officers. She'd needed him.

He nodded. Slowly pulled out of the parking space. "Is your car still at the funeral home?"

She didn't answer so he glanced over when he pulled to a stop to check for traffic. She was watching him, her eyes dark and unreadable. "I don't want to pick up my car. I want you to take me home."

His heart did one slow roll and then he nodded. They drove in silence and, ten hellishly long minutes later, he pulled into Layne's driveway, his headlights illuminating her front door. But he didn't cut off the ignition, didn't even put his truck into Park. Strangling the steering wheel, he stared straight ahead; his jaw ached from clenching his teeth.

She shifted, undid her seat belt. "The least I can do after dragging you out of bed is offer you a drink." Her words were husky, an invitation.

He exhaled through his teeth. "No."

"Why not?"

Because it wouldn't just be a drink and they both knew it. Because she was wearing that skirt, that top. Because her hair was down and there was something raw about her, something that told him he needed to keep his distance.

But then he made the mistake of meeting her eyes. And he was lost. He shifted into Park, turned off the truck. "One drink."

"I don't have my keys so I'll have to get the spare I have hidden out back. You can wait on the porch."

She slid out of the truck and, as she disappeared into the dark between the small garage and the two-story house, he once again took ahold of the keys in his ignition. But he couldn't turn it, couldn't make himself leave. He'd just go in, make sure she really was all right, maybe pour some coffee into her…listen to her if that's what she needed. Then, when he was convinced her dangerous mood had passed, he'd go. His conscience clear, his good deed for the day done.

He made his way up the walk. Her house was large, traditional with a porch that spanned the entire width, square windows with pale green shutters. The door was a deeper green.

It didn't look like her at all.

The windows on either side of the door flooded with light as he stepped onto the porch. Inside, what sounded like a large dog started barking excitedly, continued barking though the sound became muted then started up again from out back. A minute later, the door opened.

Moving aside, she held the door, sweeping her arm for him to come in. He hesitated just long enough for her to raise her eyebrows in question. Or challenge.

He went in.

She closed the door behind him then turned and walked to the right of a stairway in the center of the house, her heels clicking on the wood floor. He followed slowly. There was a living room to the left, dining room complete with a huge glossy table and one of those china cabinets, to the right. He passed another short, dark hallway then stepped into a brightly lit kitchen. It opened into a family room that had a sofa, two chairs and a large-screen TV on the wall. Dog toys were scattered on the floor, a crate was pushed against the wall between a fireplace and a set of French doors.

And on the other side of those doors, a black dog watched them, its breath fogging the glass.

"You live here alone?" he asked as she pulled two bottles of beer from the fridge, handed him one.

She twisted the top off hers, took a drink, her eyes lit with humor as she watched him over the bottle. "Do I strike you as someone who wants to live with a roomie?"

No, she didn't. She struck him as someone used to getting her own way, doing her own thing. Someone private and guarded. "This is a lot of house for one person."

She paused in the act of raising her bottle back to her mouth. "It wasn't always just me. This is the house where we grew up, me and my sisters. When Dad and Celeste decided to move in together a few years back, I bought it from him." She nodded toward the dog. "And now it's just me and Bobby O."

Bobby O? "You named your dog after Bobby Orr, the hockey player?"

"Not me. I let Brandon, my nephew, name him to make up for the fact that Tori won't let him get a dog of his own." She tossed her cap into a garbage can in the corner. Regarding him intently, she stepped forward, stopped before she could brush against him—thank God. "It's just the two of us here."

His throat went dry. He set his unopened beer on the counter. "How about I make us some coffee?" He used his most patient, soothing tone, the one he employed when questioning a victim of a crime. "Or maybe food would be better," he said, sidestepping her to get to her refrigerator. She needed something in her system, something other than beer and whatever was eating her up inside. "When was the last time you ate?"

He felt her come up behind him. Everything in him stilled: his breathing, his heart, his thoughts.

"I don't want any food," she said, her voice tinged with suggestion.

She touched him, her fingers trailing down his spine so lightly that for a moment, he thought he imagined it. But then she did it again, this time going up his back, her hand flat, her palm dragging his T-shirt up. Sweat broke out along his hairline, his heart pounded.

He bit back a groan, stopped himself from bouncing his forehead off the freezer door a few times.

When her nails scraped along the skin at his lower back, he jerked upright and spun around. She reached for him and he grabbed her wrists, her pulse drummed heavily under his fingers. He leaned close, felt mild satisfaction when uncertainty entered her eyes. When her tongue darted out to wet her lips.

"Don't play with me, Layne," he warned roughly.

She tugged on her hands and he let her go. His shoulders loosened when she took a small step back.

But then she blew his mind when she flicked open the top button of her blouse and asked, "Who's playing?"

CHAPTER THIRTEEN

HER PULSE RACING with excitement, her eyes locked on his, Layne slowly undid another button. Then another.

A muscle worked in Ross's jaw, his gaze dropped to her fingers then jerked back to her face. "It won't help."

She froze, her fingers playing with the next button. "What?"

"This." He waved a hand between them. "Sex won't solve whatever's bothering you, whatever's going on inside that stubborn head of yours."

His voice was gentle, his eyes kind. It almost undid her. He understood her so well, it was scary.

"I don't expect it to solve anything," she said, slipping the next button loose. Then another. "But I don't want to think tonight. And I don't want to be alone." She didn't want to deal with the emotions churning inside her, all her doubts and fears. She pulled the shirt from her skirt, slid the last button open. The material parted, exposing her bare stomach and the utilitarian beige bra she'd put on. His gaze lowered, heated. Desire pooled in her stomach. Her nipples pebbled, jutted against the fabric, showing him what he did to her. How he made her feel.

She wished she'd worn something fancier. Something sexy with lace or silk. Wished she had the words, the moves, to show him how much she wanted to be with him, how much she needed him tonight.

Instead all she had to offer him was the truth.

"I want your hands on me," she continued, her voice dropping. She closed the distance between them, noting how he went stone still. "All I want, just once, just for tonight, is you."

Then she kissed him. His mouth was unyielding under hers; his hands went to her waist as if to push her away. She increased the pressure of her lips against his while she caressed the soft skin at his nape; her other hand delved into the thick strands of his hair. Pressing her body against his, she poured everything she had into that kiss, everything she was.

Everything she couldn't say.

His fingers tightened on her waist, his thumbs pushing against her hip bones. And finally, thankfully, he groaned and kissed her back, his tongue rasping against hers.

She clutched his shoulders, molding her body to his when he tore his mouth from hers, set her away. Snatched his hands back as if she'd burned him.

But his breathing was ragged and his hands were clenched at his sides as if he didn't trust himself to touch her.

Layne laid her hands flat against his chest. His heart pounded beneath her fingers, his muscles tensed. "Tell me you don't want this," she said, repeating the words he'd given her the day before when he'd kissed her. "Tell me you don't want me."

He trembled. The strongest, most controlled man she'd ever known trembled because she touched him. Because she wanted him. She felt powerful. Beautiful.

He shut his eyes as if in prayer. Opening them, he breathed, "Damn."

Then he kissed her. No, it was more like an attack.

His mouth was voracious, seeking. Demanding. She had no choice but to respond, to lose herself in him.

He gripped her shirt and used the tails of it to pull her even tighter against him. Her breasts brushed against the solid planes of his chest, her stomach against the cool buckle of his belt.

She lifted her leg as far as her skirt would allow, wound it around his calf and pressed her core against him. He growled and deepened the kiss, his hands gripping her ass. She wanted to wrap herself around him. To breathe him in, to make him the only thing she knew.

Ross lifted his head, walked her backward until she was trapped between the hard edge of the kitchen island and his body, the counter digging into her lower back. He kissed her again. His hands slid under her shirt, his touch rough and bordering on desperate as he stroked the curve of her waist, her stomach.

That was what she wanted. She didn't want it slow or gentle. No, she craved the flash of heat, the hard and fast flame of desire. The kind that left you breathless and mindless, that burned through everything leaving nothing in its wake except pleasure.

She arched into him, ran her hands over his shoulders, down his arms and back again. Needing to feel the warmth of his skin, she clawed at his shirt. He broke the kiss long enough to reach behind him, pull the shirt over his head and toss it aside. Her heart lodged in her throat. He was gorgeous, leanly muscled with golden hair on his chest that tapered, grew darker as it traveled down his flat stomach, disappearing into the waistband of his jeans. She touched him there, just above his jeans. His hair was a rough, enticing contrast against the softness of his skin. His stomach contracted and he yanked her against him, her hands caught between them.

Kissing her, he pushed her shirt from her shoulders, made quick work of her bra. Bending his head, he flicked the tip of his tongue over one taut nipple. Her body jerked. He licked her breast into his mouth and sucked hard. The sound of his low grunt of satisfaction vibrated through her veins. He kept one hand at her back, holding her lower half against him. His other hand came up to pinch and tug the nipple of her other breast.

She couldn't catch her breath. Pressure mounted, built until she thought she'd go mad if he didn't stop. That she'd go mad if he did. Freeing her hands, she speared her fingers into his hair, held his mouth to her breast as he nipped and sucked. Liquid heat pooled low in her belly, dampened her panties.

She rubbed against him. He kissed his way to her other breast as he used both hands to shove her skirt up over her hips. His fingers skimmed between her legs where she most ached for him, where she was wet for him. He curled his fingers around the front of her panties, his nails scraping her skin, his knuckles pressed against her hip bones as he pulled, ripping the delicate fabric.

She gasped, excitement spiraling through her. And when he finally touched her, his fingers warm and sure on her most intimate part, she lifted her hips in a silent plea. More. Harder. Faster.

Lifting his head from her breast, he stroked her. He fisted his other hand in her hair, wrapped it around his knuckles and tugged her head back. Her eyes closed as she waited for his mouth, his touch on her neck, her aching breasts. He tightened his hold on her hair and her eyes flew open, met his.

"Say my name." His voice was gravelly, his expression hard. Savage. "I want you to say my name when I make you come."

She shook her head. She couldn't speak, could barely think. Her limbs were heavy, her mind hazy.

He slowed his touch, slid one finger inside her. Out. Then in again. Her body heated, her muscles contracted around him. She whimpered.

"Goddamn it, Layne," he growled. "Say it."

He added a second finger, stretching her. And all the while he watched her. Waited. He flicked his thumb over her center. Bent his head and scraped his whiskered cheeks against her breast, then caught her nipple between his teeth and tugged, his eyes on her. He bit her gently.

"Ross," she breathed, as the pleasure built, coiled tighter and tighter until she fell apart. Her world exploded into a million pieces. Her muscles went lax, her mind emptied of all thoughts but one.

His name.

Sweat slithered down Ross's back and his muscles trembled as he tried to find control. Control that was hard to come by seeing as how Layne was wet and ready for him.

"Ross," Layne repeated as she came down from her orgasm. He'd never seen anything as beautiful as her, had never been as turned on as he'd been touching her, giving her pleasure. And watching her as she came, hearing his name from her for the first time? Amazing.

She was amazing.

And she tested his willpower, his resolve, like no woman ever had. But even if he hadn't already surrendered to her, to his own desire for her, he wouldn't have been able to hold out now. Not when she was all flushed and warm, her skin pink, her eyes unfocused.

He loosened the hold he had on her hair but didn't let her go. Pulled her head to him and kissed her, his tongue sweeping into her mouth. All he knew was Layne. Her scent clung to his fingers, her touch burned him, her taste hadn't abated his hunger for her. It only grew sharper, edgier with each kiss, each touch.

He kissed her hard, used his teeth and lips and tongue until she writhed against him once more. Panted into his mouth, her hands streaking over him as if she couldn't get enough of him. Wedging an arm between them, she lowered her hand and cupped his erection through his jeans. He shuddered. Moaned. He was hard and hot and aching for her. Only her.

She pushed against him, turning them so that they reversed positions. Giving her control. He spun them again. So did she, so that when they reached the end of the island, he was against the counter and she stood between his legs, her lush breasts molded to his chest, her long, lean arms wrapped around his neck. He smoothed his hands up the silky skin on her inner thighs. Their harsh breathing filled the silence. And when he cupped her firm ass, rolled his hips against her, she went off like a gun in his arms, scratching his back, dragging him toward the kitchen table.

They came together violently, grappled for position, their hands racing over each other. He couldn't get enough of her. Her hair was like silk hanging down her back, her skin was warm satin covering lean muscles, subtle curves. She reached for the button on his jeans, dragged his zipper down. Together they shoved his jeans and underwear to his ankles.

Before he could take his boots off, she pushed him, hard, onto a chair.

He was already reaching for her when she straddled him. Her warmth surrounded him. He lifted his hips, kissing her shoulders, the long line of her neck. Sucked at the pulse beating heavily at the base of her throat. She moved, rubbing against him until he knew he'd go insane if he wasn't inside of her. Now.

"Condom," he managed to mumble, but he couldn't stop touching her, his lips moving over her face, her collarbone, the tops of her breasts. His tongue tasting the salt of her skin. "Wallet. Back pocket."

Leaning back slightly, she fumbled for his jeans, her movements against him making him insane. Finally, thankfully, she straightened, his wallet in her hand. She pulled out the foil packet, ripped it open and, reaching between them, her knuckles brushing his stomach, covered him.

He paused, the tip of his erection at her entrance, her soft, seeking hands on his shoulders. Only when she met his eyes did he slide into her.

The sound she made when he entered her almost drove him over the edge. Clenching his teeth, he gripped her waist, pumped into her. She met him thrust for thrust, her feet—still encased in those sexy shoes—flat on the floor as she rode him. He cupped her breasts, kissed that mobile mouth of hers. Their skin grew slick with sweat, their movements frenzied, frantic.

Her breath hitched and she bowed back, her body tightening around him. Her hips worked like pistons, her hands clutched his thighs. She looked at him, right at him, while her orgasm swept through her, while she tumbled and fell. Her eyes went dark, her mouth parting on a soft cry of pleasure.

His own release hit him hard and fast and with his eyes still locked on hers, he emptied himself while deep inside her.

LAYNE DIDN'T WANT to move. Ever.

Collapsed against Ross, her head on his shoulder, his heart beating against her own, her body felt boneless, pleasantly sore and immensely satisfied. She was content to stay there, right there in his arms, breathing in the scent of his skin, of their sex.

He stirred, lifted her away from him. Standing next to her small kitchen table, her skin chilled, her legs unsteady, she watched as he yanked his pants up, his movements rigid with barely concealed fury. So much for her contentment. She should know by now it was nothing but a fantasy anyway.

What had she expected? she thought as she worked her skirt back down and glanced around for her shirt. Tender words? A soft touch or maybe a gentle kiss? This hadn't been a date, hadn't been some romantic scene from a movie.

He turned and scooped his shirt off the floor. As he put it on, the muscles of his back contracted, his skin marred by her scratch marks. He faced her, his hair mussed from her fingers, his eyes hooded. "We need to talk."

Feeling cold, exposed, she covered her breasts with her arms. "I think we've said everything there is to say." She was glad her voice came out snide, so proud it didn't break, that none of her hurt had leaked into her words.

She spied her shirt on the floor and swept it up, shoved her arms into the sleeves and buttoned it, her fingers cold and stiff. Really, what could they possibly have to discuss? They'd had quick, semirough sex. That was all. It'd been a release and, for her, an escape.

Her fingers fumbled. She'd had quick, semirough sex with her boss, had thrown herself at him, had practically goaded him into it. Her throat closed.

No doubt about it. She was an idiot.

"I don't like being used," he said.

She met his eyes and wished she hadn't. She could've happily lived the rest of her life without seeing the coldness there. Rubbing her hands over her chilled arms, she tossed her hair back. "You sure didn't seem to mind my using you a few minutes ago. I didn't exactly hold a gun to your head."

He flushed but his eyes were hard as his gaze slid over her. "No, you didn't need a gun to get what you wanted."

"What we both wanted," she snapped, crossing to pick up her beer. She took a long drink but it did nothing to ease the rawness of her throat. She'd pushed him. Worse, she'd manipulated his feelings for her. She'd known he was attracted to her and she'd used that to her advantage.

But there was one truth he couldn't deny.

"You could've walked away," she told him. She held up her bottle, tipped it toward the back door. "You still can."

You could've walked away.

And that was what pissed him off the most, Ross realized. He hadn't been able to walk away. Hadn't been able to resist her. Instead of taking responsibility for his actions, he was blaming her.

Hell. When it came to her, he couldn't think straight. He scrubbed a hand down his face.

"Is that what you want?" he asked quietly. "Do you want me to walk away?"

She regarded him warily, her hair a tangled, dark mass around her face. The delicate skin around her mouth was pink from his whiskers. She was all rumpled in her wrinkled shirt, the buttons mismatched, the material thin enough to remind him she wore nothing underneath.

"I don't know what you want me to say," she finally admitted. "Do you want me to regret what happened? Because I don't. But I am sorry if you do."

Regret it? He wasn't sure about that any longer.

"I want you to tell me what's going on." She averted her gaze, took another drink of beer. "You said you didn't want to be alone," he continued, walking toward her. "Is that all this was?"

She lifted a shoulder. "What do you think?"

He closed the distance between them, set his hands on the counter on either side of her waist. "I think you could have your pick of any number of eligible men. And that you chose me." It confused him. Humbled him. "I think something's got you all turned around in here—" He tapped his finger against her temple. "And in here." Sliding his fingers down her cheek, her neck, he rested his hand over her heart.

She shuddered. "I…I told her I hated her." Her words came out in a rush, her voice unsteady. "My mom. The last thing I told her was that I hated her."

"You were angry. Upset. And you were just a kid. Kids say they hate their parents all the time and don't mean it. Hell, Jess tells me on an almost daily basis how much she can't stand me."

Not that she'd said it to him lately seeing as how she

hadn't spoken to him since he'd made such a mess of things at the café.

"Oh, I meant it," Layne said, picking at the label on her beer. She met his eyes. "I meant it because I knew about the affair."

He narrowed his eyes. "I thought no one knew until after Valerie and Dale disappeared."

"No one else knew. At least, not that I'm aware of."

"Did she admit she was leaving your father for Dale?"

"Not in so many words. When she told me she was going to stay with Celeste, I called her a liar and told her that I'd seen her and Dale together." Reaching to the side, she set the bottle on the counter. "How I'd come home early one afternoon because volleyball practice had been canceled." Her mouth flattened. "They were in her bedroom, in the bed she shared with my father."

"She didn't see you?"

"Oh, she was way too busy to notice me," Layne said sardonically, but her eyes were miserable. "When I told her I knew she was going to be with her lover, she didn't even try to deny it. She told me that sometimes you had to do what was best for you. That when you wanted something, you had to reach out and grab it and not let go. And that's what she was doing. She was grabbing ahold of the life she wanted. And that one day, I'd understand."

Layne pushed away from the counter and he stepped aside. She crossed to the chair where they'd made love, sat and took off a shoe. "I still don't understand it," she said, rubbing her foot before taking off the second shoe, letting it dangle by the strap from her finger. "To-night, at the memorial, with all those people offering their sympathy and Dad being so heartbroken after all these years and Nora insisting that Mom hadn't really left us, that she would've come back…" Layne sighed. Raised her head. "I had to get away. And then my night got even crappier when I saw Griffin, looking so much like his father, acting like such an ass…"

"So you called me," Ross said, thinking he understood her a bit better now. "Because you didn't want to be alone."

"I didn't want to be alone," she repeated, getting to her feet, "but more than that, I wanted to see you. I wanted to be with you."

He hadn't been able to walk away from her before when it would've been the smart, the safe thing to do. And he couldn't do it now. He opened his arms and after a brief hesitation, she stepped into them. He kissed the top of her head, pulled her closer and hoped like hell he hadn't inadvertently given his heart to this woman.

SATURDAY NIGHT, Layne felt Ross arrive at the café before actually seeing him. Seated at a table in the back, she raised her head. Yep. There he was, standing just inside the door, scanning the room, his handsome face unreadable, a white bakery box in his hand. His gaze landed on her. She straightened, lifted her chin. She may be avoiding him but that didn't mean she was going to hide.

Besides, it was too late to hide. He was making his way over to her.

"Layne," he said when he reached her table.

She twirled pasta onto her fork but didn't lift it. "Chief."

His eyes flashed. Yes, she was back to calling him Chief, despite the fact that they'd had sex, that he'd held her after she'd told him she'd known about her mother's affair. Despite her then taking him by the hand and leading him up to her bedroom where they'd made love again, slowly that time, before he'd gone home.

He was still her boss, though. And they were in public. Except she wasn't worried about people getting the wrong idea about her, about her reputation.

She was worried about his. About his position at the police department.

"Mind if I sit down?" he asked when it was obvious she wasn't going to extend the invitation herself.

"Go ahead. But if you're looking for dinner, you might be too late. I think they've already closed the kitchen."

"I'm not here to eat." He set the box off to the side as he sat across from her. "I see you're keeping yourself busy during your time off."

She paused, a bite of pasta halfway to her mouth. "Doing my best."

Setting the fork back down, she instead sipped from her glass of ice water. The day after her mom's memorial service, Layne had called the station and asked to take the full week allotted for her mother's death. She'd claimed it was to help her father settle her mother's affairs, things that had been left in flux for far too long. But she suspected Ross knew the real reason she hadn't wanted to return to work until she had to.

She was a coward. But she wasn't ready to face him every day. Not when her feelings were so mixed up when it came to him.

"What's in the box?" she asked, not really caring but needing to say something, anything, to fill the silence.

"A cake."

"You know, they sell desserts here. You don't have to bring your own."

"It's for Jess. Today's her birthday." He pushed the corner of the box so that it lined up with the edge of the table. Looked uncomfortable. "I thought she might like it if we had cake here since she seems to be making friends with the other waitresses."

"That's actually kind of sweet," she said, earning herself one of his flat looks. She bit back a smile. "But Jess isn't here."

He frowned. "She told me she was working tonight until eleven."

"She's talking to you again?"

"Bits and pieces. Enough for me to know she's still pissed."

And he was still making the effort, trying to do something nice for his niece. He may not know what he was doing when it came to Jess but it was clear to Layne he cared about the kid. She just wasn't sure that was clear to him—or Jess—yet.

"I've been here for over an hour," Layne said, "and I haven't seen her. Keira," she called when the redhead came out to clear a table. "Could you come here?"

"Hi, Chief Taylor," Keira said with a sunny smile when she reached their table. "I'm sorry but the kitchen's closed. I could get you a drink, though."

"Where's Jessica?" he asked.

"Don't growl at her," Layne told him in exasperation when Keira's smile faltered. "Was Jess scheduled to work tonight?" Layne asked.

"I'm not sure," the teen hedged.

"Seeing as how I can walk into the break room and check the schedule myself," Layne said, "why don't you save me a trip and just tell us?"

Keira shifted her weight. "I don't want to get her into any trouble…"

"Why not?" Ross asked dryly. "She's so good at it."

Layne kicked him under the table. Shooting her a death glare, he rubbed his shin.

"She's not supposed to work until tomorrow," Keira said quickly—probably afraid she'd be next on Layne's kick list.

"Do you have any idea where she is now?" Layne asked.

"Probably with her boyfriend."

"Boyfriend?" Ross repeated in his best hard-ass cop tone. "What boyfriend?"

Keira's eyes were wide. She stuck her thumbnail in her mouth. Chewed. "Uh…maybe he's not her boyfriend. I mean, she never said he was…"

Layne patted the back of the girl's hand. "Relax. Just give us his name so we can straighten this all out."

"It's Anthony," she said around her nail.

Oh, crap. "My Anthony?" Layne asked, sitting up straighter.

Please say no. Please, please say no.

Keira nodded.

And crap once again.

"Okay," Layne said with a sigh, knowing instinctively that Anthony had no idea who Jess really was. How old she really was. "Thanks."

"Who the hell is your Anthony?" Ross asked as Keira hurried off.

"My cousin."

"You think Jess is with him?"

She thought Jess was lying to him and could possibly get him into a boatload of trouble.

"Only one way to find out," she muttered, speed dialing Anthony's number on her cell phone. After two rings, it went to voice mail. She hung up. "He's not answering."

Ross pulled his phone from his pocket, called a number and held it to his ear, his scowl darkening with each passing second. "It's me," he barked into the phone, obviously leaving his niece a message. "Call me. Now." He drummed his fingers on the table then pushed out of his chair. "I'm going to find her."

"And how are you going to do that when you have no idea where she is?"

"I'll drive around. She's probably at another party."

Layne could let him go. He'd be wasting his time but that wasn't any of her concern. Plus, she didn't want to help him. She wanted to keep her distance from him, especially when it came to personal matters.

But he'd bought the kid a cake. He'd shown up there wanting to surprise his niece on her birthday and she'd lied to him. And Layne had a feeling Ross wasn't the only man she was lying to.

"Here's the deal," Layne said as she stood. "I have a pretty good idea where Jess could be."

"Where?" he demanded.

"I could tell you," she said, grabbing her purse and tossing enough cash onto the table to cover her bill and tip, "but in this case, I think it'd be much better if I just showed you."

SITTING IN THE BUBBLING WATER of Anthony's family's hot tub, Jess's eyes drifted closed as he kissed her. She linked her hands around his neck, her fingers in his damp curls. His lips were firm, his hands on her bare shoulders, his fingers splayed across her upper back. He kept playing with her hair and sliding his finger along the strap of her bikini top where it tied behind her neck. His kiss was warm, seductive. And when he lightly traced the seam of her lips with the tip of his tongue, she gasped softly, opening for him.

He kept the kiss slow and lazy until her brain felt hazy, her head heavy. He caressed her upper arms, trailing down to her elbows and back up again leaving goose bumps in his wake. And still he continued to move his mouth over hers in that mind-numbing way.

He was a grade-A top-notch kisser, that was for sure. He was sweet and funny and he'd cooked for her. She still couldn't believe it. His parents were out of town and he'd invited her to his house and made her dinner. Okay, it was just steaks on the grill, baked potatoes and a salad, not exactly the most difficult meal to make. But he'd put in the effort. And no one had ever put in the effort when it came to her before.

His hand went to her upper chest, his thumb at the base of her neck, his fingers spread against her collarbone. Her heart thumped wildly and she opened her eyes to see if he noticed. But his eyes were still shut and the way he looked when he kissed her only made her heart race faster. Made her hands tighten on his strong shoulders.

He groaned and deepened the kiss, pressing her back against the smooth edge of the hot tub. Water sloshed. The scent of chlorine mixed with his cologne. His other hand went to her waist, his fingers trailing across her stomach. Her muscles quivered, she tensed but he kept his touch light as he smoothed his palms up to her ribs, around to her lower back and then across her stomach again.

Usually when she made out with a guy, she let him set the pace, kept her hands mostly to herself. But with Anthony she couldn't stop from running her hands down the hard muscles of his arms, across his upper back. He slid his mouth across her jaw, down the length of her throat and back up to settle behind her ear. He kissed her there, his whiskers scratching her in a way that made her stomach flutter, his tongue slipping out to trace the shell of her ear.

She knew what he wanted. Sex. It was what all guys wanted from her. Just because Anthony had been nice to her, had listened to her when she'd told him her dreams for the future, had talked with her for hours on the phone, wasn't any reason to think he was different.

But she wanted him to be different. Wanted to be different with him.

His hand crept up over her rib cage, his thumb skating across her skin, just beneath her top. It felt… nice. Everything he did to her felt good, like how she imagined it was supposed to be when you were with a guy. Almost as if they were meant to be together. So why shouldn't she let him do what he wanted? Why shouldn't she, for once, be with a nice guy?

He shifted closer, his erection brushing her thigh.

"Wait," she gasped, pushing against his chest with both hands.

His hand stilled as he leaned back. "What's wrong?" His voice was deep, concerned. He couldn't be faking that, could he? "You okay?"

"I…" She licked her lips but her heart was beating so fast, she felt like she couldn't catch her breath. "I like you," she blurted, her face heating.

His blue eyes warmed. He smiled and touched the ends of her hair. "I like you, too."

She exhaled. Okay, good. That was good. "I just…I don't want to do anything to mess this up."

Like lying about her age, going to college and being

a normal teenager with a normal family. Guilt lodged itself painfully in her chest. She couldn't tell him the truth. Not tonight. But she could tell him part of it.

He covered her hands on his chest, squeezed gently. "What is it, Jess?"

God, he was so sweet. So much more than she deserved. "I've…done some things…I'm not proud of, been with guys so they'd like me—"

"Hey," he said quietly, "I don't care about your past. None of that matters to me."

"It matters to me. For the first time ever, it matters." She inhaled deeply, met his eyes. "I want you to like me for me, not because I…because we…"

"You want to slow down?"

She rolled her eyes, felt like a complete moron. "Guess I could've just said that, huh?"

"You could have," he agreed with that grin that made her stomach feel all twisty inside, "but I'm glad you didn't. I'm glad you told me how you feel."

"You're not mad?" she asked then held her breath. Was she going to lose him?

"I'm not going to lie. I want to make love with you," he said, his voice husky, his eyes heated. "But I'm not in any hurry, Jess, and I'm not going anywhere." He traced a finger down her cheek. "I'm willing to wait for you, for as long as it takes."

Tears burned her eyes, her throat. She swallowed them. She wanted to see him clearly, to etch this moment, his face, his words, in her memory. Because she knew, better than most, that perfect moments like this didn't last.

So she'd just have to make the most of this one.

She kissed him, let her lips linger on his and poured

her heart into that kiss. When they broke apart, she smiled.

"I never get tired of that," he murmured.

"Kissing?" she asked lightly.

"No." But he pressed another kiss to her mouth. Then the tip of her nose before leaning back to meet her eyes. "Your smile."

She laughed, unable to hold back the pure joy bubbling inside her. Flinging her arms around him, she smiled against his mouth. "I don't see why I can't do both."

He held her head as they kissed, his hands on her ears. Maybe that's why she didn't hear the gate open, didn't realize they were no longer alone until her uncle growled, "Son, you need to take your hands—and your mouth—off my niece."

Anthony jerked upright and for a second, Jess worried Uncle Ross had finally lost it and had yanked him away from her by the hair. But her uncle stood in front of the double doors leading into the house, his arms crossed, his legs apart, his expression scary mad, even for him.

She squeezed her eyes shut but when she opened them, he was still there. Worse, Layne was next to him looking at Jess with such disappointment, she had to avert her gaze.

"What's going on?" Anthony asked, looking so confused. "Layne, what are you doing here?"

"Sir," Uncle Ross said in his cop voice, "could you get out of the hot tub?" His hard gaze flicked to her. "You, too."

Anthony hesitated. Blushed. "Uh…" He cleared his throat. "I'm not sure that's a good idea…"

"Out," Uncle Ross said, taking a menacing step forward as if he was going to go Bad Cop after all. Layne laid a hand on his arm and he stopped but ground out, "Now."

With a defeated sigh, Anthony rose. His swim trunks were tented from his erection. Jess looked away, bile rising in her throat.

With a soft sound, Layne grabbed one of the large, white towels Anthony had brought out and tossed it to him. He caught it against his chest, got out and wrapped the towel around his waist.

"What's going on?" he asked again. "Is it my parents? Did something happen?"

His mom and dad had gone out of the town for the weekend, some political fundraiser thing in New York.

"Uncle Kenny and Aunt Astor are fine," Layne told him as Jess climbed out, her arms trembling, her legs unsteady.

Uncle? Aunt? Jess groaned. She should've realized Layne and Anthony were related. God, wasn't everyone in this stupid town connected to everyone else?

"This is Chief Taylor," Layne told Anthony as she held out a second towel, but Jess could only stare at it blindly. "He's Jess's uncle."

Anthony dragged a hand down his face, smiled sheepishly as he held out his hand. "Nice to meet you, sir."

Uncle Ross kept his hands at his sides, nodded at the bottle of beer on the edge of the hot tub. "That yours?"

Slowly lowering his hand, Anthony glanced at Layne. "Yes, sir."

"And did you provide any alcohol to my niece?"

Shivering in her red bikini, Jess stepped forward, the deck cold under her bare feet. "Uncle Ross—"

"No, sir," Anthony said. "Is that what this is about?" he asked Layne. "You thought I let her have a beer?"

"She's a minor," Layne said.

He frowned. "You mean she's underage."

Jess met Layne's eyes, shook her head, silently pleading with her not to say anything. Not to tell him. Not to ruin the one good thing she had in her life.

"Anthony," Layne said quietly, looking away from Jess, "she's fifteen."

CHAPTER FOURTEEN

ANTHONY LAUGHED. "WHAT?" He glanced around and his smile faded, was replaced by a confused frown. He shook his head. "No. No," he repeated more firmly.

But when he looked at her, he didn't seem as convinced.

"Actually," Uncle Ross said, "today's her birthday. Her sixteenth."

Jess opened her mouth but all that came out was a sound of distress. She needed to figure out a way to fix this, to make it right before she lost the best thing ever to happen to her. But she had no words, no idea what to do, what to say.

"Jess?" Anthony asked stepping closer. He smiled at her, a hopeful tell-me-they're-yanking-my-chain smile but his eyes were serious. Worried. "That's not true, is it?"

Though it wasn't cold out, she couldn't stop shaking. Water dripped off her, ran in rivulets from her hair to drop onto her shoulders, raced down her arms and chest.

"Tell me it's not true," Anthony said, his voice harsher than she'd ever heard.

She forced herself to meet his eyes. "I can't," she whispered, the words feeling like broken glass in her raw throat.

His face drained of color, the hand he dragged through his hair trembled. "Jesus."

"I'm sorry," she cried, but the rest of what was in her heart stayed there.

I'm so sorry. Please don't hate me. Please, please don't leave me.

His blue eyes went flat, cold. "What was this—some sort of joke? A prank?" He stepped even closer, looking big and angry and dangerous. She scrambled back, tripping over her own feet. "What the hell was this?"

Her heart breaking, her world crumbling yet again, all she could do was shake her head.

"Anthony," Layne murmured, touching his arm. "Why don't you go inside, get dressed? We'll take Jess home."

He didn't respond, just looked at Jess with utter contempt. With pure hatred. As if he didn't know her at all—when he'd known her better than anyone. Finally he nodded stiffly then spun on his heel and went toward the house, Layne following him.

Jess watched him go, his back rigid, his stride long until he closed the door behind him. Everything inside of her, any hope she may have been dumb enough to hold on to, died.

He'd walked away from her. Left her without looking back. Without fighting for her.

Hadn't she known he was too good to be true? And she never got to keep anything good.

"Get your things," Uncle Ross ordered roughly, like he was some damned drill sergeant and she a lowly recruit. "We're leaving."

Jess's chest grew tight, her breathing quickened until she grew light-headed. Until a strange roaring sound filled her ears. He was always telling her what to do.

When to do it. It was his fault Anthony had found out the truth. His fault she'd lost Anthony.

Vibrating with fury, with a rage unlike she'd ever known, she faced her uncle. "I hate you," she spat, her hands fisted by her sides, her nails digging into her palms.

He didn't even blink. "Okay," he said as if it didn't matter, as if she didn't matter. "But you can hate me at home just as easily as you can here, so let's go."

He didn't care. He'd never care.

"I hate you," she repeated, something inside her snapping. She caught a glimpse of shock on his face as she launched herself at him. "I hate you!" she screamed, pummeling him with her fists wherever she could reach. His chest, his shoulders. "You ruined it! You ruin everything."

"Knock it off," he ground out, trying to grab her hands. "Damn it, Jess, calm down."

But she wouldn't, couldn't. She caught him low in the stomach and he grunted. Satisfaction poured through her, gave her renewed strength. She wanted to hurt him, wanted him to know how it felt to suffer. To be in as much pain as she was in.

"Hey, hey!" Layne said a moment before grabbing both of Jess's upper arms from behind and dragging her off her uncle. "Cool off."

Though Layne's arms were wrapped around Jess's shoulders, she lunged at Uncle Ross again with a hoarse cry.

Layne whirled her around, held her by the shoulders and gave her one quick, rough shake. One hard enough to have Jess's teeth snapping together, the fight draining out of her. "I said cool off."

"What the hell has gotten into you?" Uncle Ross

asked, eyeing her as if she was some sort of tame pet that had suddenly gone rabid. His expression was fierce, his neck marred with angry red marks, his shirt wrinkled.

Gulping in air, Jess twisted out of Layne's hold and faced him. "You ruined my life."

"Ruined…?" He grabbed the back of his neck and looked up at the sky as if asking for some sort of heavenly intervention. "I think that's a bit of an exaggeration."

He would. Asshole. "I didn't ask you to take me in," she reminded him. "I didn't want to be dragged to this stupid town. You did that. Just like you made sure my mom was put away—"

"Your mother has a problem," he said so calmly she wanted to scream and yank her hair out. Or, better yet, yank his hair out. "She needs help and she's getting it."

"I helped her!" She hugged her arms around herself but she couldn't get warm. Didn't think she'd ever be warm again. Layne tried to press the towel into her hands but Jess stepped back. "I took care of her, took care of both of us. We were doing just fine without you."

His steely gaze flicked to Layne and then back to Jess. "We can discuss this when we get home."

"I'm not going anywhere with you." Just the thought of returning to that house, of being where she wasn't wanted, not really, made her frantic. She'd rather die than go anywhere with him. She whirled around. "I don't want to go with him," she told Layne, her voice breaking. "Please don't make me go with him."

"Of course you're going with me," he said, as if she were a bratty five-year-old and not almost an adult. "You live with me."

"You don't want me," Jess said numbly. "You never wanted me."

No one did.

Layne shifted. Sighed. "I can't believe I'm about to say this," she muttered, "but…" She exhaled heavily then met Jess's eyes. "You can stay with me."

Jess's heart kicked painfully in her chest. "Really?"

"No," Uncle Ross said at the same time Layne said, "Yes."

"Get your stuff," Layne continued as if Uncle Ross wasn't glaring at her, "and wait for me in my car while I talk to your uncle."

Jess scooped up the tank top she'd tossed onto one of the lounge chairs when Anthony had asked her to join him in the hot tub. Thank God she'd brought her bag back out here after changing into her suit inside the luxurious house. She couldn't handle bumping into Anthony now. Not when all she wanted was to escape. To curl up somewhere and pretend this whole horrible night had never happened.

But mostly, she wanted to get away from Uncle Ross.

Holding her flip-flops in one hand, clutching her bag to her chest with the other, she raced past her uncle, pretending not to hear when he quietly said her name. No one wanted her. Not her mother or her grandparents or Uncle Ross. Not Anthony. They all walked away from her without regret or guilt.

Her stomach hurt, her chest burned. All of her hopes, her dreams, were dead. She was empty.

But at least this time, this one time, she was going to be the one walking away.

It took all of Ross's self-control not to toss Jess over his shoulder and stomp off with her to his truck. To force her to do as he said. To listen to him, just this once.

He watched her disappear around the back of the

house, her hair wet and stringy, her bathing suit way too revealing for a girl her age. Damn it, why couldn't she trust that he knew what was best for her?

"You realize there's a good chance she'll just take off," Ross said, crossing his arms as he glared at Layne.

"There's always that chance," she said with a shrug. "But I doubt she's going anywhere tonight."

He wished he had her confidence. Or the ability to fool himself as well as she did. "What the hell do you think you're doing, interfering with my niece that way?"

Layne studied him, tranquil as the night air. "I'm making it possible for you and Jess to have some sort of healthy relationship in the future."

"At this point, I'd settle for going a day without her wanting to rip my head off." He rubbed at a sore spot on his side. He still couldn't believe she'd attacked him that way and blamed him for what happened here tonight. She lied and somehow it was his fault? What the hell kind of thinking was that? "And I'm not about to let her go off on some…sleepover. My God, she was fooling around with a twenty-one-year-old. A grown man. Do you know what could have happened to her?"

His stomach cramped just thinking about it.

"I know what could've happened if it'd been someone other than Anthony," Layne said in her brisk, no-nonsense way as she crossed to the hot tub. "She put herself in a dangerous situation, there's no doubt about that. Plus, don't think I'm too thrilled with how she deceived my cousin."

"But you still want to reward her by letting her get her way in this?"

"It's not a reward and I'm not saying she shouldn't

face the consequences of her actions. But you saw her. She's hurting, Ross," she said quietly.

"What she is," he scoffed, "is pissed she got caught. She wasn't even crying."

Kneeling, Layne shut the jets off then glanced up at him. "Only because what happened was too painful for her to cry."

He rubbed the back of his neck, wished this whole crappy night was over already. "That makes no sense."

She sighed and rose, crossed to him. "You said yourself that she didn't cry when her mom was sentenced, that when she was ready to face those feelings, she would. She'll mourn in her own time. And you're right. But sometimes what we're dealing with is so painful, you can't let yourself have the luxury of tears." Her voice dropped, her eyes were somber. "Because if you cry, you may never stop." She inhaled deeply. "That's why I didn't cry when my mom left."

He reached for her. "Layne—"

Shaking her head, she stepped back. "I just want you to try to understand what Jess is going through. To see her side."

"Her side? The only thing I see is that my niece is out of control."

"Possibly. But what good is it going to do for you to force her to go home with you? And let's be honest, some distance between you two will do you both good."

He was afraid she was right. More than that, he was terrified he'd messed things up with Jess so badly he'd never be able to fix it. "I don't know." And damn it, he hated admitting he was so unsure.

"You can fight me on this," Layne said, the lights from the house casting her face in shadows. "Or you can trust me. Jess needs some space. You're not giving in to her or letting her get away with anything by doing what she needs."

He bristled. "Every decision I've made in the past six months, every choice, has been for her. I've done everything in my power to do what's right by her."

"You've done what you thought was best for her."

"What's wrong with that? Isn't that my job as her guardian?"

"That's part of it," Layne agreed, "but Jess doesn't need you making decisions for her."

"Then what the hell does she need from me?" he asked exasperated and completely baffled.

"That's easy," Layne said. "She needs you to put her first."

And Layne walked off before he could ask her what she meant, how he could possibly do any more for Jess than he'd already done. He reached the driveway just as Layne pulled away. There was a pang under his breastbone as he watched them go.

You don't want me. You never wanted me.

He blew out a heavy breath. When she'd said that, he'd thought she was just being overly dramatic but now he realized she really thought that.

And he hadn't said anything. Hadn't told her that wasn't true, that of course he wanted her with him. He slid into his truck, leaned his head back against the seat wearily. He'd messed up with Jess, and if he wasn't careful, he'd lose her.

It was time for him to decide what he wanted. And to go after it, no matter what it cost him.

"GOOD TO SEE THE EVENTS of last night haven't affected your appetite," Layne said the next morning as Jess poured herself a second bowl of cereal.

Jess added milk then scooped up a spoonful. "I'm a growing girl."

"Hmm" was all Layne said. She sipped her coffee, watching Jess over the rim of the cup. "You sleep okay?"

She lifted a shoulder. Shoveled more cereal into her mouth. She'd tossed and turned all night. Her eyes felt gritty, burned from lack of sleep. She hadn't been able to stop thinking of Anthony, of how he'd smiled at her. How he'd said he'd wait for her.

Except, he hadn't meant that. Because now he wouldn't even take her phone calls, wouldn't answer her texts.

She'd lost him.

Her throat closed and she tossed her spoon down as Layne's dog started barking. A moment later someone knocked on the back door.

Jess glanced behind her, stiffened to see Uncle Ross standing outside the glass door. He was in his uniform, his hair damp from the drizzling rain.

Layne stood. "You ready for this?"

"Why not?" Jess asked with a sigh. "It's not like my life could possibly get any crappier."

"Don't be such a pessimist," Layne said, lightly swatting her arm. "Of course it can."

Jess rolled her eyes but then gave up and smiled. "Great. Well then. I guess I have something to look forward to."

"That's the old can-do spirit."

Jess remained hunched over her bowl, her gaze on the table, while Layne answered the door. "Morning, Chief," she said over Bobby's excited yapping.

"Captain," her uncle said in his deep voice. "I was wondering if I could have a few minutes with Jess?"

"Sure. Why don't I just take Bobby here for a quick walk. Give you two some privacy?"

Now Jess whirled around. "You can stay."

Layne, holding on to a quivering Bobby as he strained to get to Uncle Ross, glanced Jess's way. "You sure?"

"I mean, if you want, you can stay," she said as nonchalantly as possible so Layne wouldn't think Jess cared one way or the other what she decided. "It's raining out, anyway."

Layne and Uncle Ross exchanged a look. "If Jess wants you to stay," he said, "I don't have a problem with it."

"Okay, but it's too early in the morning for me to referee any fights." She raised her eyebrows at them both. "Understood?"

Ross nodded. Jess jerked up a shoulder. She wasn't about to fight with him. She wasn't even going to talk to him. Ever.

Layne put Bobby out back where he could hang out on the patio under the awning without getting wet. She shut the door and the poor dog pressed his nose against the glass looking all sad and pitiful and lonely.

She knew how he felt.

"Have a seat, Chief," Layne told Uncle Ross as she gestured to the table. "Can I get you a cup of coffee?"

"No. Thank you." He stood at the head of the table while Layne sat down at the chair across from Jess. "Morning, Jess," he said, looking all stiff and formal in his stupid uniform and so uncomfortable to be standing there facing her, Jess wanted to cheer.

Instead she sneered then deliberately averted her gaze and forced down another bite of cereal.

"Remember what we talked about last night," Layne said in a singsong voice.

Jess rolled her eyes. Yeah, she remembered. When

they got to Layne's house, all Jess had wanted was to crash. To be alone so she could call Anthony or maybe even sneak back to his house.

But Layne had insisted they hang out on the front porch. And though it'd been, like, seventy degrees outside, she'd made hot chocolate. Nothing fancy, just the instant kind, but she'd plopped some frozen Cool Whip on top and even stuck a couple rectangles of Hershey bar on it.

So while sitting there, sipping cocoa with some adult—a cop—at her side, a dog at her feet, had been so super dorky, it had also been kind of…nice. Comforting. Then Layne told Jess about her own childhood, how her mom had left them—or how they'd all thought she'd left except now they knew better.

All because Jess had stumbled upon those bones.

From the sounds of it, Layne's mom hadn't been much better than Jess's when it came to caring for her kids. But Layne hadn't sounded bitter as she'd explained that she learned early on that she needed to take responsibility for her own actions, the choices she made. That if she wanted to be treated with respect, she needed to treat others that way.

It was a total lecture, one disguised as some girly chitchat.

But Jess had to admit it made sense. Sort of. Not that she'd ever tell Layne that.

Uncle Ross dug something out of his front pocket then sat down next to Jess. "I wanted you to have this," he said, laying a small, square box in front of her, one wrapped in shiny, light pink paper with darker pink ribbon wrapped around it and a white and pink bow.

Frowning, she straightened. And forgot all about her plan to never talk to him again. "What is it?"

"Open it and find out," he said, watching her carefully. But not how he usually did, as if she was an alien sent down to make his life miserable. No, this time it was as if he was trying to gauge her reaction. To see how she felt about him giving her something.

"You can't bribe me into liking you," she said, her hands tucked in her lap.

"No bribe. Just a gift."

He'd gotten a gift. For her. Still not quite ready to trust his motives, she slowly pushed her cereal bowl aside and picked up the present. She wanted to hold it up to her ear and shake it but that would've made it seem as if she cared what was inside.

She pulled off the bow and then unwound the ribbon, wrapping it around her fingers to make a circle before setting it aside. Carefully picking the tape off the corner, she peeled back the edge and repeated the process with the other side before sliding her thumbnail under the last piece. Took the paper off to reveal a glossy white jeweler's box. Wondering what it could be, she smoothed out the wrapping paper and folded it in half. Then in half again.

"For God's sake," Layne said, a smile evident in her voice, "you're killing me here. Just open the box, already."

"Her mother was the same way," Uncle Ross said.

Surprised, Jess raised her eyes. "She was?"

He smiled but it didn't quite reach his eyes. "Christmas morning I tore through my presents, had them all opened and half of them played with before she even finished unwrapping hers. She said her favorite part about opening a present was the anticipation leading up to it."

Tears burned the back of Jess's throat. She cleared

them away. That was the part she liked best, too. The expectation, the hope of what could be inside.

Holding her breath, she flipped the lid of the box open. Nestled against the fluffy white bottom was a wide cuff, the deep silver of it etched with flowers. Her vision blurred, her fingers trembled as she took the bracelet from the box. It was heavy, the metal cool in her hand.

Unable to believe it, she met his eyes. "Is this…is this the bracelet I was looking at that day?"

"What day?" Layne asked leaning forward to get a better look at the present.

"A few days before we moved here, Uncle Ross took me to the mall to get some summer clothes." And, she recalled with no little amount of shame, she'd acted like a brat, acted as if she hadn't wanted anything when in truth, she'd been thrilled to have clothes that no one had ever worn before. "We walked past this jewelry store and I saw this bracelet…." She waved the cuff. "*This* bracelet and I was looking at it and…" Swallowing she shifted to face her uncle fully. "You bought this for me?"

"I went back the next day. Happy birthday," he said solemnly.

Layne held out her hand. "Let me see."

And it was all Jess could do to let go of it long enough to let Layne look at it.

"Pretty," Layne said, turning the bracelet this way and that. She handed it back to Jess who had to stop herself from clutching it to her chest the way that kid in the store last week had held on to his candy. As if afraid someone would snatch it away. "Good job, Chief. You can never go wrong with jewelry."

Jess was reeling. She couldn't stop staring at it. He'd

bought it for her over a month ago, had gone back and got it, made a special trip to buy it because he'd noticed she'd looked at it. Had figured out that she'd liked it. Wanted it.

"Try it on," Uncle Ross said, taking it from her and slipping it onto her wrist, his hand holding hers for the briefest of seconds. "Do you like it?" he asked sounding nervous. Unsure.

Like it? She loved it. More than any gift she'd ever gotten. "It's…" Perfect. "It's nice. Thank you."

He linked his hands on the table on top of the morning paper. "Jess, I spoke with Grandma last night. She and your grandpa talked about it and they said if you want to, you can move back with them."

She froze. "They…they said that?"

"There are a few stipulations of course," he said quickly. "And your behavior would have to significantly improve but…yes, they said that."

Keeping her eyes down, she traced her fingertips over the bracelet's design. "Oh."

"If that's what you want, we can go to Boston next weekend."

Of course that's what she wanted. It's what she'd been wishing for ever since he brought her to Mystic Point.

So why wasn't she jumping up and down and insisting he take her there today?

"Or…" he continued, drawing the word out, his voice sounding funny. Strained, as if he was afraid of her answer. "Or you could stay here. With me." He sat back, kept his eyes on hers. "I'd really like it if you stayed. I want you to stay."

Her breath lodged in her chest. "You…you do?"

"I do," he said, sounding so sincere, she almost believed him. Almost.

"You only want me to stay because you think it's the right thing to do."

"That's part of it," he admitted and her stomach sank. "But mostly, I want you to stay because, even though you don't need it, even though you don't need me, I want to take care of you. You deserve someone to take care of you. Now, that doesn't mean I'm not going to get on your case or punish you when you break one of my rules," he added quickly, but surprisingly, it didn't bring her down. Not when his earlier words had her feeling like she was floating. "But no matter what you do, I'm still going to want you to stay with me. I'm still going to want you in my life. I'm still going to want you. That won't change."

Hope lit in her heart. She tried to douse it. After all, she was smart enough to doubt it, jaded enough to be terrified by it. But it kept burning, growing brighter and warmer until she had no choice but to accept it. To believe that maybe, just maybe this time, things could be different.

She could be different.

Besides, if she stayed, it'd be that much easier to get Anthony back.

"Yeah, okay," she agreed, running her fingertip over the bracelet. "I mean, I guess I can stick around. Since it seems to mean so much to you and all."

His lips twitched. "It does. Thank you," he said, laying his hand over hers and squeezing her fingers gently.

And for a second—really, just the briefest of moments—she let him.

But when she slid her hand away, he didn't seem hurt or offended. More like...understanding.

"Now that we've got that settled," he said, "why don't you bring Bobby in and take him upstairs while you get your stuff?" He shot an unreadable glance at Layne before turning his attention back to Jess. "And take your time. I'm not in any hurry."

"Ohh-kay," Jess said, though she had no idea what that was supposed to mean. But then she noticed how he kept looking at Layne. And how Layne seemed to avoid looking back.

Jess's eyebrows shot up. Her uncle and Layne? She hadn't seen that one coming. But the more she thought about it—and really, she tried not to think about it too hard because…well…eww—the more she realized it made perfect sense. Her uncle needed someone to help him see there was more to life than being a cop and that it was okay to let go of that hold he had on his precious control once in a while. And Layne needed someone to take care of her once in a while. God, she couldn't believe she was actually thinking this, but they were made for each other.

Wonder if they've figured that out yet?

CHAPTER FIFTEEN

"I HAVE TO ADMIT," Layne said after Jess led the dog out of the kitchen. "I didn't think you had it in you."

"Didn't think I had what in me?" Ross asked, wondering if he really wanted to know.

She waved a hand in the air then wrapped it around her coffee cup. "The whole sensitive male thing. But you nailed it. Now, the only question is—did you mean it? Or are you a better liar than I ever gave you credit for?"

"I meant every word," he said quietly. "I want Jess." He leaned forward, noted the flare of wariness in her eyes, the way her breath hitched. "I want you, too."

Her smirk fell away as her mouth went lax. "What?"

"I. Want. You." And he wasn't about to let her go without a fight. One her reaction so far told him he'd soon be embroiled in. "I want to have a relationship with you. I want us to be together." He watched her from hooded eyes. "That clear things up?"

"What?" she repeated but louder this time, her voice cracking. "That's… You…" Shaking her head, she leaped to her feet, the sudden movement causing her chair to topple precariously before it settled on all four legs once again. "Oh, no. No."

She began to pace the length of the kitchen muttering under her breath about mistakes and men and idiotic ideas. He stretched his arms overhead then linked his hands behind his head and just watched her. No hardship that, not when she had on a pair of fuzzy, dark blue shorts and a clinging T-shirt the color of the summer sky. Her hair was down, her long legs bare and he would've liked nothing better than to take her upstairs, see if those shorts were as soft as they looked, if her skin was as warm as he remembered.

But between his niece being upstairs and Layne doing her best to wear a trench in her hardwood floor, he didn't see that happening anytime soon.

"Why no?" he asked, stepping into her path so she either had to stop, or mow him down.

Lucky for him, she chose the former. But she did look at him as if he'd lost a few brain cells at some point during the night. "Look, if this is about what happened the other night—"

"Care to be more specific?"

"Don't pull that cop routine on me," she snapped, all flustered and beautiful.

"Not a routine," he lied because of course it was. The technique of making a witness spell out exactly what she meant, to clarify every point by asking questions was something he did often. "Just making sure we're on the same page."

She glared. "Fine." She glanced at the empty hallway. "If this is about the other night when we had sex—"

"Twice."

"I can count," she said from between clenched teeth. "It…both times…was—"

"It wasn't a mistake," he said lowly, hotly.

She seemed startled. "No. Not a mistake. More like a one-time thing."

He edged closer, both amused and frustrated when

stubborn, hold-her-ground-for-anything Layne Sullivan backed up a step. "What if we want more?"

Hope, yearning, flashed in her eyes but then she lowered her gaze, firmed her mouth. "It won't work. It could never work."

Though he wanted, badly, to touch her, he kept his hands at his sides. "Why not?"

"You're my superior officer for one thing. God." She dragged her hands through her hair, held it back from her face. "What if it got around that we were... you know."

"Sleeping together?"

"Seeing each other. I'd never live it down. Every time you assigned me a case or if I were up for a promotion or commendation, everyone would think it was because I earned it in your bed. And I've worked too hard for my coworkers' respect to let that happen."

"It doesn't have to be that way."

She snorted.

Worried she was going to rip the hair right out of her head, he encircled her wrists and tugged her hands down, held firm when she tried to break free. "What if we didn't work together?" She went so still, stared at him silently for so long not so much as blinking, he shook her wrists. "Did you slip into a coma?"

"You want me to risk my career?" she asked bristling, practically vibrating with outrage. "My reputation and position in the department for sex?"

"No, damn it. I don't want you to risk anything. And it's not just sex. Not for me." He ran the pad of his thumbs over the inside of her wrists. Felt her pulse jump. "I care about you, Layne. And you care about me."

Her tongued darted out to lick her lips. "Sure, I like you well enough—"

"You're crazy about me."

"Hey, now," she said with a smirk, but her voice shook, "let's not get delusions of grandeur."

"And I feel the same way about you." She swallowed and dropped her gaze. He bent his head to look into her eyes. "Which is why I'm willing to do whatever it takes to make this work." Was ready to do whatever he had to to keep her in his life. "Including resigning as chief of police."

Her eyes went wide, her face drained of color. "No." She yanked away from him and crossed her arms. "No. I don't want you giving up your job for me. I don't want you giving up anything for me."

He wondered at the panic in her voice, the vehemence. "It wouldn't be for you. It would be for us. And it's a sacrifice I'm willing to make. I'm putting you first," he said softly, echoing her words to him last night.

But instead of seeming happy, relieved that he understood what she wanted, what she needed from him, she just looked scared. "I'm sorry. I am. But I just don't think I can—"

"Look me in the eye," he demanded gruffly, taking hold of her upper arms even as he felt his chance, felt her slipping through his fingers. "Look at me and tell me you don't want this, that you don't want to be with me. If you can do that, I'll walk out of here and we'll never speak of this again." Reaching up, he touched her cheek, slid her hair behind her ear, prayed she would choose him. That she'd take a chance on him. "Is that what you want, Layne? Do you want me to leave you alone?"

LAYNE COULDN'T ANSWER, could barely draw in a breath, not when Ross stood so close, his eyes searching, his expression somber. He was so handsome, so honorable and so damned good. He'd come through for Jess in a big way, was willing to make sacrifices for those he cared about, was willing to change, to work for what he wanted.

Do you want me to leave you alone?

No one had ever asked her that before. Not her mother when she'd chosen Dale. Not her father who still chose life on the sea. She was always left alone.

But this time, the choice was up to her.

"I don't know if I can be with you," she said, her voice hoarse. She felt too much when they were together. Wanted too much. It scared her to death.

"I can't promise things will always go smoothly, or that we'll ride off into the sunset together," he said, his accent becoming heavier, making it sound like *togetha.* "But I can promise that you can trust me with your heart." He slipped his hand behind her head, his words strong and sure. "I won't hurt you, Layne."

No, he wouldn't hurt her.

But how could she be sure she wouldn't hurt him?

She pulled his hand from her head, stepped back and crossed her arms. "I'm no good at this sort of thing. I'm too stubborn and I want everything my own way and I'm bossy and arrogant. I don't trust easily, I've never been in a long-term relationship and I come with a boatload of baggage." Couldn't he see that? Couldn't he understand she wasn't for him? "You don't want to be with me."

"I think I'm capable of deciding who I do or don't want to be with," he said, sounding as though he was quickly losing patience. That's what she did. She pushed too hard. Always pushed too far.

"And you're right," he said. "You're all those things,

not to mention cocky and argumentative. But you're also loyal and loving and funny and smart and one of the best cops I've had the pleasure of working with. And when I touch you," he continued relentlessly, stalking toward her until she was backed into the corner by the sink, "when I kiss you, I see my future." He picked up her hand, raised it to his lips and pressed a soft kiss in her palm. Met her eyes. "Be with me, Layne. Be my future."

She wanted to. So much she could almost see that future, see them together—today, tomorrow, always—sharing their lives. But it was an illusion, she thought, tugging her hand free. Because that's not how it worked. Relationships were imbalanced, imperfect. There was always one person giving. The other taking. She couldn't be like her father, loving someone to the point of self-destruction.

Would rather die than be as needy, as selfish as her mother.

"I'm sorry," she whispered, her voice raw, her hands linked in front of her. "I'm so sorry."

His expression hardened but it did nothing to disguise the hurt in his eyes. Pain she'd caused. He nodded stiffly. "I'll see myself out."

Layne turned so she wouldn't have to watch him walk away from her. Stared blindly out the window above the sink as he called up the stairs for Jess then shut the door quietly behind them as they left. And that was that. He was out of her life.

Bobby came into the kitchen and, as if sensing her mood, whined, nudging her leg with his head. Layne didn't move. Just stood there, her eyes dry, her heart breaking as she tried to convince herself she'd gotten exactly what she'd wanted.

IT WAS HERE. FINALLY.

If Jess hadn't been weaving her way through the café's packed dining room with a plastic bin filled with dirty dishes, she would've done a cartwheel. Not that she knew how to do a cartwheel, but still…

Today was something to celebrate because after two weeks of being grounded, she'd reached Freedom Day.

Or, as Uncle Ross liked to call it, The Start of Parole.

Pushing open the door to the noisy, bustling kitchen, Jess gave a mental shrug. Whatever. Hey, she'd survived two weeks without her phone, laptop or iPod. With limited access to the TV and nightly dinners with her uncle. And really, if she could survive his cooking, she could get through anything.

She set the dishes on the counter, avoided making eye contact with Luke, who still couldn't manage to look above her neck when he tried talking to her. Smiled at Joe, who sent her a wink then went back to whistling along to some old rock song on the radio.

"Order up, Jess," Celeste said, ringing the bell.

"Got it," Jess said, swinging back through the door to take the plates from the other side of the window. After setting the plates on her tray, she picked it up with two hands. While she may have gotten better and better at her job, she still lacked the skill to balance a full tray with one hand.

But at least she'd learned if she was actually pleasant and solicitous, she got bigger tips.

Luckily it was easy to be both with Mr. and Mrs. Lombardo, an elderly couple who came in several times a week for breakfast. She delivered their food, promised Mr. Lombardo she'd bring him extra cream for his coffee and headed toward the back to pick up a menu before crossing to one of the booths in the corner.

"Hi," Jess said, handing a pretty brunette, only a few years older than her, a menu. "I'm Jess. Can I start you off with something to drink?"

"I'll have coffee," she said with an easy smile. "And could you bring another menu? I'm meeting someone."

"No problem."

Jess grabbed another menu and kept it tucked under her arm while she got Mr. Lombardo's cream, took an order from a family of five and offered coffee refills to two of her tables before making her way back to the booth, the coffeepot in hand.

And about dropped the damn thing on the tile floor when she saw who was with the pretty brunette.

"Anthony."

She hadn't realized she'd said his name aloud until he faced her, the look in his eyes arctic. She blushed furiously. Cleared her throat as she poured the brunette's coffee.

"Coffee?" she asked him, her gaze on the table.

Instead of answering, he flipped the upside-down coffee cup right-side-up. She poured then, still not looking at him, handed him the menu as the brunette's phone played LMFAO's "Sexy and I Know It".

"Oops," she said, checking the caller ID. She rolled her big brown eyes. "Sorry, it's my mom."

Anthony smiled at her. "No problem."

"I'll be right back." Sliding out of the booth, the brunette held her phone up to one ear, covered the other one with her hand and answered her call.

Jess watched her go, envied her for her glossy hair and flowy summer dress. For her ability to walk in those gorgeous high heels and for her designer purse.

Envied her for being with Anthony. For being on the receiving end of his smiles.

Jess shifted. Anthony still wouldn't look at her. "I… uh…I'll be back in a few minutes to take your order."

He nodded, his jaw tight, his brow lowered.

And she wanted to scream. To rail at him to look at her. To stop pretending he hadn't liked her, hadn't kissed her and told her she was pretty. She whirled on her heel only to spin back around.

"I'm sorry," she blurted breathlessly. "Please, Anthony, I'm so sorry."

"Don't," he said, his lips barely moving. "Not here. Not now."

But she knew she had to do this now, while she had the chance. She slid into the booth, set the pot on the table.

He bristled. "I'm not interested—"

"I'm sorry," she repeated, leaning forward, "for lying about my age. It wasn't a trick or a joke."

"No? What was it?"

"I just…I really liked you. And I wanted, for once, to have something good in my life." Her heart raced, her palms were damp. She tucked her hands under the edge of the table onto her lap. "With you I didn't…I didn't feel so…alone. And I just…I really wanted that to last." She held her breath but he didn't say anything so she barreled on. "For so long it was like I was going down this dark road and the farther I went, the darker it got until it surrounded me and I…I got lost," she admitted on a whisper. "Until I met you."

"You lied to me," he said fiercely, glancing around before shifting forward. "You made me look like an idiot. Made me—" He pressed his lips together, shook his head. "What do you want from me?"

The only thing she could ever get from him. What

she didn't deserve. "I want you to forgive me," she said, unable to stop her eyes from welling with tears.

"Don't," he said, looking disgusted. With her. "You don't get to cry. Not after what you did." He straightened, his expression hard. "You want forgiveness? Talk to a priest because I'm not ready to absolve you of anything. Not yet. Now, if you don't mind, I'd like you to leave before my date gets back."

Numb, Jess slid to the edge of the seat and picked up the coffeepot. "I am sorry," she said again, softly this time as she stood there feeling awkward and so unsure of herself. "I'm sorry I lied about my age but that's the only thing I lied about. My…feelings for you? Those were the truth. Just as it's true that when I was with you, I felt more like myself than I ever have in my entire life."

A muscle worked in his cheek and he lowered his head, his hands wrapped around his coffee cup. She waited…she waited for what seemed like hours but was probably only a minute.

He didn't look up.

Her throat tight, she walked away, kept it together until she reached the restroom, only then did she let her tears fall.

"I DON'T CARE WHO is on the other side of that door," Layne told Bobby with her most serious tone, "you are not to jump on them. Do you understand?"

Bobby barked twice, leaped into the air then barked again upon landing.

Clearly they had a communication problem.

Layne opened her front door. "Ross," she said, so surprised to see him standing there, the afternoon sun glinting off his badge, his hair recently trimmed, that

Bobby raced past her. "Bobby," she said, snapping her fingers. "No."

"Heel," Ross ordered in his deep and yes, commanding voice.

Bobby heeled.

"What are you?" she muttered half impressed, half irritated. "The dog whisperer?"

"I'm sorry to interrupt your Saturday off, Captain. But I need to speak with you."

He hadn't called her by her name since he'd walked out of her house two weeks ago. Hadn't spoken to her, looked at her, with anything other than professional courtesy and respect. Hadn't smiled at her once.

It was exactly what she'd wanted when she'd sent him on his way.

She hated it.

"Well then," she said, moving aside and gesturing widely, "by all means, do come on in. Chief."

Ross stepped inside and instantly the foyer felt crowded. Intimate. She stepped back, pretended she just wanted to lean against the wall. "Can I get you something to drink?" she asked as Bobby sniffed Ross's shoes.

"No, thank you."

Him being there made her edgy and nervous and reminded her of what she'd thrown away. The chance to have him in her life, to possibly have that future— that bright, fictional future he'd proposed. One where she wasn't alone, where she had a partner to lean on, to share her burdens with. Someone to celebrate the good times with and hold her hand when things got bad.

What a fantasy. She was too responsible, too sensible to believe in it. Even if she did find herself wishing she could.

Crossing her arms, she lifted her chin. "If this is about that defense attorney's claim that I didn't have the proper warrant—"

"It's not." He took off his sunglasses, hooked them onto his pocket. "It's about your mother's murder investigation."

Her heart stopped only to resume its natural rhythm with a vengeance. "Did you find him?" she asked, afraid to hope but wanting so badly to do just that. "Did you find Dale?"

"No." His expression softened, his voice gentled. "I'm sorry."

She nodded numbly. In the past two weeks there had been no new leads, nothing at all to point to Dale York's whereabouts. And while her father and sisters still believed Valerie's killer would be found, Layne knew better.

Life didn't always have happy endings.

And chances were, her mother's murder would never be solved.

Her head spun, her knees went weak so that she started sliding down the length of the wall. "I'm okay," she said when Ross reached out to steady her. He immediately dropped his hands and stepped back and she could've bitten her tongue. But she didn't need anyone's support. Never had.

"The case will remain open," he said. "We'll keep searching for Dale."

"Even if you do find him, there's no guarantee you'll find enough evidence to convict him…hell…to bring him to trial for Mom's murder."

"No. There's no guarantee," he said in his calm, rational way as his phone buzzed. "There are never any guarantees. But that's no reason to give up. Or not move forward. Excuse me," he said, clicking on his phone. "Chief Taylor."

There are never any guarantees. But that's no reason to give up. Or not move forward.

"Are Keira's parents going to be home?" he asked whoever was on the other end of the line—Jess obviously. "And you'll stay there all night? No going out?" Pause. "Why don't you give me Keira's parents' number?" Another pause, a longer one that had Ross pinching the bridge of his nose. "Yes, I think we've already established that I'm anal." He exhaled heavily. "It has nothing to do with not trusting you and everything to do with trying to help you make the right choices on your first night of freedom in two weeks." Pause. "No, just text me the number when you're done with work. And, Jess? Thanks."

"Keira's a good kid," Layne said as he put the phone back in his pocket.

He slid her an unreadable glance. "I'm sure she is."

"She is." Layne winced. Okay, she'd already said that. Because she had no idea what to do with her hands, she snapped her fingers for Bobby. Scratched his head when he sat by her feet. "If you want, I could call Keira's dad. Andy works with my brother-in-law... my ex-brother-in-law over at—"

"That won't be necessary."

"Right," she couldn't stop herself from snapping. "Because that would be crossing that boundary again, the one between professional and personal."

His eyes narrowed. "I seem to recall you're the one who wanted that boundary back firmly in place."

She was. She did. She just hadn't realized how hard it would be to keep from leaping over it. Hadn't realized how much she'd miss him.

"Would you like me to accompany you while you inform your family about the status of the investigation?" he asked, back to being all-cop.

She laughed harshly. "God, no. I think I can handle it on my own."

His expression didn't change. "I'm sure you can." He crossed to the door, opened it and paused. "I want you to know," he said quietly, "I'm not giving up."

Her heart stuttered. She swallowed in an attempt to work moisture back into her mouth. "You're not?"

"No. No matter what, I'll keep looking for your mother's murderer."

He meant the case. Not that he wasn't giving up on her.

She could've cried.

"I appreciate that," she said.

With one last, unreadable look, he walked out.

There are never any guarantees. But that's no reason to give up. Or not move forward.

She stiffened as his words ran through her mind. No, he wouldn't give up. But she did. She always gave up instead of fighting for what she wanted. Her throat tightened. She couldn't breathe. She'd let him leave. Again.

Oh, God.

"Wait," she cried, flinging open the door. Bobby barked and raced after her as she flew down the front walk, the concrete warm on her bare feet. "Ross!"

He was already pulling away from the curb. Frantic, knowing only that she had to get to him, that this time she had to stop him, she leaped over the low bushes lining her yard, crossed the sidewalk and jumped out into the street.

He stopped the vehicle inches from hitting her, tires squealing, his door opening before he'd come to a complete stop. "Are you insane?" he yelled as he stalked up to her. Him. Chief Cool, Calm and Collected Taylor was yelling at her. It was great. "I could've killed you!"

She bent forward, tried to catch her breath. "I want… to move…forward."

He scowled at her, no longer stoic. No longer impassive. "What?"

"You were right," she said, straightening to meet his eyes. "I am crazy about you. Please don't go. Please don't leave me."

"No." He shook his head, his posture rigid. "No. You don't get to do this to me. Not again."

"I'm sorry. I'm so sorry I hurt you." Bobby raced around them, quivering with excitement. "I was just… God…I was so scared. Am so scared." And admitting that was one of the hardest things she'd ever done. But Ross was worth the hard. Worth any sacrifice she had to make because she knew he'd sacrifice anything for her, too.

"I'm so tired of not moving forward," she continued, clutching his hand, emboldened, hopeful when he didn't tug away. "It seems like I've been at a standstill all my life, living in my mother's house, waiting for her to come back…" She had to stop. To swallow past the tears thickening her voice. "I don't need a guarantee or for everything to be perfect. All I need…all I want…is you."

His fingers tightened on hers. "Layne, I don't—"

"Please," she whispered, knuckling away a tear. But she stood on her own two feet and she looked into the eyes of the man she loved and she knew she was making the right decision. "I know I can handle whatever happens with Mom's case on my own, but I don't want to. I don't want to be alone anymore. I love you, Ross.

You offered to be my future and I was too stubborn, too scared to accept. Please don't tell me I'm too late."

He wiped moisture from her cheek with the pad of his thumb then cupped her face in his large, warm hand. "I love you, too. And I'll be your future, as long as you promise to always be mine."

Her heart leaped with joy, with a relief so profound she couldn't catch her breath. Then Ross kissed her and she forgot all about breathing, all about anything, everything except him.

When he leaned back, she smiled at him and linked her hands around his neck. "I can definitely promise you that."

* * * * *

HEART & HOME

Harlequin®
Super Romance

COMING NEXT MONTH
AVAILABLE JULY 2, 2012

#1788 UNDER THE AUTUMN SKY
The Boys of Bayou Bridge
Liz Talley
One night with Louise Boyd and Abram Dufrene wants more. Then he finds out she's the guardian for a recruit and his job as coach is on the line. Yet walking away is impossible!

#1789 ISLAND HAVEN
The Texas Firefighters
Amy Knupp
Weeks before paramedic Scott Pataki's escape from San Amaro Island, Mercedes Stone shows up with the half sister he's never met. But he's determined to leave, no matter how tempting it is to stay.

#1790 THE OTHER SOLDIER
In Uniform
Kathy Altman
Corporal Reid Macfarland can't live with the mistake he made. But if he can convince a soldier's widow, Parker Dean, to forgive him, maybe Reid can learn to forgive himself.

#1791 HIDDEN AGENDA
Project Justice
Kara Lennox
Jillian Baxter is undercover on her first assignment. But she can't keep her cool when she learns her new boss, Conner Blake, is the boy from her past responsible for the most humiliating incident of her life.

#1792 THE COMPANY YOU KEEP
School Ties
Tracy Kelleher
Surely Mimi Lodge and Vic Golinski have put their past behind them. But when they meet at their college reunion, it seems the sparks are flying just as high!

#1793 A SON'S TALE
It Happened in Comfort Cove
Tara Taylor Quinn
When Morgan Lowen's son goes missing, Caleb Whittier finds himself reliving the nightmare of a similar case. This time he'll do all he can to make sure this boy comes home.

You can find more information on upcoming Harlequin® titles, free excerpts and more at www.Harlequin.com.

HSRCNM0612

REQUEST YOUR FREE BOOKS!
2 FREE NOVELS PLUS 2 FREE GIFTS!

Harlequin

Super Romance®

Exciting, emotional, unexpected!

Harlequin
Super Romance

Debut author

Kathy Altman

takes you on a moving journey
of forgiveness and second chances.

One year after losing her husband in Afghanistan,
Parker Dean finds Corporal Reid Macfarland at her
door with a heartfelt confession and a promise to save
her family business. Although Reid is the last person
Parker should trust her livelihood to, she finds herself
captivated by his silent courage. Together,
can they learn to forgive and love again?

The Other Soldier

Available July 2012 wherever books are sold.

This summer, celebrate everything Western
with Harlequin® Books!

www.Harlequin.com/Western

HSR71790

Harlequin® American Romance® presents a brand-new miniseries HARTS OF THE RODEO.

Enjoy a sneak peek at AIDAN: LOYAL COWBOY from favorite author Cathy McDavid.

Ace walked unscathed to the gate and sighed quietly. On the other side he paused to look at Midnight.

The horse bobbed his head.

Yeah, I agree. Ace grinned to himself, feeling as if he, too, had passed a test. *You're coming home to Thunder Ranch with me.*

Scanning the nearby vicinity, he searched out his mother. She wasn't standing where he'd left her. He spotted her several feet away, conversing with his uncle Joshua and cousin Duke who'd accompanied Ace and his mother to the sale.

He'd barely started toward them when Flynn McKinley crossed his path.

A jolt of alarm brought him to a grinding halt. She'd come to the auction after all!

What now?

"Hi." He tried to move and couldn't. The soft ground pulled at him, sucking his boots down into the muck. He was trapped.

Served him right.

She stared at him in silence, tendrils of corn-silk-yellow hair peeking out from under her cowboy hat.

Memories surfaced. Ace had sifted his hands through that hair and watched, mesmerized, as the soft strands coiled around his fingers like spun gold.

Then, not two hours later, he'd abruptly left her bedside, hurting her with his transparent excuses.

She stared at him now with the same pained expression she'd worn that morning.

"Flynn, I'm sorry," he offered lamely.

"For what exactly?" She crossed her arms in front of her, glaring at him through slitted blue eyes. "Slinking out of my room before my father discovered you'd spent the night or acting like it never happened?"

What exactly is Ace sorry for? Find out in
AIDAN: LOYAL COWBOY.

Available this July wherever books are sold.